DARK

MATTER

TRANSIT

(TWO)

(The Journey Continues)

VERNON J. YARKER

[handwritten dedication:] For ... with all best wishes, Vernon Yarker, December 2019.

First Edition

Typesetting by Ryan Ashcroft

Feedback welcomed mail to:
darkmattertransit@writeme.com
www.darkmattertransit.com

For Rosalind

ACKNOWLEDGMENTS

The cover photograph of this book is reproduced by the kind permission of:

SPACE TELESCOPE SCIENCE INSTITUTE (STScI)

Steven Muller Building
3700 San Martin Drive
Baltimore, MD 21218
USA

28 August 2019

Foreword

For those who have read the previous book Dark Matter Transit, they will know that Geoffrey Holder, by accident of nature and technology, was transported from an airfield in Southern England to the Qee van Ongle (QvO) which was a giant spaceship lurking hull down behind the moon. It was studying Earth's flora and fauna and public service channels through its' Discan T which they had mounted at the rim of the moon. Historically, the species crewing the QvO spaceship are humans who are the descendants of slaves originally spirited away from Earth, mostly from ships of sail, by the Rap Foundation. The Raps forcibly bred their human captives to produce yet more slaves, but eventually the slaves became organised and they overthrew their masters and assumed control of the Rap Foundation planets which they renamed as the 'Ongle System of Planets.' There was no way back from the giant spaceship for Geoffrey and he became a crew member of the QvO and he proved his worth on many occasions during their deep space adventures.

The QvO employs Dark Matter Transit (DMT) which enables it to move limitlessly through the cosmos. Physics, Geoff comes to understand, is by no means universal in space. Dark matter has no form, no width, no depth, no height and it pervades the universe. Because dark matter has no dimensions you do not travel through it as in going from A to B because there is no measurable distance in it. To employ DMT you set the biases applicable to where you wish to go before you submerge into dark matter and you instantaneously re-emerge from it at your destination.

Initially, in Book 1, dark matter transit was sometimes a hit or miss affair because there are eddy currents in it and they can result in a spaceship being ejected billions of kilometres from where it had hoped to emerge. However, by the end of the first book a new and stable method of DMT had been discovered and DMT has become a reliable method for journeys in the firmament. Of course this also endangers the Earth itself which does not have the technology nor even a space fleet. Moreover, when the manufacturing capability of whole planetary systems are involved in making war or preparing for defence, fleets of more than one-hundred thousand vessels are not uncommon.

This book is a continuation of the first book which ended when the combined Rap-Terrabot fleet had been defeated in their threat to annihilate the planet Earth. They were using Earth as a bait to bring the fleets of the Ongle System of Planets and the Ambrocognia Mundi system into a battle where they would be vastly outnumbered.

In this book you are able to follow the continued journey to new worlds and new experiences, to meet new species and to engage with them. Once more Earth is threatened with extinction.

Chapter 1

THE HUNTING PARTY

As a result of a combined accident of nature and technology, Geoffrey Holder had been transported through space to the giant space craft, the Qee van Ongle (QvO), where he met and married Imogen who was originally assigned to guide him through a transitional rehabilitation from Earth culture to the more advanced culture and technology of the Ongle system of planets. He had experienced many incidents and adventures as a crew member of the spaceship. The most terrifying, for him, being the vastly superior, in numbers, Rap-Terrabot fleet which had unsuccessfully sought to avenge previous defeats by annihilating the defenceless planet Earth. In this case the Earth was merely the bait; the intention of the Rap-Terrabot fleet was to draw the Ongle and Ambrocognia-Mundi fleets in a fight to the finish in circumstances where the Rap-Terrabot fleet would be numerically superior.

Following on their outstanding and brave service, both Geoffrey and his wife Imogen had been awarded the highest level of commendation by the Supreme Council For The Ongle System of Planets. The way in which awards were given differed from Earth in that the

1

awardees were asked to make a wish which, if reasonable in its' expectation, would be translated into a gift by the Government. The award ceremony also contained an option to defer taking up their gifts to a later date. Geoffrey and Imogen had chosen this alternative and their wishes were sealed in gold dusted envelopes and were locked away until such time as they felt able to accept their awards.

When, at the request of Geoff and Imogen, the envelopes were later opened their enclosed wishes were identical and they had asked the Ongle government to establish them in the post of joint Wardens for the planet Marina. Hitherto, Marina had been declared a galactic Nature Reserve and nobody was allowed to live there permanently, although there was one habitable building, called the Grande Lodge, which had been built years earlier as temporary accommodation for an official scientific expedition to the planet.

It was not an easy decision for the Ongle Supreme Council to take because the rules of no permanent residence had been enshrined in law; but it was successfully argued by members of the government that dramatic changes had been made in the application of dark matter transit which rendered it a reliable form of transit in the cosmos. The consequence of the changes meant that no part of the universe was more than a milli second from any other part of the universe and spaceships belonging to other worlds could arrive at, and on, Marina without warning. It was, therefore, necessary to establish legal ownership of the planet by virtue of it having human beings in residence upon it who were nominated as being responsible for its' management on behalf of the Supreme Council of the Ongle System of Planets.

By now Geoff and Imogen had two children resulting from their union; both of them were girls and they could probably have a no more protected and environmental friendly place in the universe in which to grow up. The planet, in every aspect, was just stunning. Most of all the animals of the planet held no fear of humans nor of each other. Most favourite for the children were the mimicmees; these were long haired, sooty, black animals about the size of a Scot's terrier. To look at them you would probably think that they needed a good brushing or, in the children's perspective, constant hugging.

The mimicmees took it all in their stride and their expressionless black eyes portrayed no hint of being for or against being picked up and hugged although their actions were to snuggle down against the person doing the hugging. When replaced on the ground they immediately resumed what they had been doing before the interlude. Their most endearing quality was their ability to copy precisely any sounds that they had previously heard and the children delighted in telling the mimicmees tit-bits of information such as 'mummy is in the shower' or 'daddy has stubbed his toe getting out of bed'. Then, with the gravity of somebody announcing very serious news, the mimicmees repeated the phrase and other mimicmees repeated it on, until it was the news of the valley. Later it was forgotten by them and replaced by a more recent, up to date, piece of tittle-tattle although, at times, they recalled earlier snippets and mixed them into their current news with hilarious results. Needless to say, the children had individual mimicmee pets and they rarely went to sleep at night without at least two mimicmees in their bedroom.

Sometimes, as a part of Geoff and Imogen's shared duties as Wardens, the whole family went out on observation and recreational trips to other parts of the planet. Today, they were to have a picnic at the family favourite location of Jewel Bed Creek, as it was known, which ran through some of the lushest vegetation imaginable. Over the years the creek bed had cut down into the crust of Marina to reveal a plateau of diamonds fused into a solid sheet by a distant geological event. The constant wash of river sands had polished the diamond sheet so that it reflected light back up from the bed of the stream; and when this reflected light passed through the ripples of the water above, it was a sight to be seen and unmatched. Even by Marina standards it could be described as outstanding. Diamonds, of course, were not uncommon in the galaxy and some of them could be as large as boulders. Thus, with industry able to obtain what it wanted closer to home, this, together with the nature reserve status of Marina, ensured that this particular deposit remained untouched.

Imogen was setting out a picnic table and Geoffrey was busy making photographic recordings when they were startled to hear a hiss and crackle usually associated with the discharge of an energy beam weapon and it appeared to be coming from the centre of a small thicket.

Carefully, Geoff edged up to the thicket and parted the branches to permit him a view of the inside of it and found himself staring at the unwinking eyes of a mimicmee. "Oh, hello." He mimicked a cut glass Oxford accent.

"Oh hello," the mimicmee repeated agreeably and so perfectly that Imogen laughed, but then it tacked on the sound of a weapon discharge which had caused Geoff to investigate.

"Firearms are not permitted on Marina, so I can't think where you may have heard that!" he smiled as the mimicmee inevitably reversed his statement back to him.

Geoff beckoned Imogen over and together they discussed the mimicmee. "Well, I suppose it could have invented the sounds," Imogen tried to reason, "but they were much too realistic to me."

"Yes, I agree," Geoff nodded. "It is too much of a coincidence. I think we will have to take this one with us for observation, to see if it recalls any more sounds." With that he squeezed into the thicket to capture the entirely willing beast. The girls came over to see what their parents were doing, and they immediately set about stroking and pampering the mimicmee who confirmed in its' own mind that it had found its' way to heaven by giving out little sighs of contentment.

"Churuka," it announced loudly as its eyelids closed; and it was sound asleep almost before they were fully shut.

Imogen was searching through their language indexes as they piloted their way home and she was interacting with their transportation runabout's basic language programmes. Then she informed Geoff. "I can find no exact match for the word Churuka; but the speech pattern facility reports that words of similar sound are commonly used to indicate that one has found something or somebody. Eureka on Earth, is an example."

The sizzle and crackle of energy beams came again from the corner of the flight deck and the word 'help,' loud and clear, heralded that their mimicmee had woken up and it came over and hopped up upon the navigational console. For a while it stared out of the forward windows trying, fathomless, to understand why the countryside was flashing by beneath it. "Churuka," it muttered again, before it decided that this was too much mental exercise for a mimicmee and it sought a darkened area below the console to continue its' nap.

On arrival back at the Grande Lodge they decided to keep the mimicmee indoors in the hope of more snippets of information being recalled but it appeared to be more interested in sleeping, eating, and biting at the terminals of the batteries which Geoff had placed on the floor for that purpose so that it could top up its' internal source of energy from them. It was then, when Geoffrey had the idea of logging into a programme about the history of Ongle military hardware, that they achieved a breakthrough. Once the sounds of weapon discharges was reached, the mimicmee came alert instantly and dived behind a sofa from where a very clear conversation ensued.

'I've got one!'

'Missed it', said another voice.

'Let's get after it,' the first voice urged. 'You go that way and I will go straight across. We should be able to cut it off.'

"They seem to be hunting something," Geoff surveyed the ceiling as if for inspiration.

"There is nothing here to hunt," Imogen rejoined. "The animals of Marina just walk up to you, not run away. So who can they be. We have had no notification nor have we detected a craft of any type approaching the planet?"

"Hunting sounds as good as any explanation," Geoff replied, 'but who are they and what could they be hunting?" He shrugged his shoulders to express the expanse of possibilities. "I think I will go out there tomorrow and set up some automatic cameras to record people or movement."

Imogen was taking the children to school the next morning and she hoped to combine it with a shopping spree, so on this occasion they would not all be able to go out to Jewel Bed Creek with him, but she had still thoughtfully packed sandwiches for his trip. In the event, he also decided to take along a watch-over-me robot, described as a WHOMER in 'stores jargon.' This type of robot carried out surveillance on behalf of those they were assigned to; and they were especially useful for the elderly and the chronically ill or they could be used for just plain guard duty which was what Geoff had in mind on this occasion. The robot was already on the craft when he arrived and it respectfully watched him come aboard. No doubt it was noting and recording his respiration, pulse rate and skin tone, perhaps even measuring his face for an exact fit for an oxygen mask, should needs be, Geoff laughed to himself.

Geoff moved up to the craft's navigation centre and punched in Jewel Bed Creek then, as an after thought, he added 'discrete-mode' to his instruction. He knew that this would commit the 'in-atmosphere' (INAT) craft he was in to select a cloaked approach and to quietly land in a shallow ravine or copse up to a kilometre away from the grid ref that he had directed it to. Discrete mode was really a military application but it had been retro fitted to the vehicle because it was very useful when tracking animals that may, otherwise, be alarmed to see and hear a noisy leviathan screaming in overhead. Although, of course, the animals of Marina held no fear of other animals, they did understand that clumsy actions of another creature could cause death or injury, so they would be apt to react in panic to an uncloaked arrival of a monster from above.

The journey took him half an hour, during which time Geoff grew self conscious of the WHOMER's constant maternal gaze so he switched it off for his own comfort. Even then the robot had a last word by issuing a verbal warning that to switch it off may endanger his security. "I can manage for a little while," he replied.

Nevertheless, the robot made a doleful bell sound every five minutes to remind anybody in hearing range that it was present but deactivated. But now they were at their destination and Geoff reached over and switched the WHOMER back on. "Stay on guard here and keep within the cloaked area of the ship. Report to me anything untoward." His instruction was relayed by direct interface to the robot's brain through his hucom and acknowledged by return. Hucoms were a very useful piece of equipment for just such activities; they were worn in a band of a baseball design cap. Their use allowed humans to interact mind to mind with each other and to interact with computers and robots as well as having the ability to instantaneously translate via their interaction with mainframe computers, or 'transpolate,' which was the Ongle in-house term for it.

Geoff found that the hucom was a wonderful piece of technology but very hard to get to grips with by somebody, such as himself, who had been brought up with vocal intercourse between people. The human mind has a natural tendency to wander off subject and it took years of practice to prevent this. In consequence it required all his concentration to not be showing people pictures of his last holiday when, in fact, he had a serious technical matter to discuss. The only way he had found was to work as if reading the words from a book. Just the same, he could never be as good as Imogen or even his own children who had used hucoms from birth. Luckily, Imogen understood this and at home they usually relied upon vocal exchange.

But, now that he was wearing it, he decided to

9

contact Imogen via a hucom-linked live DMT message transfer dart to see that she was ok. Such devices overcame the delay that a radio signal would suffer to reach her which in this case would be four years, and communication with her now became almost instant. "Yes," she assured him, "but you will not believe this; by sheer accident I turned left when I should have turned right and I have ended up in a wonderful dress shop and I am lost!"

"You poor thing," Geoffrey commiserated." Do you think that you can ever find your way back out alright. Shall I ask the police to mount a search party?"

"Oh, you are a dear to worry about me like that," she replied sweetly. "It is a really complex shopping centre and the way out of one shop can sometimes be the entrance to another."

"That's my girl, ever resourceful."

"It might make me a minute or two late home tonight, though."

"Oh, a minute or two is fine." Geoff fell into her trap.

"Oh dear," Imogen sounded contrite. "I think I have picked up the wrong wrist watch. This one I am wearing is an Ambrocognia Mundi watch. How long is an Ambrocognia minute?"

"I see," he laughed, "you have me completely beguiled. Let's make that an hour or two late."

"Oh, you are such an understanding man," said

Imogen as she closed the conversation.

All was quiet as Geoffrey made his way, on foot, to the creek that the family had visited the day before. He never ceased to wonder about this spot. Year in, year out-and historically for millions of years-nobody had chanced this way to be struck with awe by the light patterns that danced across these waters. What is the point of such beauty, he mused to himself, if there is nobody to see it and admire it.

Geoff now was nearing the creek when he noticed that the upper branches of a group of trees in the middle distance were waving together in unison and then splaying outwards like a shuttle cock only to wave back in before they returned to an unwavering upright. A puff of air reached him and sent its' cooling breeze over his body. In an instant Geoffrey was in connection with the WHOMER and directing it to switch on the ship's sensors to check for other INAT vehicles in the vicinity; and he was not surprised to learn that a magnetic trail, comparable to that emitted by an INAT vehicle, was present, but whatever had created the trail was invisible to the sensors.

Geoffrey's near forgotten Ground Defence Training in the RAF, to avoid personal disclosure through sound, shape shine, or shadow, came back to him and he hit the deck. But then he saw an access route to where he judged the craft to have departed; and by getting behind a curving line of low shrubs he was able to cautiously approach the copse where he had witnessed the disturbance. At the very juncture, when he was about to enter the area from where

11

the unknown vehicle had ascended, he crouched down to observe, fortuitously in fact because as he watched a shrub on the far side of the site was being thrust aside, a robot brandishing a weapon ran into view. He saw it glance upwards and then bring the weapon it was carrying into the aim and it fired a volley of short laser bursts into the sky above.

As he continued to watch, an apparently cloaked craft had been taken by surprise by the onslaught and momentarily its' cloaking screen was overwhelmed and dissipated to reveal a small needle pointed craft hovering above. Probably a suitable size for the transport of roughly ten passengers, thought Geoff, mentally summing up its' likely capabilities. The craft had perhaps suffered a few direct hits from the robot's fire or possibly it was unable to retaliate from a cloaked situation and it now fully emerged and three energy bolts tore down from it. The first bolt dismembered the robot altogether and the second and third buried themselves in the earth and created small craters, each about one metre deep. The WHOMER came back on the air and told him that the craft had emitted another magnetic trail and seemed to have departed from Marina. This left Geoff with the remains of a robot and a big mystery to solve.

That night when he returned home to Imogen, they decided to go into conference with the overly long titled Government Department Of Natural History and Prehistoric Mapping to the Supreme Council for the Ongle System of Planets." Surely we don't have to call them that every time that we speak to them?" Geoff looked in askance to Imogen.

"Of course not, we would never get anything done bar exchanging titles," she assured him.

"I have dealt with them before, they are perfectly happy with Nat-hist."

"Thank God for that," Geoffrey sighed.

Once they had set up a secure channel with Nat-Hist, the screen cleared quickly and they were informed that they were speaking to the deputy director of that department who turned out to be a woman by the name of Angela and she listened very carefully to what Geoffrey told her. Then she asked for a break so that she could check with the Ministry of Defence of any craft known to be in the area of Marina earlier that day. After a while she came back and said that as a result of her question to the Ministry they had confirmed that with the exception of Imogen's domestic trip the results were negative. She also pointed out that Geoffrey and Imogen had no baneful weaponry with them on Marina, with the exception of a stun gun, which was a very short range weapon and specially used to pacify animals before a veterinary procedure could be carried out on them. She had, therefore, asked the Ministry to review the latter urgently. As a result an unmanned craft would be with them shortly with personal weapons on board, in case they were needed.

It was felt that whoever it was who visited Marina would probably return because they would have to have been blind or deaf not to have picked up the ownership beacons on the surface and in near space around the planet. Therefore, they had visited regardless of them. A plan evolved that Geoff would give it a break for a day or two and then check the same area and recover his cameras to see if there had been another visit. If there had been, then the Ministry of Defence would send a military detachment to provide protection, detection and security for the planet.

In fact Geoff and Imogen were busy locally and it was four days before they were able to schedule a return to Jewel Bed Creek; and this time they approached the location with enhanced stealth. They had also received an interesting piece of kit from the Ministry of Defence along with personal small arms and they decided to put it into use immediately. To do this they had to fly around their target area dropping self righting posts at its' extremities. When in place the posts switched themselves on and radiated a virtual grid which, if it could be seen, would look like a graph paper filling the inner fifty-kilometre diameter circle between the posts. Imogen's job was then to fire two explosive electromagnetic wave source projectiles (EMWPs) to the edge of space directly above the grid. "Ready?" she asked.

"As ever we can be," Geoff nodded and blew her a kiss across the cabin. "Wait a second though. We have to switch off all of our electronic magnetic systems to prevent overloading our own circuits when the source goes off."

"Gosh, In my excitement I had forgotten to do that."

"Me, too," Geoff smiled as he slammed down a series of circuit breakers. "Go now," he called out.

"Yes, sir!" Imogen mocked him with a laugh as she pressed the two switches and two slim rockets arched up into the sky leaving long trails of silver vapour as they watched them ascend to the edge of the planet's atmosphere. "Detonating source now." Imogen sounded cool and professional but the truth was that it was the first time that she had ever had to deploy an EMWP.

In response to Imogen's further depression of two different buttons, the two EMWPs exploded in unison with a light, initially as bright as the sun for a few seconds, before it died down; whereafter she switched the ship's previously abated EM systems back on. During the period of the intense electromagnetic waves being given off by the EMWPs, the computers integrated with the posts of the virtual grid and were engaged in working out if any magnetic shadows had been detected. The presence of shadows would reveal that there were solid objects suspended between the EMWP's burst and the grid below.

Geoff watched a screen as it flickered into life and the grid reports started to come in.

"Imogen, look at this!" he exclaimed and she came over to share his screen. As she looked the figures started to spill out along the bottom of the screen.'Object 20 metres long, 10 metres wide in size, elevation 10,000 metres, moving from grid ref F6 towards G9.'

"Well, who can that be?" Imogen asked, but her question went unanswered as their WHOME robot stationed outside of their ship advised everybody to take cover. There was not much Geoff and Imogen could do because they were probably in the safest place onboard their ship and they gazed upwards from out of their forward screen.

They didn't see it at first, but then they saw an alien craft fluttering and dipping from side to side and descending quite quickly. For a while it went nose-up as if attempting to scramble its' way up but it finally lost its' battle with gravity and plunged into the earth, half of a kilometre away, with a loud explosion and a pall of smoke; and within seconds clods of earth and stones rained down on the ship sheltering Geoff and Imogen.

Imogen gasped but was the first to go to the locker room and fetch their anti radiation suits, wisely, too, because she knew that there were not many ships that were able to operate both inside and outside of the atmosphere of a planet which would not give off some kind of radiation if they were severely damaged. They were stopped from going out to look at the crash when it started to create a light display of exploding ammunition and ghostly balls of fire arched out of the crash site. This was followed by another explosion and the needles of their radiation detector devices started to gyrate, indicating moderate but unsafe levels of radiation.

"We could go in if we wished?" Geoff put the question to Imogen, "but there is nothing to say that it is going to be the last explosion."

"I think not," she said "Nothing could have survived

that explosion, best leave it to the experts. We can let the WHOMER go in and reconnoitre and it can report back if assistance is required. When the military arrive they have all the equipment necessary to decontaminate it."

"I am wondering," Imogen was pensive, "who and what was aboard that ship. They were maybe not prepared for our EMWP devices; they could have wrecked their control systems, they were closer to them than us."

"Yes, that is a thought," Geoff praised her. "I have a feeling that you may be right; they would have had all of their computers switched on."

"You can kiss me there then," she pointed to her cheek, "but I do hope that they were not friendly people."

"Oh, they were a bunch of absolute bounders," he reassured her as he planted a kiss on the cheek where she had indicated. "There, is that better?"

There was a silence for reflection, by both of them, broken by Imogen.

"But I would hate to think that I had killed people who bore me no malice!"

"Well, for a start they were cloaked which suggests that they were up to no good. Secondly, they have ignored our warnings to stay away from Marina. The evidence we have suggests that they were on a covert mission and that rarely stems from good intent."

"Thank you, darling," she smiled again "I am going to seek counsel with you after all my murders," but then she still looked slightly glum.

The encounter, of course, brought the military to Marina posthaste and the Grande Lodge was soon at the centre of a military encampment, as well as there being detachments in far flung areas of the planet. Heavily clothed in anti-radiation suits, they painstakingly inspected the site of the explosion and recovered one body that had apparently been thrown well clear of the crashing craft. Surprisingly, it was almost a replica of an Earth chimpanzee but it bore all the hall marks of a warrior,wearing a reflective flak jacket and bandoliers containing fully charged energy weapons that could be drawn and fired instantly. Geoff went with them and he inspected the remains of the downed ship.It seemed a bit dated, he thought, but there was nothing much to inspect and there were many radio active fragments scattered over a wide area. The military industriously started to gather these oddments up, to be later taken up to a passing starship in sealed radiation proof containers and these would be fired into the corona of a star, at a convenient part of its'journey. The chimp-like body was highly radio active and that would suffer the same fate but would be afforded a Christian service beforehand.

Geoff was really only in the role of an observer as he moved around the site. The military all had jobs to do, but in a private amble amongst the debris he caught sight of something reflecting the sun's rays and picked it up; it turned out to be a fairly ancient looking camcorder. The Colonel came over to look at the object and immediately declared that this could be 'the something' that they had been looking for and he sent it to a lab set up near the Grande Lodge with his instructions to decontaminate it 'carefully'! When this had been done the lab technicians had levered the camcorder open and found that it was a recording system employing a conventional disk and the strong metal shell of the recorder had prevented the disk from being damaged by radiation. With a few adaptions they also discovered that they could recover the recorded data and play it over one of their computer projectors.

The Colonel, who did not believe in keeping secrets from his men, decided that the disk should be played, open air cinema style, to them all that very evening. Not knowing what was on the disk, he wisely cautioned Imogen that the two girls ought not to see it and he directed that the cinema be set up at a distance from the lodge. There were not enough natural seats around and the military dragged in some of the fallen trees they found in the forest and set them up in a semi-circle for the audience to sit on. Strangely, a group of mimicries came out of the surrounding jungle. Then, as if they seemed to understand that there was to be a film show, they hopped up onto one of the logs and waited patiently. "Shall I sell them ice creams?" One of the soldiers quipped to Geoff and they both laughed at the incongruous row of mimicries.

Chapter 2

THE CHIMP PEOPLE

"Lights, action, roll!" Somebody called out light-heartedly and a beam of light lanced out from a film projector to hit the bedsheet screen. What they saw was a planet of chimpanzees, but intelligent ones that could fly planes, drive cars, use computers and manufacture things; and they had developed a social system and a democracy; and they had conquered their near space with advanced chemical powered, sub-light speed rockets. The mimicries on the log also saw them and had reared up on their hind-legs looking like a bunch of scruffy cats and to the mirth of the human audience they gave a unified shriek and shot off into the forest. All witnessed by the Colonel sitting near Geoff who conveyed his feeling to him that it could be interpreted that they had acted with fear rather than surprise.

The clips showing the chimp creatures portrayed the female of the species as docile and feminine. The males, on the other hand, were extremely macho and nearly always wore bandoliers of weapons similar to those that they had seen on the dead body found at the wreck. The hucoms of the audience were having some difficulty in translating but they gradually improved as they were able to match words to action. Then the video moved on to a hunt in which the males slipped through quite savage terrain and undergrowth to creep up on frightening looking animals. The chimp people apparently took great pride in bringing a ferocious beast down, but it was clear that they were sufficiently armed to ensure that their encounters were very one sided affairs.

The audience's hucoms were now increasingly able to make more sense of the chimp language that they had been struggling with; and the gathering learned that despite strict government controls the warrior chimps had hunted to extinction all of the dangerous and even not very dangerous animals on their home world and they had then ventured out to other worlds on private hunting expeditions. The Marian party had discovered an abandoned Terrabot vessel adrift in space. They didn't know that it could have been a victim of the earlier battles between the Rap-Terrabot fleet and the combined fleets of Ongle and Ambrocognia-Mundi. Nor that the Rap-Terrabots had met their spiritual fate in the glowing plasma hands of a far away coronal mass ejection when they had attempted to annihilate the planet Earth. Whatever the reason, the Terrabot ship had been vacated Marie Celeste like; the question 'why' was not something that the chimp hunting party found at all necessary to solve. By sheer luck in a limitless cosmos they had found a ship far in advance of any of their own and it had holds large enough to accommodate all three of their INAT ships. It also included a cloaking mechanism, superior to that of their own craft, and to them the, hitherto, unknown ability to transit through dark matter and there were several working computers which explained to them how to use it.

The hunting party that had found the Terrabot ship did not pass it on to their own government but kept it a secret and used it as a means to extend their hunting across the universe. In time they discovered Marina but they were disappointed that the animals there came right up to them. This brought forth their streak of cruelty. The chimps exploited their dominance over other creatures and they took delight in harassing the animals they found on Marina, objective to instilling fear and subservience; and they habitually took random potshots at them to illustrate their mastery. Their trait had obviously been spread as a word picture among the mimicmees and that was the undoubted reason why they had left the screening of the video so abruptly.

Although the hunting party was the indisputable master over the animal kingdom of Marina, it did not satisfy their natural desire to hunt; and it was then that they came up with a whole new form of hunting and one in which there would be real risks as well as personal kudos for success. Possibilities started to unfold to them during their initial inspection of the Terrabot ship and the chimp hunting party came upon a hold tightly packed with robots. Logic dictated, to those who were watching the video, that these were probably a part of the old Rap-Terrabot invasion force. The chimp hunting party's trial and error experiments with the robots led them to discover that these were not domestic robots but military infantry modules. After that, it dawned upon them that they had chanced upon a sophisticated potential adversary to make their hunts real. They knew of the Grande Lodge because they had reconnoitred it one dark night and they had adjudged it to be an insignificant hazard. In any event, they always had the fall-back of a fully cloaked ship to escape in if a serious objection to their presence was mounted.

They had chosen Marina because it had an insignificant sentient life presence, far less than any other planet that they had previously encountered. The planet was lush, too, with a photogenic virgin environment and the diverse hunting territory that the chimp people needed as a back drop in which they could prove their personal bravery to their fellow chimp people. The film of hunts that they took there would be highly prized when they returned with the pictorial evidence. There was even a suggestion that they should go into business with hunting tours but the robots they had would soon be used up on such ventures and they lacked the manufacturing capability to clone them to the very high standard of perfection of those they had discovered.

The chimps were aware of Ongle's claims to Marina and they relied implicitly on their own ship's cloaking ability and the distance of their operations from the Grande Lodge. Moreover, their activities to date had remained unchallenged, which could be taken as an indication of tolerance or ignorance of their activities. They set about re-educating the robots they had found on the deserted Terrabot ship. Then they told them that they were to be set free but that there were other chimps who disagreed with this policy and they may come to Marina and try to take them back. Their best means of defence, therefore, was by ingenuity, to avoid all contact with any chimp people by hiding from them but to be ready to defend their right to freedom against hunting parties. Three of the reprogrammed robots were armed and then set down and directed to infiltrate the jungle and scrub lands; and the next day the hunt for them began. The chimp hunting party fanned out across a wide swathe of countryside and after a week of intensive tracking they had, at last, made contact with the robots.

The video then showed a rocky outcrop and the metallic head of a robot looked around a rock then withdrew. Albeit momentarily, the robot's movement had been observed by the chimp hunters and they commenced to move out to the sides, objective to encircling their prey. The robots, versed in military tactics, went on the defensive and the chimps were soon to find that it would be no walk over because the three robots had formed a wide V formation in which the two tails were abutted by rocks behind them. This allowed them to back one another up with firepower across a triangle. This formation, together with their digital accuracy with small arms, made it very hard for the chimp people to close upon them, and a roasting fire from both sides effortlessly cut swathes through the lower scrub. In time, two of the chimps were dead and burning and only one of the robots had been felled by the chimps so far. But there were more chimps than robots and it became easier for them to divide the fire of the two remaining robots; and yet another robot was obliterated and the remaining robot made off and had still not been traced by nightfall. That, of course, must have been the robot that Geoff had seen emerge from the undergrowth to attack the cloaked chimp space craft which, in turn, had responded with ship borne weapons that were technically canons rather than the lightweight pistol that the robot possessed. The unequal confrontation was a no win scenario for the robot whose demise had been witnessed by Geoffrey.

"Well done," the Colonel came up to Geoffrey. "Your find of the video recorder has explained a lot to us and I am going to confer with Ongle to see what we can do."

"One thing that I did note" Geoff answered. "They only have one ship with the qualities that enable them to travel through dark matter and they have hidden it from their government. No attempt has been made to examine it to see if it can be duplicated. If we can somehow prise it from their possession it would be game set, match to us."

"That is a good thought," the Colonel nodded. "I will include your observation in my conversation with the Ministry. What also occurs to me is that it is a little unpalatable to blow the chimps out of space and consequently kill all on board. That would be quite OTT when their primary sin is to be a bunch of macho hoodlums."

"I agree," said Geoff, "killing for insufficient reason becomes murder when you come to dwell upon it in the months and years to come. Let's see what Ongle can come up with."

Imogen had come out of the Lodge now and stood beside Geoffrey as they watched the Colonel return to be re-absorbed in his world of uniformed people sitting in front of computer screens in their brightly lit temporary Operations Centre in a tent on the lawn of the Lodge. They both turned to go indoors where Geoffrey found the two girls still wide awake and demanding that he read them a story before they would even try to go to sleep.

"That is blackmail," he said trying to sound stern.

"Yes, daddy, we know," Vivienne innocently replied.

"It's' a deal then," and he turned to remove a mimicmee that was sitting on the chair between the two children's beds and sat on the chair himself and opened the book of children's stories. Their eyelids were already heavy as he commenced in a hushed voice with: -

"Once upon a time in a country a long, long way from here, there lived a beautiful princess."

"Beautiful princess," in matched hushed tones the mimicmee confirmed from a corner of the room. Geoff never managed to finish the story, he rarely could before they had dropped off to sleep and were pursuing their own fairy stories in the land of dreams. As he got up to leave he smiled because the mimicmee had dropped off to sleep as well.

"I wonder what you dream about he asked?" But the soft contented rising and falling sigh of the breathing of a mimicmee asleep was his only answer. Imogen came and linked her arm through his.

"I hope that you have not been frightening them with tales of Earthly dragons eating people," she nudged him.

"We never do get as far as the dragons. They usually nod off around the time that the handsome prince, seated on a white horse with the sun glancing brightly from his polished armour, gallops up to the gates of the castle. I don't know whether it is the prince or the white horse but one of them seems to be the ultimate cure for their insomnia." Then he pointed to the Colonel who was just emerging from the shadows into the light thrown by the veranda lights. "I guess that he has got something to tell us."

The Colonel came up the steps to where they were seated and sat down and cleared his throat, "There is a lot to tell you," he said.

"I'll get some drinks then," said Imogen, but she was back in a moment with glasses and a jug of fruit juice from the fridge. "I hope I haven't missed anything." She gave a fake concerned expression in the direction of the Colonel.

"Nothing, yet," the Colonel laughed. "Ongle have pointed out that there are security risks if we get involved with this species if things do not work out as we want them to. They could take revenge on this planet and your family would be the obvious targets for them to vent their revenge upon. The other possibility is your abduction and they would use you as a bargaining chip. There yet another consideration, too. It is possible that they could treat you as they did the robots and arm you and then hunt you down. So with immediate effect there will be an armed guard around the Lodge and in due time you are to be evacuated.

"Oh!" There were tears in Imogen's eyes and Geoff hugged her close.

"I am sure it won't be for long," he said and she nodded that she fully understood the need, but she was still sad all the same.

"Why did they have to pick our planet for their brutal hunting?" She bit her lip.

Chapter 3

NOAH'S ARK

G eoffrey and Imogen were delighted to learn that Peter Berry, formerly the Captain of the QvO, had been asked to extend his service career and he was now Rear Admiral Berry of the Ongle Home Fleet. The QvO had been chosen because of the facilities it had to offer to assist in an evacuation plan for Marina in a Noah's Ark style operation; and Rear Admiral Berry would have his offices aboard the QvO during the period of the Operation.

The plan was to press into service the QvO's empty quarter, so called because it was almost a complete deck of the ship and measuring several hundred square kilometres of free space. Normally the area was cleaned and inspected only once per year. In particular it contained every facility in offices and open spaces. Its' historical use had been to house transiting military formations and civil populations rescued from natural disasters in the Ongle home worlds. The last time it had been used in earnest was when the Ongle System Of Planets had been involved in military containment of the robot home world, named Terrabot, which with the race of Raps had sought to annihilate the planet Earth. In this instance the complete military divisions for the incursion had been carried to Terrabot, in a single lift, and although its' robot population of Terrabot had vacated it before they arrived, the military remained there to make the planet uninhabitable for them should they ever attempt to return.

"She has pretty much proved her worth over the years," Imogen remarked.

"It was quite forward thinking, too," Geoff agreed.

The QvO had arrived off Marina and was cloaked in orbit around the planet and Rear Admiral Berry signalled that he intended to visit to hold a conference with the army and with the two Wardens who were in place. Geoff laughed when he heard a foot soldier complaining that this was an army matter, they didn't need help or instructions from the flyboys. The comment could have been imported directly from Earth, but it confirmed that military rivalry between the different services existed even galaxies apart. Rear Admiral Peter Berry was Imogen's uncle and he was going to drop in on them at the Grande Lodge; and while he was there they looked forward to enjoying a relaxed family get together with him.

They heard the sound of a guard coming to attention outside the Lodge; and Geoff remarked that Peter was approaching and went to open the door to the Rear Admiral who was resplendent in his full formal dress, but once inside he started to unbutton the tight jacket.

"Thats better," he said with relief, "another ten minutes in that would have seen me out in this heat,' and

Imogen rushed to get him a cold drink. "Good," he said while rummaging in his brief case, "we can have a slice of this; your mother gave it to me to give to you," he confirmed as he presented the tempting looking cake to Imogen. Then he shook hands with Geoffrey and hugged Imogen and their two daughters. Mostly they engaged in chit chat about the family but then it turned to matters in hand.

"I guess that you will be disappointed that you're about to be removed from Marina but it is the safest course of action that we can think of. They could take out their frustrations on you or against the entire planet, so before we do anything about them we are going to take you back to the QvO for safety. After that, the military are going to round up a large cross section of the wild life and seeds and plants and these will be shipped to Ongle by cloaked vessels. We hope that you two will supervise the welfare aspects. We are going to need fodder for the animals also, so before you go I would like you to point out to the military just what they should collect and ship over. The Noah's Ark aspect of the Operation is scheduled to take two weeks and perhaps another week to gather extra food for our guests. At the moment the Supply Branch are creating pens and other structures, in the empty quarter, for the creatures to live in when they arrive. We expect to settle this thing one way or another within the next few weeks."

Geoff got up and went into a bedroom and returned with a thick folder.

"This was left by the original scientific party that

came to Marina, the one the Lodge was built for. It contains descriptions of the food various animals eat and photographs of all of the main animals. Luckily all the animals here are vegetarian, otherwise we would have to catch buckets of insects to feed them," he said as he gave the folder to Peter who glanced at it.

"Just what we needed; that is going to help a lot."

"Churuka," added the mimicmee from beneath the dining room table.

"It keeps saying that," Imogen exclaimed. "We think it equates to eureka and is used by the chimp hunters when they have discovered hidden game."

"Well, it has been a long day, "Peter Berry said, rising to his feet. "I'm going to turn in, if that is ok by you?"

"Your bed is made up and ready." Imogen reassured her uncle. "We are delighted that you are staying with us."

The next morning the Rear Admiral left early for a meeting with a much expanded army presence on Marina; and his opposite number had, overnight, been replaced by a General and together they formulated plans for the evacuation of Marina. A part of that plan was that Geoff and Imogen were to be informed that they were to leave for quarters on the QvO the next morning. Other things were happening, too, and military parties were out cornering and stunning a selection of Marina's animals and sending them back to be transported up to the QvO. It was painstaking work but the military solved it by simply throwing man power at the problem and things were soon flowing efficiently.

Geoff and Imogen were an integral part of the operation and they were desperately needed on the QvO to advise on the rehabilitation of the thousands of animals that were being penned in the ship. When they arrived there, they were aghast to be met with a sea of crates and cages and a rather worried staff who were doing their best but were not trained in animal care. Imogen stepped into the role of supervising the provision of food and water for the captive animals and birds. Geoff busied himself with cataloguing and categorising the seeds that had arrived in packets, with nothing more than digital photographs of the mother plants attached to each packet.

For Imogen it was more demanding because she had found things quite chaotic in the cages when she first arrived. It was not really the fault of the staff because looking after unfamiliar animals had not been anticipated in the space ship curriculums. Eventually she enlisted some of the ship's robots who could then electronically brief other robots and humans in a blink of an eye. After that she relegated the humans to overseeing that there were no glitches in the system and to observe and adjust where any of their charges showed signs of distress. In the meantime, down at the ship's main lake they had created large fish tanks, some saline, some fresh water, to house hatchlings and fertilised eggs gleaned from the waters of Marina the aquatic adults of which were often too large to consider for shipment.

After seven days things had settled down but the

QvO had remained cloaked at some distance from Marina and all transports to and from it were also cloaked. Thus to an observer of Marina's near space, all looked to be serene excepting the military presence on Marina which was professionally adept at concealing the full scope of their operations. As a part of the subterfuge, a lone uncloaked ship continued to make its daily scheduled journey to and from Marina. It was during the Rear Admiral's visit to the animal pens to see that everything was organised and attended to that Geoff mentioned the problem of finding the chimp people's hidden ship.

"I would guess we could never find it unless we crashed into it, so somehow we have got to find a way to make it advertise its' location," he opined.

"Exactly," the Admiral replied, "and that is the problem that has been puzzling my experts these past few days."

"We need to get a radio beacon onto their ship somehow," Imogen volunteered.

"Brilliant! Great minds think alike: I married a genius. That only leads us to how we can achieve that?" Geoff smiled.

"Oh, I know already," Imogen gave them both one of her most attractive smiles, then continued. "Remember the radio active contaminated WHOMER that you left at Jewel Bed Creek. It is still there. The military didn't have time to decontaminate it and they reasoned that it was not too much of a problem because it was only fouled by surface dust and, left alone, the rain would wash it off.

The contaminant would then be so thinly dispersed it would be no worse than the surrounding terrain where the downed chimp ship exploded." Imogen paused to collect her ideas.

"Do you see what I am suggesting?" she said.

"Yes, but not fully, Imogen," Rear Admiral Berry replied. "I can see something developing from it though, please go on."

"My idea is that if we leave the WHOMER there, when the chimp people come back, they will see it as another robot that they can teach to be a hunted quarry. I believe that they will take it back to their spacecraft to reprogram it. However, if we get there first we can install a secret radio beacon in it. Once they have it on their mother ship we can broadcast a code to trigger a squawk response from the WHOMER's secreted radio transponder and we can then triangulate its location." Geoff slipped an arm around Imogen's waist.

"That's my wife," he said with genuine pride.

"Well done," Peter Berry enthused, "let's get onto that right away. "Geoff, can you make the device?"

"I am sure it won't be very difficult," Geoff replied with conviction. "It probably wouldn't be a good idea to have the robot squawking for very long after it received an activation code. Say a one second burst, each time it receives the code. Initially, they will probably look for the robot's normal short range radio locator and once they have disabled it they would likely not think to look for any other devices."

It was left that Geoff should present himself to the Electrical Anomalies Workshop which was where he had originally worked when he first came onboard the QvO, and he was pleased to see that Crusty was still there, although Brian had retired. Of course Crusty was delighted to see Geoff again and welcomed him warmly. Geoff couldn't help but glance at Crusty's claws and pincers and saw that they were indistinguishable from each other since he had lost and regrown one after his mishap in the lake by the tidal wave which had been created when the ship had almost collided with the planet Ambricognia-Mundi.

"Yes, it is as good as it ever was." Crusty had followed his gaze to the previously damaged limb and he clicked its' pincers to demonstrate their effectiveness. Then with his crab stalk eyes he regarded Geoffrey steadily.

"A secret mission, eh! That is the first time that I can ever recall that the Electrical Anomalies Workshop ever became involved with the affairs of State."

"Oh, come on Crusty," Geoff said with a laugh. "This workshop has some of the best brains in electrical engineering in the planetary system; who else would they choose." Unusual for Crusty the praise caught him off guard and he seemed to be flabbergasted and slightly embarrassed.

"You know, in all the time that I have been here in this workshop, we have have had polite words such as please and thank you, even well done, but never praise running to a whole sentence. I will tell the staff!" It was obvious that Crusty was delighted by the tribute to his team.

"Well you can add to that, that the words came from the Rear Admiral, although I fully endorse them myself." Crusty listened without comment as Geoffrey outlined the plan to use the WHOMER as a trojan horse to infiltrate a radio transponder beacon, hidden within its' body, into the chimp people's mother ship.

"Come back tomorrow," he said. "I will get my staff together now and see what we can come up with." When Geoff returned the next day Crusty came out of his office to meet him.

"We think we have a solution for you. Come on, lets meet the think-tank." With that he took Geoff round and introduced him to the present staff and then to his shop floor foreman. "This is Nathan. The brains of the workshop," he explained.

"Ok Nathan, tell Geoff what we have come up with." He clicked a pincer and then rested back by folding his rear legs and Nathan took up the invitation and commenced.

"We looked at the problem overall. First concealment is a major prerequisite which means that the transponder could not be buried in the body or the legs, nor the arms, and certainly not in the head So we have had come up with something that we consider pretty novel. We suggest it should be concealed within the top of the robot's little finger."

"Incredible!" Geoff remarked, "but please explain the method."

"As you know," Nathan continued, "the fingertips of this type of robot are screwed into the finger stump. The only active part of the fingertip is a pressure pad to determine the amount of grip it needs to apply to an object in order to carry out a task with it. There is a metal sensory nerve in the pad that terminates in the robot's brain. We have construed that this nerve can also be used from the finger to the brain of the robot as an internal aerial for it to receive your interrogation code and transmit a one second featureless burst in reply." He looked around the circle of other staff members to assure himself that he was on message.

Witnessing their affirmative nods, Nathan continued with his explanation. "The very instant that the transponder sends its' first response to your coded interrogation it will have simultaneously burnt out the fingertip nerve ending where it connects with the robots brain but the metallic nerve itself will still be in situ and available as radio aerial. The transponder will draw its' power from the power takeoff stud within the stump of the finger where the fingertip screws into it. The fact that you only want the transponder to make a one second burst, when requested, helps a lot, because for the transponder to have any real range it would need to be considerably larger than what can be fitted into a robot's fingertip. But, we can overdrive a smaller device to produce more output power, provided it is not for long, but you must leave a break of at least thirty seconds to allow it to cool down between transmissions," and from a container the size of a match box on Earth, he produced a metallic robot's fingertip. "There you are, the finished article," he handed it to Geoff who glanced down at the small bronze fingertip in the box, perfect even down to the false robot finger nail with a standard non-slip finger print film on the finger pad, authentically copied from the files.

"It's absolutely brilliant," he praised. "I would never have thought of using a fingertip of a robot to hide transponder beacon. How on Earth did you come to that?"

"A joint effort, if you will excuse the pun," said Crusty with his deep booming laugh. "We started with a knee cap as the repository, but we felt that would be more obvious and gradually we moved on to the hand and then the fingertip. Nobody would suspect such a small item could house a transmitter of any appreciable output, but it has been made possible because of the limitations that you have placed on the duration of its transmissions."

The time frame allowed was, of course, critical because the chimp people could find and remove the WHOMER at anytime and Rear Admiral Berry was delighted with the fingertip transponder beacon and moved it on quickly by passing it onto Captain Michael Martin who was the new captain of the QvO with instructions to work with Geoff to get this to the WHOMER marooned at Jewel Bed Creek as a matter of urgency. Rear Admiral Berry further used his overall authority over the operation by suspending all Ongle military activity in that area of Marina for the duration of the venture.

One hour later, Geoffrey found his feet once again treading a familiar Marina territory. Indeed, he discovered that the WHOMER had been found by the chimp people and they had moved it to a position where they had piled up their camping gear, with the probable intention to thwart air surveillance by concealing it under a heap of hewn brushwood. It was clear that they intended to recover all of the items stacked there when their current hunting trip was over. That was not quite yet, they discovered, because sensors on Geoff's cloaked ship had picked up energy discharges about ten kilometres from where the WHOMER and their equipment was stashed, waiting to be backloaded when they returned. There was a danger that the military would also detect and react to the energy weapons being fired so Geoff got through to them urgently to stop the master plan being put in jeopardy by their intervention.

Chapter 4.

COVERT OPERATIONS

For at least the tenth time Geoff checked in his pocket and reassured himself that he still had the box containing the robot fingertip and together with a squad of four soldiers they moved into the clearing but they all dived for cover when a laser beam zipped out from a clump of trees injuring one of the soldiers in their party. At first they could not see their assailant in the undergrowth ahead but then Geoff saw it - a darker mass moving purposefully through the canopy of a tree, with its' hand holding a pistol silhouetted as it intersected an unmasked patch of blue sky. Geoff's reaction was instant and he took aim and fired at the centre of the dark clump with the pistol he was carrying. His bolt missed the chimp which demonstrated its' agility among the trees by scampering down a tree trunk. Now that they had been seen their mission would be irretrievably compromised if it were able to relate their presence to the others of its' kind when they returned. With that in mind, Geoff instantly started running towards where he had seen the chimp descend. His swift reaction was rewarded because he cleared a patch of low scrub before the copse to find a woodland glade behind it and the chimp was making across it to one side, pistol in hand, probably intent upon setting up an ambush position on the far side. Because of the urgency of the changed circumstances, Geoff had no time to stop and press the target acquire button on his pistol so he held back the trigger on his pistol and a continuous stream of short beams of light shot out and he was able to sweep the area with them to interdict the chimp's line of escape.

"Luckily I didn't kill it," Geoff remarked to the others as they caught him up where he stood surveying the injured chimp which was bearing its teeth and screeching at him; and he raised his pistol again and shot it with a stun charge. That should keep it quiet for at least ten minutes; we can temporarily activate the WHOMER to attend to its' wounds and then take our new friend back with us. A glance at the WHOMER showed that it had been tampered with and an inspection panel on one of its' arms had not been secured properly after it had been unclipped but it was still serviceable and when they directed it to do so it took bandages and an anti-bacterial spray from cavities which it opened in its' metal torso and professionally attended to the chimp's wounded leg.

"Give it an anaesthetic, too, enough to last twenty minutes," Geoff instructed; and in compliance the robot produced a syringe and a bottle of opiate from yet another cavity in its' body and did his bidding.

"Now," Geoff spoke to the robot, "please assume the exact position where you were standing before we reactivated you." He knew that the instruction would be carried to the nearest millimetre, even down to the incline of the head and the position of its' arms and legs. "So far so good," Geoff muttered. "We can't take a chance in you remembering these last few minutes, so please purge your memory of everything that has happened in the past hour and then deactivate yourself completely. Acknowledge."

"I am deactivating now," it said as all of its' indicator lights faded to black. Geoff came forward and switched off the reminder bell which would otherwise toll every five minutes to draw attention to the fact that the robot was switched off. From a pocket he produced a pair of pliers and removed the tip of the little finger of the robot and replaced it with the tip that had been fabricated for him by Crusty's workshop.

"A pity we had to shoot him," the military commander of the party came forward and pointed to the sedated chimp. "We have to take him back with us or he would give the game away. We don't have a stretcher on-board so we will have to use a blanket to carry it." Any further discussion regarding the chimp was cut short by the crackle of an energy discharge, much closer this time than when they had first landed.

"They must be on their way back," Geoff cautioned, "we had better move out." Any observing, medical student would have been somewhat shocked to see the chimp carried away quite so roughly by his military bearers, but the military had other priorities in mind and the chimp was bundled unceremoniously into their waiting cloaked vessel which took off at once in the silent mode. Geoffrey looked back at the WHOMER that they had left there and felt a pang of remorse at having deserted an old friend in the face of enemy and to an unknown fate. But common sense asserted itself and reminded him that it was a calculated risk towards a greater goal.

"We'll give the medics a day to fix his injury, then we will see if our captive can help us with our enquiries!" Captain Martin grimaced. "Then perhaps we can get a handle on their ship with or without its' help." Those involved in the plan assembled the next morning on the bridge where Geoff had keyed the responder code into an external radio transmitter. "It requires using two separate directional receiving aerials," "he informed the group as the requisite vessels slipped in stealth mode out of the QvO's hanger bay and positioned themselves in the segment of space where it was assumed that the chimp ship could be concealed. By mid-morning they had got a positive response and a bearing and a cheer went up on the bridge of the QvO. The readings had confirmed, as they had suspected, that the alien ship was in a synchronous orbit above Jewel Bed Creek. "Maintain your positions," the Captain instructed the vessels.

"Please do a triangulation every thirty minutes and report any movements of the alien ship."

Rear Admiral Berry was back from a trip to Ongle and together with Captain Martin they were pawing over the readings. Captain Martin informed Geoffrey that the chimp ship was only five-hundred kilometres above Marina and because of the danger of causing earthquakes or atmospheric disorder it was too close to take the QvO in, so measures to subordinate the chimp vessel would have to be accomplished by smaller craft. It followed that the Rear Admiral called for a conference to be convened to form a think-tank."The problem is, the military have rightly advised, at the slightest suspicion of coming under attack by a superior force, the chimps will engage their dark matter transit and be anywhere in universe within a millisecond, so it would have to be attacked with an instant and overwhelming force sufficient to downgrade its' DM capability. There are rules," however he said "regarding launching an attack upon what may be a defenceless vessel. In the main, the rules stipulate that life would be endangered if an action were not taken. They have, so far, only proved themselves to be a nuisance to us and they have an apparent total disregard for the wildlife of Marina which is probably a cultural attitude but they have never carried out a premeditated act of hostility towards us."

The meeting regrettably became bogged down with the amount of force that could reasonably be justified in the circumstances, before Imogen intervened. As if in deep thought, she said slowly.

"I wonder about our captive. Could he perhaps give us some pointers? I understand that he has come round and he is being kept in locked quarters but so far it has accepted its' fate without remonstration. It has not been regarded as likely to voluntarily render us information of vital importance so no attempt has been made to question it." The chimp was surprised to receive company and backed against one of the walls of its' quarters and bared its teeth at the ugly humans, from its own point of view, as they filed in through into the space outside of its' cell.

They sat down on the chairs which two robots had carried in and plaeed in a semi circle around the now open cell entrance. Objective to not creating alarm, Geoffrey unhurriedly approached the chimp and pointed to his hucom and to the one that he was carrying and indicated that the chimp should put it on its' head in the same manner that he was wearing it. It could not be said that the chimp appeared willing but Geoff went around and pointed to all the people there and to their headbands and the chimp, with its' eyes betraying mistrust, slipped the headband over its' head, the wrong way round, and there followed a humorous period of gesticulation causing everybody to laugh.

Geoffrey gently projected his thoughts towards the chimp which reacted fiercely and tore off the hucom and smashed it to the floor and jumped on it. Then, in a single bound, it sought refuge on a shelf above the audience and berated them with screams and gestures. "It's too much," Geoff remarked. "It is receiving all of your thoughts at once. Everyone else, please switch your hucoms to receive only. I suggest that Imogen asks it the questions; she is rather good at that!" Imogen looked quizzically at him. "That is praise, not criticism darling," Geoff assured her. "You have a gentler method than I; and I don't think our guest would respond to being bullied."

The chimp brightened at Imogen's approach with outstretched arm and her dazzling smile and she swept an arm around to indicate the two chairs placed facing the row of representatives from the QvO and it grudgingly perched on the edge of one and allowed Imogen to replace a hucom over its' head. Through their hucoms the rest of the group could see that the chimp had immediately trusted Imogen's gentle manner and a kaleidoscope of images and life on its' own planet and hunting expeditions flashed through the minds of the audience.

"We welcome you and we are sorry that you were injured." Imogen opened the conversation. "We wish you no harm." The chimp was taken aback at her voice speaking to him in its' head and it barred its' teeth towards her but she held up her hand in a sign of peace and it settled down to watch her.

"My name is Imogen." she pointed to herself and then to him. He looked at her uncertainly for a moment then pointed to himself.

"I am the much decorated 'Ace Hunter' Mogid."

"For brevity I will call you just Mogid," Imogen said sincerely. "Well, Mogid," she said. "The planet you were hunting on belongs to the Chief Minister For The Supreme Council of the Ongle System Of Planets on behalf of its' people. We do not allow hunting there." Mogid grimaced.

"Our understanding is that it is populated by two adults and two children. They cannot use a whole planet themselves. We feel entitled to hunt there if we wish."

"You are aware of the principle of ownership on your own planet, Morgid?"

"Of course," Mogid replied.

"Then please understand, Mogid, the owner may do what they like with their own property, provided in doing so they do not harm or endanger other people," Imogen asserted.

"That does not apply to animals," Mogid shot back. "The purpose of animals is for us to hunt. That is our express right, who says that it is not?"

"We all say it is not," Imogen censured. "We hunt animals, too, but in a controlled way and we keep them for certain purposes, but we do not take more than we need and we try to attend to the welfare of wild animals and consider that they have rights to live their lives naturally and not to be hunted for sport. The planet Marina is a nature reserve and we allow its' animals to roam and develop freely."

"Twaddle," Morgid replied. "Your men are not manly then."

"I wouldn't say that." Imogen was quick to reply. "You are the decorated Ace Hunter Mogid, yet you were bested by one of our men in a firefight; and our man has never hunted animals and believes that they should be allowed to live free and independent lives on Marina and elsewhere. You were beaten, so you are not an Ace Hunter after all, Mogid. Our people prove their abilities in other ways, none of which involve killing, unless they are first attacked. We are strong when we are required to be strong but we do not spend all of our lives proving that we are heroic."

For a while Mogid sat there in front of his audience

refusing to engage in conversation so Rear Admiral Berry dissolved the meeting and asked Geoffrey and Imogen to stay behind and see if they could get anywhere with their charge. With a sudden brainwave, Geoff logged into the ship's archives via his hucom and began to relay a video over it of the battle that Ongle and the AMC had fought against the Rap-Terrabot fleet. Missiles and exploding ships were everywhere and the Ongle fleet was in peril of defeat. Then the Ambrocognia-Mundi fleet arrived. Their timely arrival reversed what had been a sure win for Rap-Terrabot who were routed and chased away. From having been initially dismissive, Mogid began to take an interest as cameras panned in to record the bodies and debris from both sides of the conflict drifting in space across the area of conflict.. Mogrid looked at them in awe.

"That is how you hunt?"

"No, not at all." Geoff confirmed. "That is how we defend ourselves if we are attacked. The men, and women, too, on those ships do not set out to prove that they are brave, although they are. Their principle is that they are defending what they believe to be right and their right to be free and not hunted down and treated as you would treat animals."

"I see," Mogid frowned." Can I see more."

"Of course you can; we will teach you how to use the hucom that you are wearing to access the ship's archives and we will call and see you tomorrow."

When they got back into their cottage in English village Imogen was rather taken aback to see Geoffrey make a beeline for a computer. Seeing her glance, he stopped and explained. "I won't be a minute," he excused himself, "I have just realised that Mogid is using a guest hucom so its' use is monitored and every search he makes will be recorded." He turned and tapped a security password into a computer. "Aha, he is looking at the insurrection and Tom Wong. That won't do him any harm. I think we can leave him to it."

"Good, I have hardly touched my man all day, but we first must collect the children from Angela. We are really lucky, you know, to have Angela; she is so good with them sometimes I have to nearly prise them apart."

"Come on then," he grabbed her hand, "let's get our kids back," and they ran laughing together from the cottage to the Manor where Angela lived and from where she ran a thriving day nursery for working parents. They learned, as told to the children by Angela, that the Scottish haggis had two short legs on one side of its' body which enables it to run around steep hillsides without toppling over. Imogen caught the slow wink that Geoffrey gave her and giggled.

The news that Captain Martin told them next morning was that Rear Admiral Berry had left the QvO and returned to his offices on Ongle. Captain Martin also requested them to drop in on Mogid to see if any progress had been made; and indeed it had, they learned when they paid their visit to him. He was still using the hucom and reports confirmed that he had been doing so all through the night and he could barely drag himself away from it when they entered his quarters.

"A remarkable device," he enthused as he turned towards them. "I have learned much about your people and your worlds."

"Did you sleep well?" Imogen enquired, although she knew that he had not slept at all; but she hoped to draw out the reason, objectively to see if there was anything extra that they could do to improve his comfort.

"Sleep," Mogid answered. "No, I did not sleep. My sleep cycle starts tomorrow and then I shall sleep for three of your days. You will not be able to contact me at all."

"How extraordinary!" Imogen exclaimed. "Do all of your people go to sleep for the same three days?"

"Certainly not, all at one time, it is elective which days you will sleep and it tends to mirror your occupation, so people engaged in a similar project such as working in a factory all select the same days, this prevents disruption. My colleagues on our hunting party will also sleep at the same time as myself so that we can face all of the challenges as a group."

"Do you need anything, food, etc. during your sleep?" Geoffrey was inquisitive.

"I need nothing at all because I will not wake up until my regenerative sleep is over."

"Oh well, then," Geoffrey replied, "do call us now if you need anything today."

"I am more than happy with this hucom and I have found some quite palatable food prepared by one of your catering robots; but what is to happen to me?"

"It has not been fully decided yet," Geoff briefed him, "but the consensus of opinion is that you are to be returned to your home world."

"That was the sort of information that we were looking for," Geoff affirmed to Imogen as they sped to a meeting with Captain Martin. "It seems that the entire hunting party will be out like a light for three days. That is probably the reason they have stayed on in orbit and they will be very difficult to reawaken. I think that we have found their weak spot." The Captain was delighted with their information.

"We have pinpointed the exact location of their mother ship but we have not approached it for fear of forcing them to do a DMT. I am sure that we can make good use of the information that you have given us," he told them.

The plan, as it evolved, was simple. They would continue to clandestinely observe Mogid until he was judged to be sound asleep and then Geoffrey and four military crew members and an engineering robot (engbot) would take a scout craft over to the chimp ship. Of the present they only had an approximate fixed position made several minutes ago but space craft tend to pitch and yaw when they are in a fixed orbit so there was a risk of a collision with it if they were too close. Geoff suggested firing an invisible wide angle maser beam at the cloaked ship so that its' bulk would intersect it. Another craft, positioned behind the target could monitor and report its' stability to them. Then it was to be a case of men donning space walk kits and taking tools and a portable airlock and jetting over to the hull of the chimp's vessel to force an entry into it.

For the raid, their space suits and helmets had been especially blackened making them sinister and all but invisible against the backdrop of the universe. For propulsion they were powered by one single jet pack, with each member of the party holding on to a single long line from the leader and they drifted over in this strung-out formation towards the cloaked chimp ship. Once there they first erected a substantial air lock on the hull. The engineering robot with them used its specially designed fingers to electrically weld the air lock airtight to the hull. It was a lengthy operation and more than once Geoffrey had to switch his helmet blowers on to dry out the sweat which trickled down his face. From inside the airlock the engbot was again employing its' ability to melt metal with its' fingers and it cut out a lid into the hull, leaving just a tongue of metal to stop it crashing down into the ship. The versatility of the robot did not stop there because it was also scheduled, as per plan, to be first into the airlock. On command 'ready' it then applied its' mechanical strength to lever the lid up so that it was now upright and supported only by the bent back tongue and the robot looked down through the opening and signified all was clear by dropping down inside.

It a was great feeling of relief that things had gone so well as they set about organising a 'should it be needed' defendable escape route. Once they had gained access the commander of the party signalled to the QvO, requesting the remainder of the military occupation force to be despatched to secure the ship; and when they arrived they seeped silently through it. Essentially, they could see that it was a ship designed to be crewed by robots because it offered no crew comforts at all, not even a chair, although the chimps had strategically placed boxes to sit on where it was essential for a biological body to maintain a stationary position before the computers and the guidance systems. It took them several hours to methodically work their way through the ship, room by room, until they at last discovered a dormitory with the chimp crew all sound asleep on mattresses on the floor, the mattresses apparently stuffed with vegetation gleaned from Marina.

The party soundlessly tiptoed through the sleeping chimps, slipping manacles over their wrists and feet and moved on to continue to search the rest of the craft. In the holds they found the two remaining chimp INAT vessels which they had employed to descend to Marina for their hunts. That done, Geoff studied the bridge control console. The task was made particularly difficult because its' previous robot owners had no need of identification symbols on the switches because they could address their own internal memory regarding their functions. The chimps, he envisaged, with time on their side, had worked it out. But judging the likely use of the switches by their position, he made a few tentative stabs at lowering the cloak and after trial and error he was successful when a screen lit up to show a real time picture of the ship's hull emerging from a virtual mist. As it did so, unheard by him, a round of cheering and clapping resounded on the bridge of the distant QvO.

"Well done," Captain Martin signalled. "We are now going to de-cloak and close your position. We propose to drag the Rap-Terrabot ship into our main hanger bay, prisoners included. Please stay there while we fix the grapple and complete the procedure." Even in space the colossus of the one-hundred and seventy kilometre ship was mind blowing and, as Geoff looked, the great mouth of the hanger deck opened widely for them. From somewhere in the recesses of the hanger two grapples wavered snake-like out towards them with a robot astride each grapple. As the grapples neared the chimp ship the two robots vacated their perches and hand guided the grapples to the most likely strong points of the chimp ship and with a minimum of fuss the ship was drawn into the jaws of the QvO. Once they were inside, the massive doors closed and air hissed in through nozzles to recharge the hanger deck to normal atmospheric pressure. With that, Geoff and his recent companions egressed the chimp ship as a relief security and a scientific team entered through the same doorways. Within minutes they were, no doubt, busily inspecting the pre-owned Rap-Terrabot warship in minute detail.

Two days later, all of the chimps woke in a very different world to the one that they were accustomed to and, on finding their hands and legs manacled, gave loud voice to their displeasure and fears by screaming their anger at their human captors whenever they appeared. In the end, at Imogen's suggestion, they fetched Mogid. The sight of him walking in unfettered silenced the chimps but they were sullen and probably regarding him as a traitor to their kind. Yet, calmly he sat amid them relating what he had seen and been told of their captors who wished them no personal harm but whose strange ways forbade them from hunting for pleasure. The hardest pill for them to swallow was that to prevent them ever returning to this planet the humans would confiscate the vessel that the chimps had found and availed as their own. The humans were not going to repurpose it as their own, he told them. When they had learned its' secrets they were going to destroy it by projecting it into a star.

In the coming week the chimps, to a greater or lesser extent, accepted that, even if unmanly in their eyes, the humans were honest and they had allowed them liberty in their own quarters but they were not permitted to visit any other part of the ship. They were all provided with hucoms so that, under Mogid's instructions, they were able to electrically tour the QvO's archives and they even grudgingly admitted that the battles that the searches uncovered were infinitely more dangerous than hunting, but hunting was in their blood and culture.

Later, in general conversation, Geoffrey ventured the subject of sport to them. It was an alien concept to them. 'Why would anybody waste energy competing in something which yielded no return and no cultural status on their planet?' they asked. So he showed them videos copied from Earth television of track events, cycle racing, skiing and football, even cricket and baseball. They were definitely interested in that; and they were very excited by the Olympic Games.

"It appeals to them because if they could win they would get to stand on a podium as victors in front of thousands of other chimps and receive homage; they would also get a medal to wear. I wouldn't mind betting that they will have a version of the Olympic Games before long." Geoff ventured his opinion.

"That would be nice," Imogen agreed, "but I feel they would include hunting as one of the events somewhere down the line."

When their studies of the Chimp's Rap-Terrabot ship was complete they permitted the chimp people to witness its' destruction as it was towed out near a star. It would become too radioactive in decay, they told the chimps. If it were left in space like that it could, one day, crash onto an inhabited planet. They watched it solemnly as its' flight path described a figure of eight to align itself to point at the star's churning surface and then it made its' fatal dive; and in one bright flash of light it was gone. From there they made a DMT jump to Zalfn which the chimps had pointed out on star charts as being their home world. The Captain addressed their guests and told them that he was soon to ask them to board their two ships which had been hauled out to docking bays of the QvO. The Rap-Terrabot ship itself, he told them, had been deemed a technological leap too far. If they had continued to use it in the manner that they had, they would antagonise other races many which would have the full means of making war on Zalfn. He urged them to think of the videos that they had watched on the ship and understand the illustration they gave of just how devastating wars between worlds could be; and they would simply not be able to defend themselves against a technologically advanced species. In such a war even the innocents would be slaughtered en masse and the very atmosphere of their planets would become deadly to their own inhabitants.

The chimps were quiet as they filed into their ships through the docking tubes. Their silence made obvious that they did not like losing their mother ship, but at the same time they were grateful that they had not been mistreated and they were still alive. "It seems a pity to deprive them of their ship," Geoff whispered the words to Imogen.

"I know what you mean," she said, "but it wasn't really theirs and it was cutting-edge technologically streets ahead of their present evolutionary status, but I feel justified mainly because they were using its' special dark matter transit facility to enable them to hunt animals across the cosmos. They still have some growing up to do before they are able to venture out into deep space again."

"You are right, of course," Geoff agreed."I didn't tell you before but before they went Mogid asked me for a whole raft of videos, especially back copies of Olympic Games and World Games recorded by the QvO from Earth television channels; and he also asked for copies of the great battles we had against the Rap-Terrabot armadas and even some of the broadcast wildlife films which we had recorded. I asked him what he wanted them for and he is obviously an individual always open to the main chance. There was nothing like them on Zalfn, he told me, so he is going to go into business copying and selling them. You figure in quite a few of them, so you are probably going to become the first ever inter galactic actress."

"Oh, gosh!" she put her hand to her mouth. "I don't wish to appear racist but the thought of some of those spidery looking creatures pawing over me doesn't thrill me at all."

"Wait until you get their fan mail," Geoff laughed, and dug her in the ribs playfully.

"DMT jump to Marina imminent," the message came to them via their hucoms, then additional information followed. "Please be advised. Rear Admiral Berry has left instructions to the effect that two military detachments are to be put down on Marina. One detachment will be located in the forest near to the Grande Lodge and the other will be situated at Jewel Bed Creek. The detachments will continue with roulement of four months until it is decided that they are no longer required on Marina."

"I think they are really looking forward to it," Imogen confided to Geoff. "I have heard that they had to put their names in the hat, with a prize of being selected for detachment to Marina."

"Probably the fact that they will also be drawing untaxable deep space allowance was an added motivation. It is also a once in a lifetime experience as well, so something they will never forget." Geoff mimicked their possible look of delight.

"That, too." Imogen agreed. "Initially they will help with the repatriation of the animals that we brought on board to protect their species in the event of bad turning to even worse."

Chapter 5

AMC AMSTAR

Their return to Marina was touched with sadness because in a way they felt that their planet had been violated. It still looked the same, the animals were just the same, but the notion of innocence lost troubled their minds. The chimp people had imported and demonstrated their ability to wantonly destroy and kill. Now, albeit for their protection, the weaponry of the military was present on Marina. It was machinery which had the sole purpose to kill and it was secreted in jungle glades around the Lodge. Its' lethality, if anything, multiplied the new unease and the most recent addition to the Lodge was an arms chest. Imogen felt it more than most; the children had new things to explore amongst the army equipment but Imogen was saddened because she felt more deeply the loss of the purity that had existed before the chimps came.

The military also made it clear that their presence there as Wardens of the planet added additional security concerns and commitments to their task which they would rather not have to take onboard. It would also mean a loss of privacy for them because their roving patrols would include the Grande Lodge in their daily and nightly sweeps, not to mention IR beam intruder alerts focused across walkways and other, considered to be, weak point approaches to the Lodge. So, the feeling grew in them that they had had the best of Marina for the present.

Thus, after a lot of soul searching Geoffrey and Imogen put their case for a respite from Marina, until it was returned to normality, to the Supreme Council (military section) for Ongle and it was agreed by them, but they pointed out that Geoffrey was still a paid Officer of the Space Fleet and he would either have to resign or be available for duty with them if he returned to Ongle. There were some serious family discussions with Imogen and the girls and they decided to opt for Geoff remaining in Space Fleet. It was not that they relished the prospect of more separations but, at the moment, Marina seemed tarnished and they took the decision to return to Ongle for a while until things had settled down. They were mostly silent as they packed their bags and walked to the landing pad to await a pilotless shuttle to let down and the conversation they had was mostly to placate their two girls with promises of a return one day.

If that was not enough for their minds to deal with, they were also running slide rules through their thoughts to measure the ups and downs of their decision. They both knew that each of them was wavering constantly above and below the 'must commit line.' But always, the general consensus of their thoughts coalesced around the fact that only a part of Geoff's time would be spent in space and at any time they wished to resume life on Marina they could, if it were safe to do so. Geoffrey would automatically be paid as an Officer of the Fleet, be he on Marina or elsewhere in the universe, but he would lose some pension rights if he resigned his Commission.

In the meantime they were entitled to a statutory two weeks settling in time in their new quarters at Ongle, near the Ministry of Defence complex of buildings; erstwhile Geoffrey was to receive his new posting as an exchange officer seconded to the Ambrocognian-Mundi Colligate fleet. Secondment had become a customary practice after the battles which their united fleets had fought against their common enemy. Now every substantial warship of either star system would carry a seconded officer to keep alive and continue to cement the spirit of co-operation and friendship which had been laid down between the two races in the two wars which had threatened their very existence.

When the order finally come through it was in military terms, ordering Geoffrey to report for a period of secondment to the Ambrocognia-Mundi ship the AMStar. The ship would be passing through the Ongle system of planets at some time in the next week and it would despatch a shuttle to pick him up at Spaceport, Ongle city. He would be informed later of the exact reporting time. Imogen would, of course, remain on Ongle with the two girls who needed continuity of schooling and the security of a home atmosphere, so the parting was sad when Imogen came with the girls to wave him off; and their youngest daughter Sophia, who bore her emotions heavily, was in floods of tears.

By tradition, all Colligate space shuttles were painted

absolute white and the shuttle gleamed in the sunlight as it curved down through the sky to Spaceport and landed and discharged a Colligate Officer who was to work at the Ongle Ministry of Defence, while Geoffrey replaced him on the AMStar. Geoff paused on the steps of the shuttle to wave to Imogen and the children and, as he turned and entered the craft, he observed that the pilot was a woman. When she moved to acknowledge him he saw with surprise the same wavy brown hair and brown eyes that he had glimpsed so briefly when he had made the 'first contact' between Ongle and Ambrocognia-Mundi, when she had flipped her visor just briefly to reveal that she was humanoid. At the time Geoffrey recalled he had no such option with his own visor and in any case it would have been considered far too dangerous to carry out. Their reintroduction as they welcomed each other was special because that first meeting where they had met in space.was now on-record as the kickstart for a new chapter in their respective home world's inter galactic histories. It was recorded along with their names in the history books of the two planetary systems. "Alisia," she said extending her hand which he took and told her they had all come a long way since their initial meeting.

"Yes, indeed," she said, "hardly a week went by without my being interviewed on television or by some journalist or other who wanted to write a column in their newspaper about it."

"Ah yes," Geoff retorted. "It has been much the same for Imogen and myself; the media hounded us over the smallest details."

"Imogen," Alisia smiled. "Do tell her that the women of AMC are delighted with the makeup that she introduced us to. It still sells like hotcakes in the Colligate and there is even a company that manufactures makeup under the name 'Imogen'."

"She will be delighted to hear that," Geoff rejoined, "but tell me, is the use of the acronym AMC officially approved for use instead of Ambrocognian-Mundi Colligate?"

"Indeed," Alisia smiled. "Only our government officials and your people on the Ongle system of planets tend to use the full name every time. You may certainly refer to it as AMC, we do!"

"That is of great relief," and he sounded relieved, too. "I sometimes trip over my tongue using the full title," to which Alisia giggled,

"There you are then, you have made progress already and you have not yet fully stepped into the craft." Geoff looked beneath his feet and flustered a little that he was still technically outside of the aircraft.

"All aboard now pilot," he confirmed and she waved him to a seat beside her.

The AMStar grew out of space as they approached it, first a tiny flashing beacon developing into a child's toy which you could have picked up and put in your pocket, but now as they came near it grew and grew until it was arguably the same size as the Qee van Ongle. "Like your QvO," she informed him. "The AMStar is its' equivalent in our Collegiate and it has the same variety of uses but, unlike the QvO, the AMStar has a metallic skin."

"Initially the QvO made sense to us," he said, "because space exploration was nearly always a long term project so it had to carry everything with it to survive for years without being able to return to the 'home world.' In the circumstances it had to provide as near as possible a normal life for its' crew. Of course, for us, DMT was in its' infancy then and the QvO was so expensive and so heavily populated that it was not allowed to DMT until the dark matter itself had been reported as stable every day for three months. This meant that she could be years waiting for a window of opportunity. Later events have illustrated to us that we were not wrong, but your risk-less dark matter transit update to the QvO has now made travel between galaxies routine, instantaneous and safe."

"We would agree with that," she nodded. "We have two other ships of the same size and design as the AMStar, but the AMStar is the latest addition to the Star Class ships, hence the most up to date and likewise the most expensive!"

The floodlit hanger doors of the AMStar yawned to admit the shuttle and as they converged with the ship a limpet tug came out to meet them and it magnetically attached itself to their hull and used its' own motive power to propel them into AMStar. White, Geoff noted, seemed to be a favourite with the Colligate because the interior of the hanger was white, even down to the floor. He was a little unsure when he saw it and secretly hoped that not everything was characterless white, but he was to discover that otherwise they used normal colours and hues of colours but white was lavishly applied where visibility dictated its' over-riding requirement.

They were met by the Captain of the ship, Captain Moska, who was waiting for them to alight from the shuttle. He shook hands with Geoff and welcomed him warmly and told him that he was pretty much a celebrity onboard and the crew were all eager to meet him and that he would be working as the ship's radio officer; and the Captain came with him on what the crew called a skid which was a flat open vehicle with a guardrail round it. Captain Moska explained that it was officially called 'deck transport' and these vehicles followed subfloor guidelines and they were intended for local use and in this case it would transport them to a vacuum tube centre. From there it was a ten minute journey followed by another skid at the other end of it where the Captain showed him to his quarters which were spacious and included a control console in its own right.

"Sometimes Bridge officers, as you are now, are contacted to make executive decisions when they are off duty. From your console you can contact any part of the ship and log in and monitor any communication channel and make diagnostics and command judgements, which means that you do not always have to attend to a problem in person. Luckily it is not used that often but you will discover how useful it can be, if it is. Anyway, once again, welcome on board, Geoff, I hope that you enjoy your stay and I am looking forward to working with you. I have arranged for a social robot to contact you tomorrow morning and escort you to the bridge where I can introduce you to everybody. Oh, you may hear the word Ayer mentioned. That translates to Captain in your language, but the hucoms will take care of most translations" and with a nod and a smile he left.

Geoff took stock of his quarters. He had a small kitchen, a shower, a lounge and a bedroom, but most of all he appreciated that he had a porthole to space outside. That was something missing on the QvO, he thought. True we had a screen showing us space outside but it seemed to be second hand and filtered, compared to an actual view. He stood for several moments looking out to space but was returned to the moment by the sound of a discrete knock on the door of his quarters which, when opened, revealed a robot towing a luggage cart and the five suitcases lovingly packed by Imogen. For a while he busied himself with unpacking them into the various lockers and wardrobes. In one of the cases he found a love letter and a box of his favourite chocolates and he felt his love for her welling up inside as he relocated his possessions into what he guessed were the appropriate locations. Alisia came up via hucom to remind him to eat. "Officers eat in their Messes. There are several of them spread around the ship; they have your menus prepared for us by Ongle but it is best to nominate which particular Mess that you will be using so that they can have the ingredients to hand to prepare for you. The closest Mess to you is one floor down on the lift in front of your door and you will find the Mess is right in front of you," and he thanked her.

Modernity was everywhere you looked and a far cry from the simple living on Marina and he was amused to see on a menu that they were able to supply a full English breakfast, well probably as good a copy as one could get. He chuckled inwardly over some of the copies of Earth food that he had been presented with in the past. But he reminded himself that it was still officially morning in the AMC so he went down to the Officers' Mess and had a late breakfast but, by now, everybody was at work and he had the pleasant restaurant style Mess to himself, except for the catering robots who fussed around him resetting the tables for lunch. After he had returned to his quarters he spent some of the day setting things out and getting to know the console in his room. It was so easy, he knew, to make a faux pas in an environment where the tradition of ages existed, so he allocated the rest of the day to studying the ship's routine via the console and directly through an interlink with the ship's archives.

Chapter 6

THE COMMUNE

The next morning Geoff responded to a rap at the door to his quarters and found himself looking at a robot.

"I am Henry. I am a social robot and I am here to conduct you to the ship's bridge. It is only a short walk so mechanical transport will not be required."

"Thank you, Henry," Geoff replied.

"It is my pleasure, sir," Henry responded smoothly. Henry was chatty as they walked and wanted to know if robots on Ongle had any free time and seemed to be pleased to learn that they did; and he wondered if he would ever be able to meet any of them.

"That is not beyond the bounds of possibility," Geoff assured him, "but I don't quite know how that could be arranged. What would be the advantage of it?"

"We all have different ways of doing things," Henry answered suavely. "There are lessons that could be learned which will improve efficiency for everybody on Ongle and AMC alike."

"Hmm, I wouldn't have thought of that, you may be right. Leave it with me and I will ask around and see if there are objections or difficulties and get back to you at some time in the future."

"Thank, you sir." There seemed to be a discernible warmth in Henry's reply.

Geoff was still smiling about their conversation and he smiled more widely when he entered the bridge and saw that it was a cutting edge environment, indeed, and that Captain Moska sat on a stage with screens and operators in a lowered floor well before him. Geoff humorously thought that if the Captain was given a conductor's batten it would complete the picture. But there was nothing really wrong with the set up, it was efficient. The Captain rose and came to meet Geoff and he repeated that his reputation had proceeded him and they were, indeed, lucky that he had been seconded to this ship. He then showed Geoffrey over the bridge and explained the area on it where he was to work and they talked for a while. Then the Captain said that, right now, he wanted Geoff to take the next three days off and get around the ship as much as possible so that he could learn where the major parts of it were and how they could be reached.

"Don't be afraid to ask," he added. "The Colligate has no secrets from Ongle, so go where you like. Everybody knows that you are here, so there will be no problems with regards to your identity."

Alisa had been nominated to show Geoff around if he wished and he availed himself of her help and spent most of the day visiting workshops and engineering departments. But he found that they could not visit the forward section of the ship at all.

"What is up there that is so secret?" He pointed and laughed.

"None of us are allowed up there without a permit except the Captain," she explained. "The AMStar is on a peaceful patrol around the Colligation planets. We have more room onboard than we need so the government allow people to book holidays and travel with us. They have hotel like accommodation up there at the front. It is particularly popular with students and whole schools come sometimes, so there are also educational facilities included so they can continue to educate their pupils on the journey. People get off at various planets and we pick them up weeks later, but if we are unable to do so they have to find their own way back via commercial shipping. If there was the slightest hint of trouble, requiring a military response, we would set them down on one of our planets or send them home in space runabouts. Ships of this size are expensive to run and the government can recoup some of the cost by hiring out a part of the ship."

"It is a novel idea," Geoff was amused. "I wonder what our Ministry of Defence would say if I were to suggest a similar use for the QvO!"

"We also found it distinctly odd in the beginning," Alisia remarked, "but the guests are self-contained and they have tour guides and space vehicles. We hardly see them. The pitfall for them is that the ship could come under instructions to ditch its' present schedule, in which case they could find themselves put down almost anywhere. That had not happened at all until quite recently," she added. "That time was when the Rap-Terrabot fleet invaded the Colligation; then we managed to put all of the paying passengers down on one of our home worlds before we left, so they didn't have to involuntarily partake in the war."

Geoff was gaining in confidence with the transport system and how things worked; and Alisia drove him hard to remember all the instructions and guidelines that she poured out at him like a torrent. Then she gave him a slightly worried smile and told him that she had to leave for duty, but not to forget that he could call her on his hucom if he got into difficulties. With a backward wave she ran off in the direction of the vacuum tube line and Geoffrey was pitched into fending for himself in an alien super-sized ship. It was only a few kilometres shorter than the QvO but he learned through tapping into the computers which were available everywhere, that it had less than half of the crew of the QvO but, of course, intended missions for the two ships differed. The QvO was intended for deep space penetration. Whereas, the AMStar by comparison and for historic reasons concerning AMC security, rarely ventured out of its own planetary system. The AMStar itself also relied much more on automated function controllers than did the QvO but the pluses and minuses generally evened out the capabilities of the two ships.

Inevitably Geoff took a wrong turning somewhere

and got lost. This didn't worry him a lot because he knew he could always ask for directions via his hucom, but he felt it was an adventure and a privilege to be left entirely alone to wander at will in the belly of this humongous ship. Currently he was deciding the purpose of the various ducts in the corridors and he busied his mind with studying their engineering architecture and trying to work out which ducts were doing what and why. Sometimes in his curiosity he put his ear up alongside them and was satisfied when he heard the hiss of air or spotted inset faucets. Thereafter he knew the colour codings of the water and air ducts, leaving the remainder as being probably electrical.

Engrossed in looking at the walls, he had come round a corner and found that he had reached a dead end. However, a metre square inspection plate with a wedge shaped handle on it caught his attention because it rattled, followed by the sound of hammer blows from the inside. As he drew closer he could hear voices within and more hammer blows. His immediate thought was that a workman had climbed in through the hole and that a comedy of errors had ensued in which the lid had dropped back and the wedge handle had slid down leaving the workman trapped inside. Certain that he was about to rescue somebody, he lifted the handle so that he might open the hatch, but the handle was detachable and it was only slotted into a spiral boss but not otherwise fixed to the hatch plate. It came off its' boss which caused him to lose his now unbalanced grip on the handle and it dropped out of his hand with a clatter to the floor.

He had bent down instinctively trying but failing to catch it mid-descent but he was too late. It was to be a life saving move, he was now to discover, because as he had bobbed down to catch the handle an energy bolt buzzed through the space above his head. Then a hand with a pistol in it came through the hatch and tried to shoot down the vertical wall at the foot of which Geoffrey had now taken cover. Being unarmed and at the foot of the wall left him without a cogent plan. He could attempt to run or try to close the cover plate because he now had the handle to it in his grasp, but a hand holding a pistol and half of an arm was through the inspection cover and a series of exertive grunts indicated that somebody was trying to climb through it, which limited his option of making a run for it. With the arm and pistol now through and past its' elbow, Geoff crouched down on his haunches in order to get the full power of his thigh muscles as he sprung upwards and slashed at the arm with the heavy handle. A dull crunch of breaking bone accompanied the action and there was screech of pain and the arm withdrew and the pistol clattered to the floor of the corridor and he completed his action by slamming the hatch door shut and putting the handle in the worm boss and tightening it down as far as it would go and then he stood before it.

Geoff's hucom was currently pre-set one to one with Alisia and she was aghast when he told her but also very proactive and in seconds she told him that security were on their way and would be with him in less than three minutes. Above his head Geoff could hear scrabbling sounds in the short funnel of the pipe which he had just sealed when he replaced the hatch cover but he concluded that his present position could not be compromised because he had the drop on the hatch as he fisted the recovered laser pistol and stood guard. He was still standing there pistol in hand when he heard the running footsteps of the security team. He did not have to explain anything to them because Alisia had rebroadcast the unfolding scene as she had received it on her hucom. The leader of the security group came up and produced a hand held munition from his body belt. "Open it quickly," he nodded to one of his team who obliged with rapidity and as he did so the group leader hurled the munition in through the opening. There was no delay for a primer to activate the weapon and for three seconds afterwards an intense blue light flickered back through the opening accompanied by some sparks and a sizzling sound.

"Electric grenade," the security officer appraised him. "It addles the circuits of robots and knocks out the nervous system of biological lifeforms. Anyone in there will be out for a least an hour and they will need medical supervision for several days before they are fully recovered. "We are not finished yet," he added as one of the team passed him an object reminiscent of a mortar tube which the security officer twice aimed through the opening and a fainter blue light flickered this time indicating that the grenades had gone to the further reaches of the area accessed from the plate.

There was no further activity from beyond the plate and they waited for a few minutes as the team located a workmen's storage cubicle in the corridor wall and extracted a step ladder from it. The team leader and one of his security team carefully climbed in through the opening and announced from within that there was a fixed ladder inside. All was quiet inside and the team member put his head back out of the access point and invited Geoff to come in and take a look. When he had clambered through he could see that the security team had scattered light emitting globes around them but even so the area was so vast he could not see the distant end of the cavern, but there were bodies everywhere, luridly twitching into the depths until the available light gave way to darkness.

"They seem to look like they are in pain, "Geoff observed.

'Nowhere near as painful as they would have been if we had used fragmentation grenades or as final as an energy bolt," the guard commander grinned. "They will be alright when they come round."

"Who are they?" Geoff inquired.

"Anarchists, I would think" the Commander of the security team told him. "We know from intelligence that a bunch of AMC anarchists have been looking for a ship to steal. They are in an unused reserve water tank. They must have booked in as tourists, perhaps in tranches of twenty to fifty so as not to arouse suspicion, and they must have opened up the reserve water tank to live in. In my opinion it would have needed a significant degree of insider help, so we will have to take a close look at the people who do the physical checking on and off the civil side of the ship." Returning to the duty in hand he engrossed himself in briefing the medical teams as they arrived but he asked Geoff to stay awhile until he had finished.

Later, Geoff took the time to wander around the water tank. It was a good four hundred metres long and, he observed, with more contorted and twitching bodies in the further depth. It was also pretty squalid inside with inflatable bedding and empty tins of food, bottles of water and weapons littering the floor.

"I've got the security camera report," the team leader re-engaged him. "Yesterday, according to the camera shots, an individual had walked down the corridor and had taken off the handle and the wedge from the hatch cover and then he climbed into the tank and did not reappear. It raised no suspicion because it was not a sensitive part of the ship and the camera was not set up to trigger an alert, so it was regarded as an appropriate routine activity for that area. This corridor is hardly ever used but on this rare occasion a maintenance inspector had walked along it this very morning carrying out a structural inspection. Electric clipboard in hand, he had stopped when he saw the handle and the wedge on the floor. His fingers traced over his clipboard ascertaining from it that there was no maintenance going on, nor planned, inside the tank. Drawing a blank with his search, he resorted to shouting into the opening twice but received no reply. Satisfied that it was mysterious but of little consequence because it could have been like that for months, he slipped the handle back on its' boss and tightened the cover and continued with his inspection along the corridor.

Captain Moska came through via Geoff's hucom and

inquired if he was unhurt.

"Thanks, nothing wrong, but who are the anarchists and what do they want?"

"What they really want is a good question," Captain Moska replied. "There are some anarchist groups in the Colligate. Basically they object to being governed; they are a sort of flotsam of society really, unbalanced daydreamers, unemployed, unemployable and work-shy. I am sure that you have similar people back on Earth?"

"Indeed we do," Geoff agreed. "But what is this particular group seeking?"

"Well," Captain Moska cleared his throat, "we do not yet know but we can guess in this case; usually they are seeking social simplicity. At this early stage of our investigation, as far as we can understand, they intended to take over the AMStar by force, turf off the crew and tourists and then use the ship as a commune to endlessly drift around the universe. They would plan to set down from time to time until they got tired of their surroundings and then drift off again. Apparently, they must have cut their way through the wall of the disused reserve water tank which houses the hatch cover and they intended to use that unfrequented part of the ship to expand out from the tourist area into the military area and take over all of the vital parts of the ship. Clearly there must be insufficient or inadequate security checks being carried out on shuttle craft arriving and departing at the tourist end of the ship and they have exploited that failure to their advantage. I will now have to intervene, as Captain of the ship, with the tourist administration and insist that they make changes. Your timely inquisitiveness spoilt their plan and probably saved the ship; at the very least you have probably saved the loss of life of many crew and of the anarchists."

In the subsequent clean up, they discovered that there were two-thousand, six hundred anarchists on the ship and they had boarded by arrangement from different places so as not to draw attention to themselves. A civilian on the passenger side of the ship was now under arrest for falsifying passenger manifests which were made to appear that passenger intake and putdown was evenly balanced. As they were essentially booked to be conveyed within the legal confines of the Colligation there was no check of their luggage and it was found that they had imported a variety of weapons. Their take-over of the ship was scheduled to take place that very night. Once they had gained possession of the vital parts of the ship, they had apparently planned to use its' runabouts to ferry in substantial numbers of anarchists who were already packed and awaiting for their call forward.

Geoff was later told that the cover is an access entry point for people or robots for inner tank maintenance; and it would have been properly sealed and locked if the tank behind it had contained water. Because the tank was normally full of water it had not been recognised as an evasive route from the civilian side of the ship to the military side. It was the anarchists' bad luck that the maintenance inspector had replaced the handle. As the Captain remarked to Geoff later. "Even if they had been successful, they would have learned that it requires some kind of hierarchy and discipline to run a super sized spaceship, so their freedoms would still have their limitations."

"I think it is very true," Geoff nodded. "Many movements that aim to depose a government would find that having done that they end up with - well - having to have a government, even if they give it another title."

"That is an astute observation which they tend to overlook," the Captain remarked with a laugh. "De Facto, the AMStar's journey had been a routine security check around the Colligation planets, but it could not now to be resumed until after they had made a return journey to Ambrocognia-Mundi to drop off their, now, sheepish looking prisoners." He added that Geoffrey was required to attend the Court because the prisoner who had fired a pistol at him had been easily identified by his broken wrist. In Court Geoffrey found its methodology was fair and the Court listened intently to all the evidence, including a few fanatical statements from the prisoners of their right to a free and unfettered life of their own choosing. Countered by a grave and serious prosecutor who pointed out that they could have done that but, when it came to stealing spaceships by force of arms and shooting at people, they had assumed that free and inalienable rights belonged solely on the side of anarchy.

Then the Court came to the culprit who stood accused of shooting at Geoffrey; and he lamely excused his action by saying that the pistol went off accidentally, but the Judge interceded to ask if the weapon were of standard construction. He didn't state his reason for asking that question but those in the Court knew that a standard weapon could only be fired after the deliberate sequence of first switching it on. Geoff was deeply interested in the whole procedure because he had never been in a Court room on Earth, let alone in another galaxy. In the end, the prisoners' sentences mainly followed whether they were leading or were led. Those who were led got seven years with the possibility to earn up to a one third off for good behaviour. The leaders were given ten years with the same facility to earn a remission. The prisoner who had shot at Geoffrey was given fifteen years with no remission.

It was custom in an AMC Court that the plaintive, in this case Geoffrey, was expected to make a plea for other factors to be taken into account. He rather surprised the Court by saying that he believed the culprit had pursued his belief so vigorously that it had culminated in having brain washed himself to believe that anarchy was the be all and end all of political doctrines. As a result he had obviously sidelined the normal checks and balances associated with rational thinking. Geoffrey asked that his assailant be given the same sentence as the other anarchist leaders of the group and, if appropriate, a reduction for exemplary behaviour. The Judge sat for a moment rubbing his chin and deep in thought, then cleared his throat.

"I had half expected you to ask for a longer sentence for the prisoner and you have surprised me. I am going to agree with you and make this sentence for only ten years with the possibility for earned remission; but I have also to consider that the original length of the sentence took into account a calculation to prevent reoffending. I shall make this provision. In reducing this sentence, upon release from prison, the convicted will be on pain of re-imprisonment for not less than five years if he knowingly attempts to make contact with any of these prisoners who have stood before me today." Geoffrey nodded his approval.

The AMSstar had stood off Ambrocognia-Mundi for the period of the trial but now their returning shuttle docked by the ship's and they stepped again onboard the AMStar.

"I am very sorry for that unpleasant interlude," the Captain apologised. "You had best take the next two days off to continue your tour of the ship, then report back on the morning of the third day. Try not to find any more terrorists though," he laughed and patted Geoff on the back.

"Thank you," Geoff was relieved. "It was fascinating to see how your approach to problems differs from ours but we all hope and demand to achieve the same results."

"Yes," Captain Moska smiled, "I hope one day to be able to look over your QvO for those reasons."

"When that happens, I hope to be able to guide you," Geoff replied.

Chapter 7

THE ZIYLEX

Geoffrey's next internal journey of the AMStar took him to see the colossal sub-light poenillium X fusion engines. The engines were only slightly smaller than those of the QvO but there were four of them whereas the QvO had only two. The architects of the AMC had clearly solved the conundrum of the tubing for the proton linear accelerators because they were considerably shorter than the similar purpose apparatus on the QvO. As a result the space taken up by engines at the rear of the ship was only six kilometres, in depth representing a considerable saving in deck space v/v the fifteen kilometres required by the QvO for the same operation.

On another journey of exploration Geoff espied a signpost which his hucom translated to read 'church' and he decided to follow it. When he did arrive he was amazed by the facade of the church and its' striking resemblance to those on Earth and also on Ongle. Obviously the AMC had correspondingly engaged the best stone masons and artisans at their disposal for its' creation. As he stood before it he found it was stupefying to witness that they had come up with almost identical architectural blueprints. Geoff decided to go inside and as he approached he could hear soft music and words softly spoken reassuringly, encompassing all human fears in their scope; and when they were translated by his hucom they were very familiar.

'Y*ea, though I walk through the valley*

of the shadow of death,

I will fear no evil: for thou art with me;

thy rod and thy staff, they comfort me.'

"I do wish the waring people of Earth could see and hear this." Geoff exclaimed aloud but to no one. The reading of the 23rd Psalm continued until he made his entrance to the church and it faded out as he passed over the threshold. The layout, compared to an English church, was very similar but it tended to use more colourful depictions of nature in decoration. There were even pews which were intricately carved from quarried stone slabs. It would not, to a degree, be really out of place if you could have transported it back to Greenbrook. It was one of those moments in life when you feel the presence of God; and he went to one of the church pews and sat down and prayed earnestly for the things and the people he loved; and he felt stronger in spirit and refreshed in mind when he had done so.

"You are the first outworlder who has ever visited my church," a robed figure approached with outstretched hands. "I know you from television. You are Geoffrey Holder of the starship QvO and the first contact between our two races. You are most welcome here. Geoffrey stood up and accepted the offered handshake.

"I am so pleased to see this magnificent church here. You know, wherever I go in space, there is always the church and a ribbon of belief in God running through every culture and the 23rd Psalm also appears in every language."

"How right you are," the clergy man nodded affably. "It is such a shame that especially the younger generations mistake inventions as proof that God does not exist, whereas each invention really reveals how little we know and the knowledge that there are yet further discoveries to be uncovered beyond that. We know so little about anything really."

Geoff sat and talked to the vicar who seemed to assume Geoffrey to be an expert on English Christian churches and he questioned him very closely about every aspect he knew about the Church in England. Geoff struggled with the torrent of questions often about insider politics of which he knew little and subjects such as the stipend paid to the clergy. Did they have set hours of work, at what age could they retire and was it true that he had heard that vicars of the Church on Earth could perform weddings. Geoffrey, although not disinterested, was beginning to think that he may have to spend the rest of the day there, but the vicar eventually rose and announced that he had to go.

"That was the most enjoyable and enlightening hour that I can ever recall," he said with conviction. "I do hope that I will be able to talk to you again?"

"Of course," Geoff rejoined. "I have also learned an awful lot from our chat as well; most certainly we will have to meet up again soon."

Geoff was uneasy in himself. He knew something of the problems leading to the war that the AMC had fought against the Ziylex people but he felt that he did not know enough about it. The First Secretary, of The Incllusive Government of Ambrocognia-Mundi Colligate had told them a little at their first contact. He said, at that time when they had first met the Ziylex, the planet Ambrocognia-Mundi had been called Yolanda. Geoff learned that the Yolandians' first contact was when they came across the Ziylex when they were prospecting in space. The Yolandians had landed on a planetary moon to coincidentally find the Ziylex were already there. Both parties approached each other with great caution but when the Yolandians bent down and grounded their small arms the Ziylex did likewise. It transpired that the Ziylex were looking for copper but they had broken the drive shaft of their drill and after looking at the broken part the chief engineer of the Yolandian ship said that he could effect a repair on the spot.

The logical progression from that was that this was to be the true beginning of an enduring friendship between these two planetary systems and it was set to grow with trade links and the exchange of ideas and technology. Of the two planetary systems, Yolanda was clearly the most advanced but the Ziylex were catching up. They hardly interchanged populations at all because the Ziylex explained that there was a very intolerant element in their society towards other races. Give it time, they said, and this would pass as they got used to living together. The Ziylexians seemed to be very keen anglers and they often visited the lakes of Yolanda. They had been friends now for ten years with no mishaps or misunderstandings but during this time people had started to disappear from the Yolandian perimeter societies. There were all sorts of theories, mostly centred upon the deprivation suffered through living in frontier settlements which lent itself to depression and suicide but why this should be happening now when there had been settlements in the same areas for hundreds of years, did not make sense.

The first inkling of suspicion arose when two Yolandian anglers living in a village in a remote area of Yolanda decided to go fishing at a lake some distance from their own settlement. This involved going by vehicle across virgin terrain and the last kilometre before the lake, where they intended to fish, revealed itself to be a marshy swamp. They decide to leave their vehicle some way back and walk the rest of the way but they could see that a Ziylexian space runabout was already parked by the lake. The ship, of course, could let down on marshland so it was logical that they had parked it at the water's edge. The two AMC men knew of the Ziylexian passion for fishing and thought this would be a good opportunity to exchange methods and techniques. None of this would be possible without a Yolanda- Ziylex phrase book and one of the Yolandians went back to retrieve a copy of it which they kept in their vehicle. The other Yolandian continued on to meet the two Ziylexians at the lake.

The Yolandian, who had gone back to the vehicle, decided to re select his fishing lures that he was going to use and spent a little time swapping them around with some of his 'specials', as he called them, that he kept in the vehicle. It was about fifteen minutes before he started back towards the lake. As he came to the edge of the brush he was startled to see that the two Ziylexians were on the beach of the lake and his friend was standing with them but was wrapped around in a fishing net and he seemed to be trying to untangle himself from it. The Ziylexians were making no move to help free him and remained talking to each other. Then they turned and bundled him more securely in the net and he was still struggling as they hefted him on their shoulders and pushed him roughly into their space runabout which immediately after took off. The remaining Yolandian felt that his friend must have been taken ill and was being assisted by the Ziylexians so he was not alarmed. Their space runabout could be at a hospital in minutes, whereas his terrain vehicle would take several hours across a bumpy and imperfect trackway, so it made sense. The significance of the fishing net did not make sense, however, but he would obviously get to know all about that shortly when he got back to the settlement.

When the fisherman got back to the settlement he started to ask around after his friend, but nobody knew anything about him, so he called the local hospitals, with no result and he finally contacted hospitals over great distances with still no news. Eventually, he addressed his request for news to the local police and from them the search spread over the planetary system and from there to the Ziylexian system, but nobody could shed a light on where his friend had been taken. The Ziylexans were dismissive of the report that it was one of their ships and suggested that it may have been a visitation from renegade space adventurers, whereupon robbery or slavery were the most likely motives. They added that occasionally, in the past, they had, of course, lost a few small craft in space and perhaps one had been found and repaired and was now in the hands of villains. They suggested that Yolanda await a ransom note which was almost certain to follow.

No ransom note was received and people still continued to disappear randomly from remote sites and one or two space cargo ships vanished in the firmament; and this conferred credibility to the Ziylexian renegade space pirates theory. As they did not know who they were and where these pirates came from, the security services of Yolanda started to covertly secrete motion activated movie cameras in out of the way places but they initially recorded nothing at all. Finally, one day, one of them bleeped into life and sent pictures of two Ziylexians befriending the owner of a small rowing boat on a lonely beach and then bundling him into a net and taking off with him. Again the Ziylexians denied that they had anything to do with it. They must be the same hoodlums they averred and to assist Yolanda they would task their entire space force to hunt them down.

The breakthrough in the mystery came when a Yolandan freighter, that had stopped to make urgent repairs, was boarded by Ziylexians with an offer of help but then the Ziylexian crew captured the Yolandians. So sure were the Ziylexians that their capture of the freighter was a copy book operation they boastfully told their Yolandian captives that they were to be on the menu of a feast to be held on Ziylex. In gruesome detail they told the captured Yolandians that it was a religious tradition of the Ziylexan people to eat other species and when there were no more left to gorge upon they took possession of their lands. In the case of Yolanda a direct attack had not been possible because Yolanda was militarily in advance of them, so they had planned to bide their time awhile to assimilate Yolandian military capabilities and when they caught up technically they would launch their attack.

What the Ziylexians raiders had overlooked was that there were four Yolandian engineers working on the poenilliam drive of the ship and the Captain of the Yolandian freighter had left his com-link open and they were able to hear the whole conversation and they devised a ruse. It was simple. One of the engineers was to appear at the mouth of the tunnel, look surprised, and then run away back down the tunnel. The deception, when they carried it out, went exactly to plan and the Ziylexians despatched their four armed guards to pursue him. As the Ziylexian pursuit followed the fugitive around a bend in the tunnel, three burly workmen dropped on them from its' roof. The Ziylex were no athletes and they soon succumbed to fisticuffs and hammers. Minutes later, in the hold where the Yolandian prisoners were being held, they saw what appeared to be the Ziylexian guards walking back out of the tunnel. The remaining Ziylexians who were guarding the Yolandian prisoners perhaps heard the sizzle of energy weapons before they slumped lifeless to the floor. Now there were enough weapons to go around among the crew of the normally unarmed freighter, and the Ziylexian ship which had launched the attack was still connected to the freighter by a boarding tunnel. The crew of the Yolandian vessel, with revenge in their hearts and weapons of revenge in their hands, stormed into the Ziylexian ship, shooting at anything that moved; and within a minute or two nothing could move, save themselves.

Chapter 8

ANNIHILATION

Back at Yolanda things were in turmoil and the Julate of the Inclusive Government demanded to know the reason for the attack and their true intentions towards the people of Yolanda. The response they received from the Ziylexian government was not the abject apology that they had expected. Instead they knew that they were exposed and they consequentially dropped all pretence and said curtly that they had tried to make the last days of the Yolandians as peaceful and as pleasant as they could. They had a biological need for humanoid flesh and henceforth all diplomatic relations were to be severed. Yolanda was to surrender to Ziylex immediately and if they did they would receive the special dispensation of being stunned before they were eaten. If they did not then they would be butchered alive one by one.

"What a repulsive bunch they are," Geoff muttered to himself but stayed logged into the Colligate computer. It transpired that nobody knew quite what to do at Yolanda. In their total history they had never fought a full scale war but, as a start, they commenced to recall all of the military spaceship crews that were on leave and then called up their reserve forces and raised their military threat level to the highest ever. It was a phoney war to begin with as both sides shored up their defences and tried to gather the kind of intelligence that would be advantageous when war commenced. The initial smart move by Yolanda was related to their immediate understanding of the immeasurable expanses of space that they would have to patrol. Therefore, to beef up their presence they threw everything into a crash programme to produce more ships for the military; and after six months with the whole planetary system involved, especially their industrial robots, their military space fleet had increased three-fold. Inevitably there were those that, objective to saving their own skins, reasoned that to avert war they could perhaps offer their elderly to the Ziylex. It would be the lesser of two evils they argued 'to assign their elderly to the Ziylex.'But would they have been so keen when they approached old age themselves, Geoff wondered.'

Warships were continuing to come off the Yolandian production lines in ever increasing numbers. Crews for them were recruited and trained on existing spaceships and the crews of civilian ships were directly co-opted by government decree. By the end of a year the Yolanda fleet had been increased by twenty-thousand ships and the pace of production continued. They were spurred on in this by their intelligence reports that the Ziylex were doing exactly the same. But, being inexperienced in war, the Yolandians had been thinking more in terms of defence than attack. In short, they had been waiting for it to happen instead of dictating when and where or how to degrade Ziylexian military assets and communications to render them less capable of waging war.

It was to be two years after their demand that Yolanda should surrender that Ziylex launched their preliminary offensive. Evading Yolanda picquet ships, they came out of the blackness of dark matter like a colony of bats and descended upon a more distant small, inhabited, Yolanda planet. They were initially engaged by a weak squadron of Yolandian ships patrolling in what had, hitherto, been considered to be a non-strategic backwater but they were brushed aside and decimated by the overwhelming numbers of Ziylexian ships. As a preliminary to the attack, the Ziylexians had jammed the Yolandian defence squadron's ability to communicate that they were engaged in battle and none of them lived to tell the tale. Thus, news of the attack was delayed in getting back to the Yolanda fleet and, when it was discovered, their heavy fleet units set course immediately for the beleaguered planet. But, by the time they got there in battle order, the Ziylexian fleet had disappeared into dark matter, along with thousands of Yolandians who had been herded like cattle into Ziylexan transport ships included in their fleet for that very purpose.

There had been no escape either for any remaining Yolandians. Those that the Ziylex fleet had not captured were killed off by barrages of toxic weapons as Ziylex laid waste to the planet. As a stark calling card, they left behind a small Yolandian space craft which they had captured and it contained the blood reddened skeletons of the passengers whose flesh had been stripped from them and a gory video record of their deaths had been left playing on a loop over the ship's computer screens. When this reached the news headlines on Yolanda there were riots in the capitals of the Yolanda planetary system and demands that the Ziylexians be purged from space. Rightly or wrongly, the Minister for Defence was sacked on the spot. It was not entirely his fault; through all of his service he had been a member and then the commander of peacetime defence forces. He was, to some extent, a victim of a Yolandian dearth of history into how to conduct a war, but somebody had to be blamed and the finger pointed at him.

His replacement. (General Winter) was different in his personality. He was not somebody for ceremony, ritual, Mess dinners or fine wines. His job was his profession and not the perks to be derived from it. With new broom alacrity he got down right away to looking for weaknesses in the Ziylexian strategy and their order of battle. He hit upon the problem right away and it was surprising that nobody else had, but they had been thinking in terms of defence. That is to say, the other side attacked you and you tried to defeat them. Fine, he had said, as long as they do not defeat you instead.

In the past, Ziylex had noted the ease with which Yolanda ships were able to transit dark matter so accurately. At best the Ziylexian system of DMT could only rely on an accuracy of seventy percent success. Many of their ships that had failed to make a clean DMT jump never returned, with only a few managing to make it back after years of wandering in space. In the spirit of friendship Yolanda had helped Ziylex to convert their ships to use their dark matter transit system and gave them the codes to the Yolandian dark matter beacons. When electronically challenged by one of these codes the beacons yielded the biases to be set for a ship's wire mesh envelope. There was nothing more to do but adjust the mesh to the biases and engage DMT and you emerged right where you intended to be in another part of the universe.

The Ziylex had never manufactured their own beacons and, indeed, they were not given the blue-prints for these devices because there was no need to - they were friends. Although Ziylexia had the codes for the beacons, to assist ship movements, for statistical and fleet management purposes they were given a different set of codes to those used by Yolanda. Moreover, the Ziylexian covert intent towards the Yolandians had been discovered somewhat earlier than the Ziylexia had in mind so they had not had the time nor opportunity to wheedle the secrets of the DM beacons from Yolanda. It was this omission in their master plan that now worked in the favour of Yolanda. Naturally, it had already been suggested that they turn the beacons off or reset the pass codes and there was a study going on as how best to do that, but that wouldn't stop the Ziylex from attacking them. The Ziylex were a ruthless enemy and they would revert to their earlier hit or miss system of DMT and the loss of two or three thousand ships that would fail to make it through dark matter would not deter them from making an assault on Yolanda.

At the moment, Yolanda was working on a system whereby they could eavesdrop on Ziylexian requests for explicit bias settings from the beacons. If they were successful they would be able to position Yolanda's vessels in strength to meet the Ziylexian ships the moment that they materialised from the DMT.

Mistakenly the Ziylexians misread this as a Yolandian peace offering and a weakness that they could exploit.

General Winter had told his military cabinet that he thought that they could do better than that. "Wars are not just fought with hammer blows," he said, "they had to employ guile, too. Even if we were in a position to meet their attacks," he told them, "they may well send an overwhelming force or they could employ trickery to catch us off balance." He had wondered about the codes used by the Ziylex to access the beacons. "We know the ones they use but they don't know ours." He was, as he sat there, deep in thought and a solution swirled out of the mists of his mind and he mentally ran it backwards and forwards before clearing his throat.

In his proposal to his Chiefs of Staff, the general outlined his grand scheme to use their control of the beacons to their advantage. "The nub of the plan," he said, "is that we must alter the beacons so that when they are activated by a Ziylexian code they will transmit a false bias reading and when they key it into their DMT envelope it will result in them being ejected elsewhere in the universe. To accomplish this we are going to use our own fleet as a lure." Not everybody present fully understood the plan but it sounded good and with nothing better on offer they remained silent. At least they now had a strategy other than to just slug it out with the opposing fleet until one of them ceded defeat.

It was acknowledged on Ziylex that Yolanda would now feel that it had a score to settle with them and it was a part of the Ziylexian game plan to entice Yolanda to make the move by attacking two Yolandan outposts. With much forethought Ziylexia had prepared their subterfuge for the expected reprisal. They were not surprised, therefore, to see hordes of ships materialising out of dark matter at the edges of their own planetary system. As the Yolandian armada swept in, like fire breathing dragons their concentrated fire turned Ziylexian ships into red-hot scrap. But the Ziylexian defence was defence in depth, or a 'sponge' they called it, and it was soaking up and isolating elements of the Yolanda fleet and the deeper they penetrated the sponge the more concentrated the defence would become.

A part of the Ziylex counter plan was that half of their fleet was still hidden in an asteroid belt in space and they would be unleashed behind the Yolandians as they tried to extricate themselves from the sponge. When the trap was finally sprung the Yolanda fleet would find itself outnumbered and outgunned. Already an increasing number of the Yolandian ships were exploding as they were hit from all angles. The Ziylex did not know, however, that most of the exploding Yolandian ships were dummies which even if they received a quite minor hit, would explode dramatically, giving the impression that things were going badly for the Yolandians. It was now clear to the Ziylex that if the Yolandians did not extract themselves they would surely lose the battle 'big time.' In the circumstances the Ziylexian fleet commander judged that the Yolandian fleet would make a tactical withdrawal in disarray. Thus, when the Yolandian fleet winked out into the cover of dark matter he must have been elated thinking that the Yolandian fleet would arrive in their own territory like a startled flock of birds. Now was the time to follow them to Yolanda to launch his hammer blow to finish them off, once and for all. Everything was going to plan and they would feast on Yolandians tonight.

As the Yolandian fleet passed back through the DM they sent out activation codes to the DM beacons to 'chirp' fake bias settings when they were triggered by a code used by the Ziylexian vessels. As they had rightly guessed, a large portion of the Ziylex fleet was ordered to follow them back to the Yolanda system. There was nobody and no way to record or send warnings about what was happening to the Ziylexian spaceships as eighty-thousand of them emerged from dark matter to find themselves in the swirling core of a massive black hole. In fact their ships were already being squashed to pieces and their biological bodies were being crushed to death by the ferocious gravity before their crews even knew that they had been tricked.

Once more the Yolanda fleet appeared in Ziylexian space and once more they attacked and then withdrew and more Ziylexian ships followed them expecting to engage in battle in Yolanda territory but in reality they were to suffer the same doom as their brethren before them. Of now, the Ziylexian fleet was so attenuated that an executive order was flashed out from Yolanda to its' fleet, committing them to seek, engage, and destroy Ziylex ships at will. When the main Yolanda fleet later re-entered the Ziylex system proper, it was this time to stay. The Yolandian crews found that the Ziylexians had managed to capture a few of their battle crippled ships and they were sickened by the grotesque remains of the crews of those ships and as their reports reached Yolanda a red mist of anger descended upon Yolandan's population.

The Julate, in blunt speech to his people, declared that there was to be total destruction, 'without pity' of the Ziylex system; and all of their planets were to be left irradiated to prevent their ever returning to them. The full implementation of that order was horrendous and brought out the very worst of their natures but the possible effect of not doing what they must do could be just as devastating for them, were Ziylex to ever rise again and re-invade Yolanda. Any remaining Ziylexian ships were hunted down. Surrender was not an option given to them. Those that did try to escape invariably attempted it via DMT and suffered an identical demise as the rest of their fleet in the insatiable intestines of the blackhole.

The total destruction of the Ziylex planets was given over to the giant battleships and these roved around the Ziylex system spewing malevolence in the form of streaks of fire as their devastating poenillium canons raked planet surfaces. Neither a humanoid, nor an ant, nor an earwig survived as planets blazed around them; and even sunlight was extinguished from them by the smoke of the conflagrations of whole cities and forests burning and the dust kicked up into the stratosphere by the explosions.

Lastly, they deployed their radiation bombs, just one of which, after it popped open in the upper atmosphere of a planet, would make it uninhabitable for ten million years. In the aftermath, the larger vessels remained over the Ziylexian planets for five years to ascertain that no Ziylexian life had survived or had sought to return. At the end of their vigil they had nothing to report..

Then came the feelings of guilt and the recriminations. Were they entitled to exterminate an entire life form? There had been women, children and animals on those planets. Yes, and they also ate Yolandians, was the counter and they had intended to eat us all, including our women and children. If it had been anything less than final the Ziylexians may have come back and tried again. It was ghastly but they were right to do it. The argument raged back and forth and would probably still be talked about in terms of right and wrong for a thousand years on Yolanda if something could not be done to give them a new beginning and a new history.

A system wide referendum was held of all the planets of the Yolanda system; and one of the questions on the referendum was: - 'Should Yolanda withdraw from contacting other races in space and isolate itself?' This proposal received the sweeping support of the majority and, as a start, they made using long wave radio transmissions illegal, opting instead to using short range infra-red light for communication. They changed the name Yolanda to Ambrocognia-Mundi so that even if they were chanced upon by space travellers one day, when they went back home they would not tell the people of the planet Yolanda; and lastly they sought to blot out their complete planet system in space by spreading minute refractive crystals into space around them. They decided, also, to maintain a large standing fleet of up to date space warships as a measure of insurance against their ever being attacked afresh; and modifications were made to their DM beacons to render them mute to anything other than an AMC challenge for DM information. In short, they had become reclusives in space. Only then did they begin to feel safe in their resolve of never again to be regarded as haute cuisine on the menu of another race. Neither, too, would they be called upon to commit another genocide. But their attitudes were changing after the QvO, unaware of the disguised AMC planetary system in its' flight path, had narrowly missed crashing into the capital planet of Ambrocognia-Mundi.

The subsequent alliance that they had since formed with the Ongle system of planets had given them strength in numbers and their confidence to exlore the universe had been restored.

"I never knew the whole story, blow for blow," Geoff remarked to the Captain when he was next on the bridge.

"It would be interesting to hear what you think," the Captain asked him. "What do you think that we should have done?"

"It is not really up to me to criticise nor praise," Geoff was careful, "but my personal opinion would be that Yolanda did not have any other options. If I were there I would certainly have agreed."

"Thank you," said the Captain, "for your opinion. Because you are an outlander, it is refreshing to hear that you believe that we did the only thing that we could have done." Geoff had spoken frankly what he felt but he sensed he had said the right thing and just a little more ease and a warmer smile greeted him from then onwards.

Chapter 9

SHIPS ROUTINE

Geoff fitted seamlessly into the ship's routine where he worked eight hour shifts; and the other crew members, he noted, were diligent and professional but as with all of the people of the AMC they were fond of practical jokes. Once he was offered a fake coffee. It looked normal and even had a slight ripple on its' surface but when he lifted the cup to drink it he found that the ripple was created by a small covering of liquid on the surface of a solid lump of fat underneath and the crew watched him amusedly. Another time he was given a sheet of paper laying out the order of tasks for the day but as he glanced at it the writing faded and disappeared, to a suppressed titter from the perpetrator of the practical joke.

Geoff didn't go straight back to his quarters that night and he stopped off at a fabric workshop and asked them to create an object to his design. The next time that he was on duty he waited until the jokester who had played the prank of the disappearing ink on him had left the bridge to go to the toilet. The bridge staff watched him with interest as he slipped the whoopee cushion that he had commissioned underneath the thin comfort cushion of the joker's chair. The practical joker shot up from his chair when he sat down and the crew looked at him with exaggerated expressions of distaste, until he rooted around underneath the cushion and found the source of his embarrassment.

Practical jokes, though, were not permitted to deter the crew from the seriousness of their occupations and when one of the crew on another occasion unwisely put the whoopee cushion underneath the normal cushion of the Captain's chair, the Captain, on return, sensed that everybody was looking at him. He deferred from taking his seat right away and casually inspected it instead and found the cushion and asked who had put it there. The crewman responsible virtuously and somewhat sheepishly owned up. There was no anger on the part of the Captain as he addressed the crewman. In a normal everyday run of the mill conversational tone. "Thank you, Mr Croix," he said without emphasising any word. "You can dismiss yourself back to your quarters and, in your own handwriting of not less than fifty pages, write me an essay on ship's etiquette by this time tomorrow, please." Captain Moska smiled thinly after the crew man had left, perhaps remembering that he, himself, had once been a junior crew member but the authority of command had to be visibly maintained and enforced.

It was afterwards, in conversation, that Captain Moska mentioned to Geoff that he ought to patent the whoopee cushion at the AMC patent office. Geoff thought about it for a while then with a brainwave asked if there were any charities in the Colligate and learned that indeed there were. It was well received when Geoff decided upon a ship wide questionnaire asking the whole crew which charity they would prefer to receive the manufacturing and retail distribution rights of the cushion. He was addressing a closed shop really, so he was not too surprised that the majority vote was for the Widows, Widowers and Orphans of Spacemen killed or invalided in the discharge of their duties. The plain choice was for the ship's Welfare Officer to make the necessary arrangements with the patent office and the charity. In due course an effusive message was received from the Widows, Widowers and Orphans of the Spacemen and Spacewomen Charity expressing their sincere thanks and stating that an engraved acknowledgement plaque would follow to be affixed within the AMStar, registering their generous gift of copyright.

At home on Ongle, Imogen was living the life of a housewife and mother of their two children. Time was passing slowly for them but, once a month, Geoffrey was able to take one of the AMStar's shuttles back to Ongle to visit her. Otherwise their communication in between was difficult as they had to rely upon the indirect method of dark matter transfer. Each day a dart was loaded with official and crew messages from the AMStar and it was sent through DMT and when it emerged at Ambrocognia-Mundi the messages were rerouted by post to their addresses. Or in the case of Geoff's letters they had to be sent on to Ongle via another DMT postal dart. The number of messages between the two systems was not excessive so it did not warrant a constant stream of DMT postal darts plying to and fro between them; but at least one dart per day was despatched in either direction and even after arrival at Ongle a message still had to finish its journey via the postal system. Thus, depending upon the time of despatch of a letter, its answer being received could take two to four days.

Captain Moska was aware of the programmes that Geoffrey had instigated to detect rogue robots when he was on the QvO and he asked him to conduct a similar investigation on the AMStar. Geoffrey found himself teamed up with a taller than average AMC flaxen haired woman named Gillian. As on the QvO they introduced discreet radio frequency scanners in various parts of the ship and it was not long before they discovered one particular robot was making regular trips to the hull of the ship and making short range broadcasts which were unintelligible to any code cracking systems that they had on board the ship.

When they took the robot in and examined it thoroughly they located a transmitter concealed in the ring collar through which its' approximation of a head extended. The modification plate inside the robot showed that it was a very old model and it had been patched up many times in its' history, but to whom and where and why was it transmitting on a daily basis was a mystery. The effect of the discovery was instant and the ship went into lock down and the remaining civilian holiday makers were transported to the nearest planet. Military establishments went on to high alert and armed soldiers appeared around major government buildings.

Eventually the security net zeroed in on a quite elderly man who had once worked in the government Ship Provisions Department when they discovered that he had actually signed the issue voucher transferring that robot to the AMStar. He was a bit bemused to be rushed to the Department of Defence and put into contact with Captain Moska and he asked him for a description of the robot.

"Ah," he said, "I remember them now. Some years ago the Department purchased a job lot of robots from a collapsed mining venture. This particular job lot were specialist laboratory assistants used to assay mining spoils and some of them were sent out alone into wild countryside to radio back what that they had found. When these robots came to us we de-tooled them and reprogrammed them for their new tasks. I just wonder if there was some small part of the programme we missed. It seems sad to think that perhaps this lonely robot has all down the years been assaying anything it come across on the floor of the ship and it has faithfully continued its' daily reports to the non existent radio receivers of a defunct company headquarters. I would leave it alone if I were you; it will do no harm," he ended. A pregnant pause descended over the bridge and a bout of embarrassed coughing ensued.

The Captain was in reflective mood when he next spoke to Geoff. "I think looking into the communication habits of our robots can be discontinued now. There is no telling what we might turn up." True enough, as a cross check, they had sent recordings of the robot's unofficial daily messages to an AMC geological lab and they had reported back that they were not in a complicated military code at all. What they had sent to them was merely a data stream expressing elements and compounds which was not likely to mean much to anybody that did not have a geologist's training. The Captain and those on the bridge at the time couldn't help but chuckle. But, as is the want of the media, it had initially reported in banner headlines in terms of 'our heroic, brave, ever alert military men were being spied on by alien robots' etc. etc.. Now, they did a journalistic handstand and they were asking if this had not been a gross over reaction on the part of the government.

"Their job is to sell the newspaper, one way or the other, even if they have to contradict themselves to do it," Captain Moska remarked to his bridge officers.

The voyages around the AMC planetary system were an education for Geoffrey who had only experienced the culture of four planets so far and they were not so different from Earth; but out there, there was an abundant list of planets to pick from and they ranged in size and temperature. Some were so atomically compact that their gravitational forces were too powerful for him to visit. Anti grav suits were available but only used as a necessity because they carried with them a risk of failure and, in that event, almost certain death. Yet, strangely life on them had adapted and pictures from them showed people and animals as squat and powerful looking. Apparently, he was told acclimatisation to a slightly higher gravity planet only took a single generation. But, there were still many planets upon which a human could never stand because they be would be crushed to death by gravity instantly if they tried. Other planets were much warmer and others were covered in never thawing ice. Yet more rotated very quickly or very slowly or did not rotate at all. Yet, by sheer tenacity, biological and vegetive life had adapted to colonise many of them but they were often very strange life forms to the human eye.

It was an eye opener for Geoffrey, but there were a lot more challenges out there that had been entirely overlooked in Earthly science fiction, wherein its' heroes seemed able to step from planet to planet with ease regardless of gravity, temperature or atmosphere. There was so much to see, with geysers that shot kilometres into the sky and lava lakes stretching as far as the eye could see and canyons as dramatic, if not more so, than the Grand Canyon, and mountains that would sideline Everest to the status of being an interesting peak. Whereas, in the seas there were creatures which he shuddered to think about. In essence, the planets that he was able to visit displayed the biggest, the tallest and the widest; and just when he thought that he had seen the definitive example, he was astounded to find it redefined again!

One planet that really intrigued him contained ocean sized expanses of marshy ground. The Planet of Spirits, they had named it. There at night, on the marshy lands covering most of the planet's surface, will-o'-the-wisp like, ghostly gowned ladies danced eternally to a sound of their own symphonies. But these were not 'just' will-o'-the wisps because the scientists on the AMStar had classified them as 'B level' life forms, evidenced by reason that they sung crafted melodies rising and falling eerily as a choir as they artistically twirled and intertwined to their own music. These experiences taught him that there is no such thing as 'normal' when you spoke of the cosmos; there was always something more. It was a great leveller of all egos and of the tenets of science. It was especially in unrestricted space that he came to realise just how small and insignificant a human being really is. What is the significance of a jet engine or a super computer or walking on the moon to all this he wondered? He knew even more positively now that people needed God in their lives because their association with God lifted the human being from the audience to a part in the orchestra.

It was at this time that a message was received by Captain Moska, from the Ministry of Defence on Ongle, to the effect that Imogen had misjudged a garden step and had fallen heavily breaking a leg so badly that she would be out of action for at least two months. Ongle had asked the Colligate to release Geoff from his secondment to them, a fact which Captain Moska rued, but he accepted that Geoff had duties elsewhere at the moment. Albeit, the Captain did try to reinterpret the wording of the message and opined that it really meant that it was a temporary leave of absence. Geoff laughed at the ruse and thanked him for a wonderful enlightening voyage. It was something that he would never forget and, if at all possible, he would one day return to the AMStar. Geoff departed from the ship with an arm full of flowers for Imogen and all manner of pretty rocks and stones for the children.

Chapter 10.

REASIGNMENT

Imogen had indeed broken her leg badly and she was grateful that Geoffrey had been given time off to return home, but she was recovering slowly. They were now permitted to return to Marina for short breaks but it had not yet been declared entirely safe after the chimp people had used the planet as their hunting estate.

Their girls were maturing and on the verge of their teens and they were developing other interests. On Ongle, they combined sleep overs with their trips to school, but now they were able to invite friends back to Marina for short stays which was a facility which made them extremely popular because Marina was an otherwise prohibited planet as far as tourism was concerned. Geoff looked towards Imogen and elevated his eyes towards the sky when one of the girls asked if she could invite a boy over to stay. It was Imogen who took the lead and suggested it was a bit too early to think of such things, but when she was older, may be. However, they both received a regular supply of teenage magazines with pictures of their favourite, freshly oiled looking pop singers.

Once Imogen had fully progressed, Geoffrey was to

receive a new posting as the Radio Engineering Officer on the Ongle Star Class warship the Passing Star. She was smaller and more modern than the QvO but at eighty kilometres long it was still a substantial sized ship. In truth, it represented a change in spaceship design and the new vessels required less human resources to man them. This, the joining instructions spelled out, was to be an accompanied post and he was delighted that Imogen and their two children would be able to accompany him.

The purpose of the mission of the Passing Star was one of pure exploration and a departure from previous explorations which had, on occasion, bumped into other races and recorded them. Their commission, this time, was designated the code name 'Darwin' and was to deliberately look for other intelligent life forms and to establish contact with them for the purpose of trade and cultural links and to make treaties of friendship. They knew, of course, that the mission could only ever be a pinprick in the vastness of space; there would always be something beyond and beyond that. Notwithstanding, this assignment specifically instructed them to make really deep penetrations of space, further than any ship from Ongle had ever gone. The unusual directive certainly excited the crew to be on this voyage of exploration. ".....three .....two...one. engaging DMT." They caught the last sequence of the countdown as they switched on their hucoms to hear Captain Donald's deadpan countdown for the initial DMT jump.

There was a moment of uncertainty as a glow of warmth was spreading through the ship and their bodies felt very heavy and it was difficult to stand. They heard the Captain's voice more hurriedly call for emergency engine power and for the gravity field to be detensified and they felt relief as their bodies became lighter and normal again. Usually you could not hear the engines of a spaceship but on emergency power the severe vibrations of engines under stress were converted to sound and it signified that extreme thrust had been applied by the engines and obviously something that had gone wrong. But, in this instance, the associated and very noticeably vibrations indicated to them that something had gone 'very' wrong! The residual heat died down quickly as it was wafted away by air conditioning and the Captain's voice came over the address system with the advice that they had materialised into the corona of a large star but they were clear of it and gravity had been restored to normal.

Following the mishap a series of staccato commands were rapidly issued by the Captain via their hucoms: - 'Engineering Branch, report damage to Damage Control. Hull-side Maintenance, inspect and report the integrity of the outer hull. Instruments Branch, re-optimise the settings for all instrumentation. Computer Engineering Branch run diagnostics on all computers. Geoffrey Holder report to the Bridge. Sub ship crews, check the instrumentation of all hanger based space craft.' By now Geoff was on his way to the bridge. 'Radiation safety teams to carry out ship wide sweeps for ionising ingress.' Geoff heard the last command being spoken vocally by Captain Donald as he came through the doorway of the bridge.

"Ah ha, there you are," Captain Donald exclaimed as Geoff came breathlessly through the door to the bridge. "That was a close run thing, we nearly ended up inside a star. We were just far enough out from the centre to be able to take emergency action and pull clear," he mocked, wiping sweat from his brow.

"I wonder what happened?" Geoff inquired.

"We are not too sure yet," Captain Donald informed him. "The navigator has advised me that this is the furthest DMT jump ever attempted by an Ongle ship; and even the smallest invisible discrepancy in the DMT bias settings given by a beacon could translate into a large graphical error when transiting over such a long distance. From now on we will have to limit our enthusiasm and take smaller leaps into the unknown. It seems that we are learning already and we have only just started out," he simulated a shudder. "What I wanted to see you about was that just after we pulled clear of the corona, Radio Monitoring picked up some intelligently crafted radio signals coming from somewhere nearby. Probably from one of the captive planets of the star that we nearly bumped into. Do you think that you could get a fix for me?"

"No problem," Geoff assured. "Did they record the messages?"

"Yes, they were in the HF spectrum. There were some muffled sounds which could have been audio and some high pitched random bleeps, nothing a hucom could latch onto and translate."

"Right sir, I'm on it." Geoff turned on his heel, saying "I will get down to Radio Monitoring right away and see if we can make some sense of it."

It seemed that Geoff may have judged the nuance as the end of the conversation and that the Captain had dismissed him; and he flinched when the Captain's

"Good luck with that, Geoff," came to him over his hucom as he walked out of the door. He hurried back to apologise, but his apology was brushed aside with the Captain's reassurance that these were his afterthoughts.

"I am interested in this broadcast because it may represent the first contact with an intelligent species this far out from Ongle. That would be something to put in my reports; so far I have only got down that we were nearly annihilated by a star!"

"Fine," Geoff thought back. "That was certainly interesting enough, perhaps a little too interesting, in fact. I will do my best to find them something more in line with their expectations." The Captain projected a high five, which Geoff reciprocated.

When Geoff entered the Radio Monitoring Section of the ship he noted that there were two spectre robots there and one male technical operative who he learned was called Garry; and they were painstakingly scanning the frequency over which they had heard the original transmissions. As they listened the transmissions recommenced and they heard a stream of broken sharp pips of varying lengths. It twigged something in his mind, a far off memory awakened and he listened intently. "It sounds like continuous wave Morse Code," he said, "but I don't know the Morse Code itself. Once it was a system of sending messages on Earth but it is obsolete now, just a few enthusiasts continue to use it for recreation," he squinted. "I wonder if Ongle know anything?" He was speaking to the spectre. "Let's originate an urgent DMT message to them to ask them what they know about Morse Code and how to read it." The robot nodded that it understood and it framed the request on a nearby screen. 'Earth, Morse Code, how sent, how read? All other supporting advice available is also required.' Then he touched a key on the computer keyboard. He gave it the caveat of 'urgent' which meant that a special DMT dart would be despatched immediately to Ongle and they would not have to wait to send it on a scheduled DMT dart. Their computer confirmed its' despatch almost at once.

Geoff sat back as the minutes ticked away and stifled a yawn. "We must have given them a tough one, we have got them scratching their heads no doubt," he laughed. He was cut short from further observation by the ping sound of an incoming message alert from a computer whose screen had lit up with the words.'Your question re Morse Code answered herewith. Attributed on Earth to Samuel Morse, the Morse Code was one of the earliest forms of long distance continuous wave (CW) radio communications on that planet. For Morse Code, each letter of the alphabet is converted into a unique identity described by dots and dashes. A trained operator transposes a message into Morse Code when sending a message and reverses that process when receiving a message. This was followed by the complete description of the Morse composition of every letter, number and symbol relevant to the English language. It was given at machine speed, so fast that only the spectre working with Geoff could absorb the information. Indeed, Geoffrey could see that the spectre had understood and was already practicing with its' slim metallic fingers by drumming out Morse on the desk in front of it.

The spectre's finger tapping aptly demonstrating its' digital speed of learning which would be very precise down to the micro pause between dots and dashes and the longer gap between words; and then it announced that it had assimilated Morse Code and was now proficient in it.

"Unbelievable!" Geoff blew the word through his teeth. "It would have taken a human months to learn and become proficient in it."

"It illustrates the difference in storage and application between the human mind and the digital mind; robots operate subject to machine-law. That makes us especially good at repetitious tasks and premeditated tasks." The spectre had assumed the necessity to explain. "The biological mind is good at creation and spontaneous action, at random action and at invention which, in turn, has led to the creation of robots because humans required our machine law to assist them in their endeavours. In this case, I received a full set of instructions from the Ongle data base. The instructions also contained the Morse Code and the physical movements necessary to send Morse code. There was nothing to learn on my part; the programme was simply added to my own data base. It was as if I always knew it. However, robots did not invent the Morse Code, a human did."

"I still find it breathtaking," Geoff commented. "I wonder how fast you can read it and send it? The usual speed of a trained and experienced human operator is around twenty-five to thirty words per minute." The spectre paused as it scanned over what it had recently learned.

"I have been given no actual parameters with regards to speed but I do not have the same restraints as a human because I would be translating Morse code to a digital record and not writing it down. I have checked my abilities programme and I ran a test through them. I believe that I could receive and translate to digital language nine-hundred and fifty three point five words per minute, depending upon an optimum requirement of no radio interference and the quality of the transmission."

"Extraordinary," Geoff sucked in a breath. "In old money and in the days when Morse code was used that would roughly equate to the entire daily throughput of a small communications centre."

But the larger picture was that they still did not have any idea of the scope of the language they were looking at and recording. Moreover, the information would not have been sent in Morse code but using a similar system of transmission. Geoff concluded that, using Morse as a model, there would be longer separations between words and micro silences between the letters of a word. That knowledge would enable them to isolate blocks that were words and by closer examination they could, perhaps, work out the repetition of letters within words, not much but a start.

The next thing to do was to try to isolate the vowels by virtue of their constant repetition. It was not perfect but it was creating something to work on. The outcome was a page of typed words that were a meaningless jumble. It was only when Geoff asked the question that he had, hitherto, forgotten to ask, which was whether each transmission intercepted was unique, the spectre advised him that each message was nearly identical, but not precisely so. It was this piece of information that helped Geoff to make a break-through. "Oh dear, some code breaker," he muttered glumly to himself and then he contacted Captain Donald to brief him that the message had not been broken yet but, in his opinion, because it was constantly repeated it was some kind of warning message or perhaps a frequency blocker. Frequency blockers were often sent out automatically to defend a frequency from being poached by others muscling in on it and using it for their own purposes. But one thing common to all Morse transmissions was that they invariably contained the identity of the transmitting station somewhere near the front of their message.

Geoff waited before framing a request to the Captain. "I think that we can make a guess as to the probable content based on our own habits. I would suggest that among the first few words of the text there will be one of the following, warning, danger, position, help, this is, we are at, keep off. With your permission, I would like to tap into any spare computing capacity that we have on the ship, to help speed up the search."

"That sounds a good idea," Captain Donald sounded interested. "The navigational computer is the most powerful that we have aboard. Since we are in orbit around this planet, the nav computer is hardly being used. You can have ninety percent of its' capacity but if we need it in a hurry we may grab that back without warning."

Geoff turned to the spectre and asked him if he could make the connection. When that had been established, he ran the encoded word blocks through the computer to ascertain if there were repetitions in the text which might then indicate common words.

"We have to bear in mind though," Geoff was speaking to Garry in the workstation, "our analysis shows that this is a longer alphabet than ours and the word help, for example, is not necessarily spelt with just four letters in another language."

The nav computer was a masterpiece and at the front end of Ongle computer technology and capable of 'extended random theory' and 'what if' applications. The spectre was plugged straight into the computer terminal while Geoff sat alongside it watching the computer screen tumbling through endless equations and suppositions and then with the sound of a klaxon the screen halted and in the middle of it were the words 'help'. The word demanded their attention by brightening; with a conclusion that there was an eighty percent probability that this word was the second word of the text. "Ah ha." Geoff was relieved as he turned to the spectre beside him. "As we know," he told the spectre, "the first word is ninety percent certain to be a callsign. Working on the basis that it is, it could be any jumble of letters and figures and we may never get it. Let us relegate the first group of the text as unimportant at the moment and we can assign X in lieu of each letter and repeat those as a bijection across the alien text." A new picture appeared on the screen in front of them showing random Xs and underscores for the unsolved letters between them.. "Now please biject the letters of the word 'help'." The screen refreshed and showed a mixture of X's and the letters H E L P spread around with many underscored blanks between them. Thereafter, by guesswork and intuition they moved letters around in the read outs and the nav computer constantly tried them in relation to likely consonants and vowels and a small trickle of probables for English language letters began to grow across the text and the spell check facility of the nav computer started to suggest words and substituting X's where it could not find a probable resolution " Well, we have quite a few possibles now," Geoff exclaimed, "let's get the computer to look again now for 'we are' or 'we have crashed or help needed'," he instructed the spectre. Finally they were left with six pages of A4 size print outs with gaps and letters and a welter of suggestions. Geoff and Garry looked at the jumble of words that were still little more than an incomprehensible mess.

"We could probably have arrived at these without the aid of a computer," Geoff was dour as he and a spectre stared at the jumble of letters.

"I think I can see something," Garry was exuberant. "Looking at the first words, we could jumble them around like this." He leaned forward and typed into a computer and the letters 'ON' and other letters and Xs appeared on the screen. "I have rearranged the letters in the order that you can now see them. Now split it like so and we can deduce it to be 'HELP XXXXX XE HAXE CRASHED ON. It needs a bit of a 'licence' to deduce it, but the letters 'SHED' and 'ON' at the end enables one to guess at the message. I have had to re-sequence words so that they accord with how they would be expressed in our own language!"

"Brilliant," Geoff broke in. "I think that is enough, it is a guess based upon partial evidence. I don't think that we will ever get the rest of it." The three of them gathered around the sheet of paper and they agreed that it seemed to be right. They also felt if this was the true wording of the message then continuing to try to tease out the rest of it could take another week. The originators of the message may not have that kind of time at their disposal. "We will send it to the Captain now, as it is," Geoffrey affirmed.

Geoff asked Garry to relay a hard copy of the message to Captain Donald whilst he simultaneously connected to him via his hucom.

"Hang on, Geoff, I'll just catch up," the Captain came on the line. "Your text has just come in, give me a couple of seconds." There was a small gap in the conversation as the Captain digested the message. "We have crashed on. I think we can go along with that and now we must get a radio fix on the exact location."

"We are not one-hundred percent certain," Geoff interceded, "but it is the best we can do. Their alphabet, according to our analysis, has fifty-two letters which makes it difficult to find matches to our own." Geoff sat back tensely and it was only now that he realised just how intensive their quest had been. They had been working flat out for five hours to extract just five words and even those were fifty percent guesswork; and they intently waited the Captain's reply.

"I'm up to speed now and I support your conclusion," Captain Donald confirmed. "I think that we must go down there to see if we can offer assistance. We have the bare bones and we have already triangulated their location. Go and get a coffee and unwind for a bit as I put this together. I would like you and the spectre, designator seventeen, who is with you right now, to go down with a party. You will be accompanied by a physimed and a small party of marines. Let's see if you can find out what this is all about."

Chapter 11

EMERGENCE

Geoff found that he just had time to visit Imogen before his imminent departure to the surface of the planet below and she expressed her concern that she didn't like having her husband whisked away at short notice to the surface of a planet which they knew absolutely nothing about.

"Don't worry, darling," he told her, "I am married to the most beautiful woman in the universe so I am not going to take any risk which would mean that I couldn't come back to her."

"Flattery, mmm, don't stop," she lilted. "If you can get a chance, we could do with some fresh fruit. Keep in touch when you are down there," she added wistfully. Then she touched his arm, "If you find that there are even 'more' beautiful women down there, ignore them!" she said playfully.

The assignment order came through almost as soon as Geoff had grabbed a few personal items from their apartment and it directed him to report to the Expedition Stores to be kitted with micro biological protective wear and anti-insect and 'biting animal' repellent clothing.

"How does anti-biting protection work then?" Geoff asked looking at the clothing suspiciously.

"Not many animals like an electric shock in their mouths," the store-man explained. "Mind you they may have to take a bite at you to find that out," was his unreassuring reply. As standard issue his survival suit included a full helmet fitted for air filtering and oxygen intensification; and his personal armament consisted of a poenillium pistol but the military contingent was fully armed to light combat standard. The military commander was to be in overall charge of their 'insertion,' he deadpan described it in military jargon. By now all of the nominated crew had arrived at the Expeditions Stores and the air was abuzz with their chatter and introductions as together they hefted their bags of equipment for the short walk to the hanger deck. They were delighted to see that they were to have a medium size runabout for the trip down to the planet because these larger vessels had full resources including sleeping apartments, a kitchen and other facilities and they were undoubtedly preferable to living in a tent on an unfamiliar planet. Geoff donned the expedition gear provided and the military men struggled into their armoured suits. There were six marines in the party plus, their Officer, Geoff, a spectre and a physimed. Looking around him Geoff mentally categorised the military section as business like and prepared for eventuality. The physimed and the spectre robot with them did not require special protection because of their largely metal exteriors and because they had no necessity to respirate.

"Standby for descent," a pleasant recorded female voice announced through their hucoms, followed by, "descending now." In this case, descent was to be a free fall and the bow thrusters would slow them down just before atmospheric entry. Geoff felt his stomach sink as the thrusters counteracted gravity. In the meantime the spectre accompanying him was busy pinpointing the origin of the Morse type transmissions and interacting with the robot pilot of the craft. They came in gently in the stealth mode to land three-hundred metres from the computed location of the intercepted call for help. Air analysis on entry had shown adequate oxygen levels with no mixture of harmful gases but the military indicated that they were to wear their helmets by reason that they were entering into uncharted territory. 'Prepared for surprises' as one of the marines explained.

Initially the military group alighted and Geoff and the spectre came down the ramp last. For a while they stayed invisibly within the stealth mode envelope of the ship as they surveyed the lush world outside of it. The spectre was pointing to a sheer cliff face as being the origin of the CW signal. There were trees between them and their objective so, with their military escort, they started towards the source of the distress call. The undergrowth here was particularly dense and hostile and armed with treacherous barbs which tore at the thorn proof clothing they wore. Once again the usefulness of the robotic frame was demonstrated as the spectre and the physimed used their bare mental hands to bend and twist the malignant undergrowth aside to make a pathway.

By now Geoff had established rapport with the military commander of the expedition and he learned that the officer was Lieutenant Colonel Tom Brooks, a professional man of not many words, who now turned towards Geoff and observed that he could sure do with a couple of robot hands himself. It was meant to be jocular. Geoff laughed with him and then added that they were probably good for getting things out of a hot oven as well. But now there was a new twist of events as they became aware of a murmur of sound in the background which was getting louder as they progressed through the entangled shrubbery. "It sounds like a large crowd of people," Geoff speculated.

Geoff's guess was confirmed to be accurate shortly afterwards because as the spectre parted the next group of bushes they could see out into a glade. Given that the scene which met their eyes could have been regarded as comical, it also had sinister potential because the clearing before them was packed with a metre and a half tall replicas of Earth's meerkats. Each armed with a bow or a catapult and they were concentrating their firepower in waves at a cave opening, twenty metres above them in the cliff face, from which an occasional perfunctory rock was hurled by an unseen hand from the dark depths in the direction of the meerkats who with their 'keened in the wild' reactions were nimbly able to dodge them.

"My word," Geoff uttered the words involuntarily, "these are extraordinary. I wonder what is in the cave?" Tom Brooks responded to him with the observation.

"Our binos have picked up that there is a thin wire

coming out of the mouth of that cave and I would suggest that it is the antenna for the radio transmissions that we have been receiving. The question we have to solve now is how to get to the cave without engaging the animals in front of us!" His preferred choice of a stealth approach disappeared because one of his party stepped on a fallen branch which gave a crack which, in turn, disturbed a bird which flew out of the brush squawking furiously. As meerkats do on Earth, these rose up to stand on their hind legs and they turned, as one, to face them; and Geoff was obliged to dive for cover behind a tree as arrows and catapulted stones zipped amongst them.

Observationally heroic it seemed, but in truth Tom was impervious to the arrows in his bullet proof combat uniform as he strode unhurriedly back through a volley of them to see Geoff to check that he was unharmed.

"I think I am going to have to put on some kind of a show of force. Any ideas?" Geoff thought for a moment.

"We don't know the rights and wrongs of this yet," Geoff advised. "I think we have to try not to kill any of the meerkats if it can be avoided."

"That is what I am thinking. My plan is to have my men advance into them. They will carry pistols ready to fire if necessary but when these meerkats, as you call them, see that their arrows and projectiles can't take my men down they are going to have to come up with a plan 'B' and I hope that includes talking to us."

"Seems a good idea," Geoff was supportive, "the less killing the better, we have yet to determine which side we have to back." Geoff loosed his poenillium pistol in its' holster as the Colonel moved off to martial four of his men, leaving two behind with Geoff with the instruction that they were to provide backup or be prepared to cover his party's retreat, depending on how the situation unfolded.

The two marines that were left behind set about forming a defensive triangle position with Geoff and the spectre robot and the pysimed holding one corner. It wasn't perfect but it was the best possible solution with the resources available and the human element of their party kneeled down behind the low undergrowth to observe the forward party's advance into the meerkats.

"There does not appear to be a command structure among them," Tom remarked to Geoff via his hucom. "Right now they have assessed that our weakness is our flanks and they are splitting their forces to approach us from three directions. So please keep them from closing the fourth side which is our way back if we need to retreat."

The meerkats circled warily to enclose the advancing marines from three directions and Geoff's rear guard moved closer to their defensive permitter so that the meerkats could see that they could not completely close the circle and surround the advance party without risk to themselves. There was no spoken word of command from the meerkats yet they all raised their bows in unison as they loosed off a storm of arrows at the advance party. However, the rain of arrows tailed off as they registered that their projectiles were bouncing off the suits of the marines as did the stones fired at them from their catapults. It then became apparent that the meerkats had a siege weapon hidden behind the trees and they heard a whoosh as it released a heavy boulder towards the advancing marines. Apparently, it was not a very accurate instrument and the boulder would surely have killed several of their own people as well if it had landed, but with the crackle of a poenillion rifle the ball of rock vanished mid-flight in a cloud of red dust. Now, however, with the existence and location of the siege weapon revealed, the marine immediately in front of Geoff set to work with a poenillium rifle and cleared a line of fire through the natural screen. It looked as if there was a madman with an oversized chain saw out there as trees came crashing down, left and right, until a line of sight had been levelled through them to reveal a heavily timbered siege catapult. With just one more shot by the marine the whole structure collapsed to the ground in a state of beyond immediate repair.

The arrows, aimed at the advance party, were coming in sporadic numbers now and they dwindled off completely and the meerkats sat down on the ground flummoxed or out of projectiles. Just one of their number, and closest to the Ongolan party, was left fiddling to locate an arrow on the drawstring of his bow when a marine stepped forward and wrenched the arrow away and broke it in half and then broke the bow over his knee and handed the bits back to the forlorn meerkat.

A murmur that sounded like despair went through the throng; and the meerkats sat down, as one, with their large unwinking eyes steadily regarding the marines. There was no observable hostility from them but certainly discernible anxiety as they tried to guess what the actions of these creatures with God-like powers in their midst would do next. The question was answered for them almost immediately and they were soon up and pointing at the sky above as another space runabout, despatched at the request of Colonel Brooks, hove into sight. In his request for support the Colonel had specified a show of force with a dramatic landing; and the craft with undamped thrusters, screamed in and threw up a large cloud of dust as it landed in a fluid operation. Hidden in the dust cloud a ramp had dropped and a large party of marines disembarked from the craft and commenced to form a ring around the glade; and the worried meerkats sat down again looking defeated.

On request, Geoff joined the Colonel in the centre of the meerkats and he looked around, not without sympathy, because he was disconcerted by so many anxious faces following his every move.

"There must be a leader among them somewhere," Tom wondered aloud, "but which of them do I talk to!"

"I would imagine it would have some kind of identification mark, a necklace or a badge or even a crown" Geoff conjoined as they started to wander through the meerkat gathering, looking for clues but there were none immediately evident. Then Geoff caught sight of a slow and furtive movement by one of the meerkats and he kept a corner of his eye on it and saw that it was surreptitiously attempting to pull at a loose corner of a gold threaded material to try to conceal it beneath itself.

Geoff said nothing but he drew Colonel Brooks aside and told him what what he had seen and indicated with his eyes and a nod towards the meerkat in question. To allay suspicion, the Colonel's walk was unhurried along the first row of meerkats and Geoff nodded again to indicate when he was opposite the suspect. Colonel Brooks signalled with a hand to the meerkat that it should stand up but he was met by a stoic impassive stare as if the creature was not directly involved and the Colonel must be indicating the meerkat next to him or even one three rows back perhaps! Thus, in a fell swoop, Tom bent down and pulled the meerkat to its feet and revealed that what it had been sitting on and trying to hide was a gold threaded cloak. In that instant the two thousand or more seated meerkats rose to their feet screaming abuse and gesticulating at him; and their archers, that still had arrows left, commenced to load their bows.

For a moment it had looked as if they were going to have a riot on their hands, but that was defused when the Colonel solemnly held out his hand and shook the meerkat's paw; then he bent down and picked up the cloak. With care he shook the dust off it and draped it around the meerkat's shoulders and tidied it up so that it fell neatly around its' body. By the use of hand gestures he invited the meerkat to follow him to the centre of the gathering. From there he directed a marine to get a chair out of the space runabout and he invited the meerkat to sit on it with the cloak of woven gold thread draped regally about it.

Whatever the status of the meerkat was, the others had now all resumed a sitting position and were looking just a little less anxious; but two-thousand pairs of glazed black eyes staring back at you, blankly following your every movement, was a surreal situation to be in. On a brainwave and seeing the opportunity to build on success, Geoff approached the meerkat with a hucom and showed the meerkat leader how he took it on and off his head. It was not going to be that easy, he found, because when he indicated that the meerkat should do the same it adopted the inscrutable look of its' species and stared passively through him as if he did not exist.

"Oh well, I can't force it to wear it," Geoff was frustrated, "that would certainly create an incident if I did." An idea came to Tom Brooks who rummaged in his protective suit and produced a bar of chocolate and broke a piece off and ate it and the meerkat displayed an interest. Tom next offered a piece to his highness, as he now called him, who hesitated a while and then took it very tentatively and bit a piece off and a look of sheer joy crossed its' face.

"I should have thought of that," Geoff laughed, "chocolate has been used to establish communication in first contacts throughout the cosmos by authors of books and the directors of Sci-Fi film in dozens in their works back on Earth. This is probably the first time it has been tried for real though!"

"So far so good," Tom commented. "So let's try again," and he offered a fresh piece of chocolate and this time it was readily accepted and a hand shot out for more.

Tom refused and indicated that the hucom was to be put on and then he would give him another piece of chocolate. "Well, I assume it is a him," he grinned. This time his highness had apparently become a confirmed chocoholic and he donned the hucom over its' head with alacrity and held out its' hand.

"Ok Geoff, try it out," Tom called. "I will switch it on remotely and be listening in."

"Hello," Geoff ventured, "we are from the Ongle star system and we have come here in response to a distress call from this planet." He didn't get any further because his highness was now standing on his seat gibbering away and his subjects were back on their feet gesticulating and shrieking loudly as they shuffled towards them and the distinct words came over Geoff and Tom's hucoms.

"What the bloody hell is this?" and his highness was tearing the hucom from his head.

"At least the hucom has found a language match; that's progress of sorts." Geoff stuck up his thumb towards Tom,

"But it's not much good if its' laying at its feet in the dust," Tom observed laconically. But, ever resourceful, Tom had sent a marine back to gather up all the chocolate available in the two ships and when they had done so he requested more from the Passing Star; and soon a good-natured group of marines moved among the flock distributing squares of chocolate and in doing so they were cementing friends for life!

Once again Geoffrey persuaded the meerkat to don the hucom he was holding in its' hand.

"This is a hucom," Geoff touched the band of the one he was wearing and walked over and touched the band of the one his highness was wearing. "It enables us to talk to you and for you to talk to us."

"It's witchcraft!" The reply was shot back.

"No, it is not witchcraft, it is something that we have invented and we all wear them. They enable us to speak to each other over long distances and in many languages." He followed up with another pacifying square of chocolate.

"Easy on the chocolate," Tom cautioned, "if he gets sick, those may be the last words we ever get to say to them." Meantime, out in the flock, their allegiance, paid for by chocolate, was fast switching from his highness to the finer things of life. In any case, they had observed that the headband now had the approval of their leader who was listening with a new inquisitiveness to what he must have assumed was a voice from the sky.

"My name is Geoffrey," he began in hushed thought, "may I ask who you are?"

"I am Olaf, king of the Minx people, and these are my subjects," he swept his extended clawed hands around to encompass the throng sitting on the grass. "I have never seen you or your like before. Are you from across the seas?"

"Not from the sea. I have come from further away than that," Geoff displayed his open hands and looked upwards at the expanse of the sky. "We have come from the stars, the same stars that you see at night." Olaf did not seem in the least fazed by this information and his reply revealed that his Majesty might mentally be just out of the evolutionary stone age but his mind was sharp, educated and receptive to new concepts. However, Olaf had sat expressionless as if deep in thought before he responded.

"We have long believed that there were people out in the stars but we have never seen them before until recently. Is this why you are here?" Geoff explained that it was possible to send messages over long distances and they had picked up a call for help.

"Do you know anything about it; we were thinking it had something to do with whoever is in that cave?" Geoff pointed to the cave in the cliff face.

"Oh those," Olaf pulled a face. "they look something like you, which is why we attacked you because we assume that you are of the same tribe."

"We are not of the same tribe," Geoff hastened to correct Olaf's assumption, "but a cry for help is a cry for help. We felt duty bound to respond to their call."

"Huh," Olaf didn't seek to disguise his distaste at the notion of helping the people in the cave. "They came out of the sky in that iron bird of theirs and skidded across the ground and killed five of the Minx people. They managed to get out of their bird but it caught fire. We chased them into the bush and lost them, but three days later we found them. Somehow they had scaled the cliff to that cave," he pointed to the same cave that Geoff had indicated. "Whatever they used to get up there, they took with them and we have no means of getting up there because they drop rocks down on us if we try. We are not bothered by that, they have to eat and drink, so we will stay here until they die of thirst or starve to death." He had spoken as if the matter was final and he did not anticipate any further questions on the subject.

Geoff surmised intuitively that this was a critical moment in their dialogue and resolved to choose his words very carefully.

"Where we come from we say that there are two sides to any story. What we do know from their message is that they crashed and that means that they were unable to control their iron bird. It is most probable that they did not wish to kill any of your people. I would like to go up there and see them and try to get to the bottom of what happened; I have the means to get up there. All I am trying to do is to get some answers to this and seek a solution." Olaf said nothing and sat with unblinking eyes but he was patently thinking it through.

Eventually Olaf come to a decision and said: -

"Yes, we would like to hear what they have to say but I have to address my people first."

"Please do." Geoff encouraged. With a nod of agreement Olaf stood up on his chair and gave a peculiar piercing whistle which would probably carry over a long distance and his subjects got to their feet with their large wackadoodle eyes fixated upon him as he explained the events of the past minutes to them. He told his people that their new friends were from the stars and that they had come here because the people in the cave, who they did not know, had called for help using a magical instrument which could send messages beyond their own planet.

"Ah," they murmured in unison as he explained what Geoff had told him about hearing all sides of the story and of Geoff's desire to go and meet with this other tribe and that he would come back and tell them what he had found out.

"Could they agree to that?" he asked. There was a ripple across the throng and a lot of foot shuffling in its' midst.

"I have noted that their claws are jointed like fingers and they seem to think things through better when they shuffle," Geoff used a private channel to speak to Tom.

"Might try myself then, if it helps," Tom joked back. Then one meerkat paw was raised and then another and then another and soon a wave of raised paws swept through the gathering and Olaf turned to Geoff and told him that it had been agreed.

It is not as if the Minx people had ever seen a jet pack before but they regarded it, as always, impassively as it was carried to Geoff and he stepped into it and was strapped in by a marine. They sat unwinkingly as he turned it on and they observed silently as he promptly disappeared into a cloud of dust kicked up by the downdraft. Two thousand pairs of eyes followed his every aerial manoeuvre as he re-emerged from the dust cloud and made his way to the cave entrance. Soundlessly they watched him alight on its' rim, before they turned back to avidly discuss in a hubbub of sound the wonders that they had just witnessed.

"I think you will be written down in their history as an angel," Tom's words followed him.

"They treat the unusual as just another day in the life of a meerkat," Geoff satirised.

As Geoff's eyes adjusted to the cave's dark interior he could see that there was great depth to it and there were seven silver suited humanoids gathered at the far end and as soon as he had landed they had bent down to pick up rocks and advanced towards him with the clear intent of throwing them at him. Geoff held up his hands to illustrate that he held no weapon and pressed a button on the neck of the helmet and it fell away on a lever to hang in a cradle behind him. The party stopped and looked at him with amazement, as Geoff did to them. They were tall and statuesque in the model of the Zulu race but they all had startling blue eyes.

Geoff advanced cautiously towards them holding out a hucom to the person who appeared to be their leader which he had deduced by reason of the many badges on his uniform. He pointed to the hucom that was on his own head and it was readily understood that the other person was to wear the one that was offered to him. The individual he had nominated took it and glanced over it, turning it over in his hands, intelligently gathering from his examination how to adjust the headband and then he placed it over his head. The alien was the first one to speak.

"Who are you?" he asked, although he still hadn't grasped that it was a mind to mind transfer rather than open speech. It would take some time and practice to become used to such a device as Geoff had learned from his own introduction to a hucom. Geoff consciously slowed the process down and that was one of the earlier hurdles to be overcome in mind to mind conversation.

"Well done," he complimented and the other perceived that Geoffrey's lips had not moved and took his hucom off again and re examined it more closely. He pointed to it and said something unintelligible and Geoff removed his own hucom and repeated vocally what he had just projected by thought and that was patently just as incomprehensible to the alien. Geoff re-donned his hucom and repeated what he had just said and tacked on. "It is a mind to mind communication device and it also translates languages, so it is best to keep it on. It may not be a perfect translation to begin with but it learns and its' user learns, too. You will have to fill in any gaps in the translation initially, but after a day or two there will be no problems."

The alien's large blue eyes had widened and he grinned. Then it was Geoff's turn to be startled as pictures of space and children and family events and mining facts tumbled through his mind together with a graphic rendition of their recent crash. The uncontrolled thoughts raced through the alien's mind and thence through his hucom, thence onwards to Geoff and also to Tom who was listening in, in the background. Geoff beckoned the alien over and reached out and tapped a number into the numeric keypad on the alien's hucom so that from then on his hucom would only translate and relay direct speech. "What happened?" Geoff enquired. "You have certainly upset the native people of this planet; they plan to starve you to death or kill you beforehand if you dare to venture out of this cave."

The alien's eyes were downcast with apparent sorrow and he seemed to be setting out the sequence of events in his mind,

"We are a geological survey team from the planet Suva. We found this planet and we were trying to put down on it to meet the people who live here and seek their permission to carry out a survey of their resources. We collided unnoticed with a small object. We think it was a very small meteorite that had come straight out of space and would have, otherwise, impacted this planet; instead, it hit the nose cone of our vessel. Regrettably all of the ship's external sensors and gyroscopic stabilisers were located in the nose cone and they were catastrophically damaged.

"Bad luck," Geoff interjected, that sort of thing does happen. Could you not land and effect repairs?"

"In theory that should be possible but in practice these craft are notoriously difficult to control in an atmosphere without their sensors. Still we, well myself really, decided to land to make the repairs, but the descent became very rapid, almost a vertical dive in fact, and we just managed to pull the ship into a near horizontal plane but we couldn't stop it hitting the ground quite hard and it skidded into a group of natives."

"They are called the Minx," Geoff broke in.

"Well, they were Minx and there was nothing that we could do and three of our own crew members were killed; and then fire broke out on the ship and there was a real danger of explosion. We grabbed what we could and vacated the ship. Our emergency use small arms were locked away in an arms chest and there was no time to retrieve them. We got as far away as possible. We did not hear an explosion but we could see the smoke and we believe that our ship was destroyed in a conflagration which had also ignited the surrounding brush, so we moved further away still."

Geoff temporarily stilled the conversation while he consulted with Tom to confirm that the conversation he was having was being recorded and he received his affirmative.

"Then what happened after that?" Geoff was questioning him closely. "Sorry I didn't ask if you have a name?"

"My name is Razil and I am the chief geologist on this trip. For a start we just kept a safe distance from our craft but then a party of Minx discovered us and started shooting at us with bows and arrows; and they injured one of our crew members and we couldn't get back against the swarm of arrows to save her. In our panic we had forgotten that we did have sticks of geological grade gelignite in our backpacks and when we remembered them we fused one and threw it towards where we last saw the Minx party and they ran away. We then went back to find our missing crew member but we could see that she had been dragged away and we are too small in numbers to contemplate a raid. In any event, you can see that we are now being watched day and night. We are very worried about her and feel embarrassed that we could not do anything to save her." Geoff interrupted the alien.

"Hold it there a moment. I will see what I can find out. What is her name? "

"Aprilla," Razil looked earnestly at Geoff.

"We would be most grateful if you could." Then in a lowered tone, almost fading away towards the end, he added, "We were to be married when we return to Suva." Geoff held up his hand to still the conversation and called through to Colonel Brooks in a privatised link to ask what he could find out from the Minx and if the missing crew member had survived. Geoff had expected to wait several minutes and he went to find a seat on a rock ledge. His action reminded him that his back pockets were bulging and he recalled that he still had a dozen bars of chocolate tucked in them which he had intended to distribute as largesse to the Minx. His jet-pack also had an emergency water bottle slotted into a side pocket and he produced these and offered them to the crew who took them eagerly.

"We cannot take sides at this juncture," he advised Razil, "but we can act humanely. We do not support starving people to death nor depriving them of water until they die of thirst."

"We are indebted to you," Razil was delighted.

Geoff's hucom pinged an incoming message warning.

"Hi Geoff, I have some information for you," Tom was brief, "best switch this to encrypted conversation," and they both made the necessary adjustments to their hucoms and a red light flashed three times in Geoff's mind to show that a 'secure link' was confirmed.

"Olaf is aware of Aprilla. She has recovered and she is well but she is to stand trial as an accomplice to unlawful killing. It amazes me but they have a fully functional and quite complex judicial system in place here," he added.

"Let's hope it is fair then," Geoff responded. "As you will have heard, they claim that they lost all exterior sensors on their ship due to meteorite damage and they were trying to fly in by the seat of their pants but, according to them, with no input from its' exterior sensors. It is a brute of a ship to fly by hand and they pancaked it, killing three of their crew. They made it to the cave before the irate Minx got to them."

"I was wondering about that; I must have missed something," Tom replied. "How did the Suvans get up there; it looks pretty formidable to me, even the Minx haven't tried it. You would have thought that the Minx's claws might be useful for climbing!" Geoff momentarily switched his Hucom over to Razil to ask the same question before returning to his conversation with Tom.

"As I understand," Geoff continued, "in one respect, at least, they had some luck because they are a party of geologists and there is a lot of climbing gear such as ropes and pitons and hammers in their backpacks but even then they only just made it. They had a base radio station in a backpack but the microphone was broken. However, their radio technician was able to construct a Morse key from a hacksaw blade and that was the signal which we picked up. I think there is no cover close to the cliff for the Minx to make an assault from the ground and they haven't figured out how to lower themselves from the top. As we have found out, Olaf is in no hurry to commit his subjects to die in an assault when nature will do the work of finishing off his unwelcome visitors for him. "You know," he added, "it does appear to be a pure accident to me, but Olaf and the Minx have no concept of piloting a space craft. They will not understand that things can go wrong over which the pilots have no control. It is rare, but it does happen."

"I agree with you," Tom confirmed, "but I think that we are going to need a, yet to be defined, capital letter 'X' solution to solve this one."

"Could you try Olaf with the faulty space ship angle and see what he says?' Geoff asked.

"Will do," Tom was business like, "keep this channel

147

open."

Geoff looked around and saw that Razil was hovering expectantly and he felt guilty for having become so engaged in speaking to Colonel Brooks, so he beckoned Razil over and switched his hucom back to general.

"I am sorry," he excused himself, "there is good and bad news. The good news is that Aprilla is alive and well but, on a serious note, they apparently want her to stand trial because of the Minx people you killed when you landed. They claim that she was an accomplice to an unlawful killing." Razil's face broke into an enormous grin, then clouded.

"But we did not set out to kill anybody; it was unavoidable. We must stop them, by all means."

Geoff sat back in thought and vainly sought inspiration but found none before he summed up the present state of play. "We can't interfere with their legal system, if that is what you mean," Geoff cautioned, "we can only try to persuade them. Their complaint against you is that they hold you all to be accomplices to unlawful killing. In the meantime, while we try to negotiate, I think you should stay here and I will tell their king Olaf that we cannot allow people to starve to death because you have not yet been found guilty of anything; and we will supply you with food and drink, medical assistance, bedding and a change of clothing,while we try to get them to cede the point that unavoidable accidents do happen sometimes with mechanical devices."

By the time he returned, Geoff found the glade where they had encountered Olaf and the Minx people was almost empty, with the exception of a Minx night watch seated in view of the cave entrance. He made his way to their ship where he and the Colonel spent a long hour discussing the situation. "What I will do in the morning," Colonel Brooks advised, "is to go and see Olaf and try to reason with him." However, when they met the next day the Colonel had the bad news to relay that Olaf had dug his heels in. He had listened to what Tom had to say but then had expressed the opinion 'that if space craft were occasionally dangerous or became uncontrollable then they had no place bringing one to his planet. In doing so they had knowingly put the lives of Minx people at risk.' He agreed, on reflection, 'that it was perhaps illegal to try to starve the crew to death but his people had been pretty angry at the time. But, despite the overwhelming evidence which, according to their law, points to their guilt, at present they only stand accused and they have not yet been convicted of anything, so he agreed that they could be sustained in their present location, provided they did not try to escape. Meantime, the legal executive on Ongle and the AMC had been briefed but they had signalled that they were still discussing the situation; but they had decided only to keep watch, their directive was that they were to continue to negotiate with Olaf.

"I noted the word 'yet' in my conversation with Olaf," Tom recalled later. "For all their exactitudes regarding the proper legal procedure, they seem to have prejudged this case."

"It can only be so," Geoff summed up. "These people are at the evolutionary equivalent of Earth's middle ages. They have buildings and they are able to make clothes and furniture and employ various mechanical constructions such as waterwheels and ploughs and grow crops. I would imagine that their laws reflect their state of evolution. With your permission I would like to go and see if we can reach some kind of compromise?" The military mind makes a decision quickly and the Colonel instantly nodded his agreement,

"Right, you've got the floor. Will you need an escort?"

"No, I think not," was Geoff's reply, "but I think I will take the spectre with me. I have a plan to use him to put on a bit of a show to impress them," he laughed.

"Good luck with it then and stay in touch by hucom; it is not far away and we can be with you in minutes if it gets nasty."

Chapter 12

DIPLOMACY

Geoff did not have much conviction that he could succeed when, with the spectre, he set out for Minx township the next morning; and when they arrived they were soon surrounded by very engaging Minx children. The children had no historic notion of a robot, so they were happy to assume that the spectre was another strain of the strange advanced species that had so recently come to visit them. At Geoff's suggestion, the robot amused the children by doing handstands and cartwheels which they all tried out for themselves, but he then spied a Minx archer and asked him to shoot an arrow at the spectre. Initially the archer demurred but Geoff asked him if he could use the bow and when that was granted he loosed off an arrow at the spectre which caught it in mid-flight as it came towards him and threw it to the ground.

It was gratifying to see the excitement this generated in the children; and adults also began to gather round as Geoff invited two bowmen to fire at the spectre; and when they did, it had the spectre leaping and jumping high into the air to permit arrows to fly beneath its' feet or twisting and turning to catch the arrows that would, otherwise, have hit it; and quite a pile of arrows was building up around the spectre until Geoff called the game to a halt. But, through making it a game, he had gained the trust of the children and their parents. He just hoped that the children would not try it on their own, but they appeared to readily accept that the robot had super powers which they, themselves, did not possess.

More and more Minx gathered until it was almost a tumult with Geoff and the spectre at its centre and Olaf was called and he came regally down the steps of a superior looking house and stood there waiting for Geoff to join him there. Geoff obliged and held out a hucom for Olaf to wear.

"Why were you doing that?" were his first words after he had donned the hucom.

"Ah, children are children wherever you go amongst the stars," Geoff related. "They have wide open minds waiting to learn, but please do tell them that what the spectre did would be very dangerous for them to try to copy. He is a special being with very special skills.

"Yes, I could see that," Olaf affirmed. "Yes, they will be told, but what brings you here today?" Geoff sucked his lips as he sought the right words to say, then suddenly brightened as random notion presented itself tohim.

"What I have been thinking is that we really know so little about one another as people and what I would like to do is to invite you and as many adults and children as we can take, to come aboard one of our ships and we could take you around your planet. There is so much to learn about it." Olaf's eyes opened wide and he rocked back on his heels until Geoff feared that he would topple over, then he recovered his composure.

"That is a splendid idea!" Olaf was enthusiastic, "but what do you want in return?"

"Nothing at all." Geoff hid his reason which was the building of trust. "The adults will be able to see their planet as they never have before and the children will learn and as they grow older they will build upon their experience and their knowledge."

"Will it not crash like the other ship did?" Olaf revealed his scepticism of space ships.

"It is very very rare that a ship crashes. Something really has to go very wrong that the crew cannot control; even then they will do all in their power to prevent it; basically they are saving their own lives as well as those of their passengers."

The trip was arranged for the next morning and a pre-selected group of eager Minx swarmed towards the space runabout which was now de-cloaked and parked in the middle of the glade; and Olaf also arrived wearing full regal regalia, probably, Geoff thought, to impress upon his people that it was 'he', their king, who had arranged this trip. Without the benefit of hucoms their conversations were a jabber which may have been apprehension or excitement but having their king along observably gave them confidence. Geoff had arranged for an address system inside the ship and he used it, through Olaf who was wearing a hucom, to translate the ship's safety procedures verbally to his subjects. The guests were taken to the hanger deck which had been cleared out and tables, some borrowed from the Minx, now had computer screens on them.

In some respects the architecture of the deck, itself, was not ideal because neither the Minx adults nor the children were tall enough to see out of the portholes without the aid of an assortment of boxes, benches and low coffee tables, rummaged by the crew of the Passing Star to compensate for the Minx lax of stature. They had also to improvise hand holds made of draped ropes for periods when the journey would be unsteady. There was no point, they found, in getting into advanced explanations about computers to a people who were yet to discover electricity. For the computer screens the term 'magic mirrors' was enough of an explanation for them to believe what they saw. The more curious of the Minx looked around the back of the screens for evidence of what they had been seeing on the other side of them. Thus, the word 'magic' they surmised was indeed the only plausible explanation.

A brief moment of panic ensued as the shuttle took off and the Minx found their stomachs queasily sinking into their abdomens and they clung desperately to the rope hand holds and they looked questioningly towards Geoffrey to ascertain if he was showing signs of distress, but they saw none. They did not know that he was already in contact with the bridge of the ship and he was calling for a more gentle touch when it came to acceleration.

Geoff continued to explain what they were seeing and Olaf translated this verbatim to the public address system. The Minx children probably thought that their king was all knowing and was wise beyond belief and as far as Geoff could tell he never heard Olaf explain that he was simply relaying what he was being told.

"Aww," they gasped as they picked up height and saw their homes dwindle in size, to be replaced by a great globe in the heavens. Geoff told them, via Olaf, that this was their planet and that was how it looked from space and they were enthralled. Then they were back in the atmosphere again and lakes, forests and villages slipped by. King Olaf was probably demonstrating to his subjects that he was the master of events and asked if the ship could make a low pass over his capital city. That was a surprise to Geoffrey, too, because, hitherto, he had prejudged Olaf's position to be little more than a local mayor which he had aggrandised to the fancy title of king. So it transpired that Olaf was, indeed, the hereditary ruler of the planet and the First Leader of the Minx government. He was only away from his capital city because of his regal duties following the crash of the space craft and the confrontation with its' crew hiding in the cave. Of the village Minx, most had never seen their capital and it was a pleasure to see their excitement as they did a very slow, low pass over it and then came in to land on a barren patch of ground in its' outskirts..

The people of Minx city were poleaxed to see a monster land in a recreational field and they peered fearfully over walls and from an area of boulders in a field nearby, but the hatch doors opened and a gaggle of their own species descended from the monster and their king Olaf was in their midst. Tom helpfully despatched one of his marines with a large box for Olaf to stand on and he climbed up on to it and gave an impromptu speech to the throng which had assembled and continued to expand rapidly before him. He told them of their new friends from a distant world amongst the stars that they could see at night and how they had humongous ships like this and they could cross the heavens at will and how they had just taken them for a journey into space and around their world. If it wasn't for the ship and the fact that they had seen Minx and then Olaf come off it they would probably have treated this landed terror as they always had done when in doubt, with flights of arrows. Then it was time to go and Olaf demonstrated his expertise of spaceships to them by posting a local guard to keep the assembled Minx back, away from the down thrust of hot gasses and possible flying debris created by the take-off.

As the Minx disembarked after their epic trip, Olaf hung back as if uncertain about something and he caught up with Geoff as he was walking back to the glade where they had first met. "You know," he said with a searching meerkat look towards Geoff, "I have been wondering about those other people in the cave. Can they do all this that you can do?"

"Undoubtedly, well probably most of it, if not more," Geoff sensed Olaf was reappraising something in his mind.

"We cannot forgive them," Olaf said carefully,

testing his words. "They came here uninvited and as a result some of my people were killed, even if they did not intend to kill them." Olaf was not giving way on that point but he was studying the sky as he spoke, as if seeking an enlightenment from it. "There is a clause in our legal processes where an accused person or group of people can reprieve their sentence on the grounds that to curtail their liberty would not be in the interests of the State. Do you think if I invoked that clause that they would stay on and educate us about our world and about space?" Geoff was inwardly ecstatic but couldn't let on his feelings of relief.

"I would have thought that they would," Geoff replied. "I will ask them for you if you wish me to, but I have to tell you that there is a pretty general acceptance by all nations in space that you cannot jump evolution and graft on thousands of years of discovery and advancements. That could lead to all sorts of social problems. I am guessing that in the circumstances they would probably provide a general education upon which your people can build and advance in their own way. Although, they would probably offer you advanced medicine at once because that is classified as humanitarian support. Your people would also learn a lot from simple observation of how they do things and about the machines they employ. That alone would effectively fast-forward your evolution. If you wish I could schedule a shuttle to take you to your capitol city right away and you can speak to your government and, if they agree, please bring them back here with you.

Olaf's toothy grin widened so much that Geoff

became worried that it might become a permanent fixture when he told him that a space craft would be put at his personal disposal so that he could go and address his government and return with them, leaving Olaf, in his own mind, inwardly experimenting with the term 'Olaf the Great,' which must surely be attributed to him in the future. "Please speak to the cave people and outline my idea," Olaf declared, "my mind is made up, I will speak to my Council. Our trip in your craft today has changed things and from now on my people will want to study in earnest and look to the wider universe."

Geoff bade Olaf goodbye and then with some haste made for the captives in the cave to advise them of Olaf's proposal.

"We could do it ourselves if necessary," he told them, "but this is more in your quadrant of space than ours." Razil took to it immediately,

"Yes, I am sure that we could do that, we have some similar arrangements with other developing worlds; but as you have rightly observed, we will not elevate them from the jungle to owning a personal computer in hours. We would eke out their advancement in accordance with our tried and tested principles."

"I am merely the gofer here," Geoff grinned. "What I propose is to get this formalised as quickly as possible and take you and Olaf and his Council to your world to get it all sewn up legally. We will use our mother ship and its DMT capability to get to your planet and back, say any time in the next two days?"

Regardless of the indications of progress, Geoff still had to get clearance for this new initiative from Captain Donald and he returned to the Passing Star to go over the minutiae with him and his request for transport. The Captain did not hesitate in giving his approval, pointing out that Ongle and the AMC would only be in the position of facilitating an agreement, but it certainly had his full approval. Then, knowing nothing could happen for a further two days, Geoff was able to spend welcome time with his family.

Olaf greeted Geoff on his return and told him that his government had agreed with his proposed solution. They were backing him one-hundred percent and his Government was here with him and they were eager to embark on their epic journey in the flying machine to outer space. Geoff chuckled and then told him of his plan to get him and his Council to their captive's planet to get a deal signed and that could be as early as tomorrow. That was not difficult for Olaf to agree, whatever the end result. It meant another trip in a space ship for him and a chance for his ministers to see space for themselves; and Geoff reflected, on his observation, that the broad smiles of a group of happy meerkats would light up any room.

When they closed up to the Passing Star the next day and the Minx saw its' sheer size they were silent and in awe. "Unusual for them," Geoff quipped. Razil and his party were with him and they had provided the coordinates for Suva and he, too, was nearly bowled over when he learned that after DMT grid alignment, which could take two or three minutes, the journey itself would take less than a second.

"It has taken us six months, with two short diversions, to get here from Suva," he observed ruefully. As it was easily construed, the visit of the Minx government caused a stir and there was much public curiosity on Suva but their visit to the planet was only a short familiarisation visit. Later, together with the front bench of the Global Parliament of Suva, they were brought back up to the Passing Star and led into the main public hall of the ship which had been adapted to accommodate this all important meeting of the planets.

"I am mystified by the Minx," Geoff remarked to Colonel Brooks as they supervised the arrangements. "Just look how imperturbable these guys are. They seem to take everything in their stride," he shook his head. "Today they have been spirited from what is essentially a medieval society and deposited five-thousand years in advance of anything they have yet to achieve."

"They must be surprised behind those unblinking expressions, but they don't show it," Tom Brooks chortled a reply. "They are undoubtedly the most unflappable species that I have ever come across and they seem to have a good sense of right and wrong and a good form of government which is something that our medievals did not particularly excel at. I feel they owe a lot to their King Olaf. He seems a pretty wise old bird."

With the meeting taking place inside a closed room, the Colonel and Geoff had nothing much to do but to sit in the lounge chairs which had been placed outside the door, and Imogen and the girls were able to join them for several hours. Then, abruptly, the doors of the public hall were thrown open by somebody on the inside and they could hear a hubbub of noise of the type usually generated by an exciting meeting coming to an end. Then Olaf emerged wearing what had become the recent norm for him - a huge smile. As he walked up to them, he opened with "I feel that I have you to thank for this," he was still beaming. "The government of Suva have agreed that, although they did not wish to harm any of my people, an accident did occur which resulted in the deaths of several of the Minx people. They have asked us to graciously accept their offer of restitution." He made to end the conversation there but Colonel Brooks came straight to the point and asked what form the restitution would take.

Olaf was suffering a personal dilemma and he declined to answer Tom's question and turned on heel and walked over to speak animately with some of the members of his own government who were standing in a group outside of the Public Hall, then he hastened back to them. "I was not sure that I could tell you," he excused himself. "The people of Minx have not been told yet, so it is on your honour that you will not discuss it with others until they know. It is a long term project and it will take a number of years to complete," he drew a breath. "Suva have offered to build five-thousand schools on my planet and to bring a core of teachers here to train selected Minx people who will, themselves, be able to educate more teachers among my people. In time, every Minx child will be able to go to school. They are also to equip us with medical know how and provide us with medicines. In return there is something which they call rare earths in the soils of my planet and they offer to trade with us for them and teach us how to mine them.

"Sounds like you got a good deal," the Colonel praised Olaf. "Congratulations," the Colonel touched Olaf on his shoulder, "You have served your people well, but sadly it was done on the backs of the death of some of your subjects."

Olaf warmed to the praise and said. "Oh, they are now officially regarded as heroes. We will pray for their souls in Church and thank them and explain to them through prayer that through the accidental loss of their lives the whole planet has benefitted; and they will be remembered in a special church service once a year, for ever!"

"You have churches?" Geoff's interest was raised.

"You do not have churches, you are irreligious then?" Olaf's eyes were wide open in bafflement.

"Yes, we do have churches," Geoff cleared up the point. "It is just where ever we go in the universe the church is ever present."

"And so it should be," Olaf replied. "Surely no matter how clever and advanced you maybe, it would be incongruous if you believed that you have done it all yourself."

"Oh, I agree with you wholeheartedly," Geoff agreed. "That is indeed so." Then came the long goodbyes and the usual promises of staying in touch but in the case of this planet, which did not have DMT technology and was so far from Ongle, they knew that it might be many years or even centuries before they were in contact again. Finally, just Olaf and his Council stood before Geoff and Tom.

"You have both done so much for my people; we will never forget you and we will pray for you in our churches as well," and a tear welled up in his eyes. But he was King Olaf and kings do not cry; and he cuffed each of them on the shoulder and whirled around dismissing himself abruptly and marched away vigorously with the curly tip of his tail swinging from side to side.

Geoff turned towards Tom. "It's funny, I never did ask how Olaf gets about. It is quite some way from his capital city to the village."

"You are not going to believe this; they have an animal a bit like a gazelle and they ride it like a horse. At speed it makes quite long jumps of something like six to seven metres at a time which gives them a speed of up to seventy kilometres an hour and they can keep that up for hours."

"Sounds fun," Geoff chortled, "I wish I could have had a go on it!"

"I am not so sure that you would enjoy it," Tom replied. "When the gazelle gets up to speed there is no restraining harness and its' passenger is thrown upwards and they spend about fifty-percent of the time either seated or in the air and hanging onto the reins for dear life." The mental picture he had of the regal Olaf engaged in such an undignified journey brought tears of laughter to Geoff's eyes.

"A curious people," Geoff remarked. "They are a mixture of the old and the new; they have gone ahead in some aspects of civilisation but are retarded in others."

"Yes, quite retarded in some aspects," Tom remarked observationally with a smile. "They don't seem, as yet, to have indulged in any civilised potty training; and I am told that the house robots are still fumigating the hanger decks of the runabout and the Passing Star!"

Chapter 13

FIRMAMENT X ENTERTAINMENTS
COMPANY INC.

Imogen and the girls were euphoric when Geoff finally came aboard after the successful outcome of their involvement with the Minx. "They are quite adorable," Imogen remarked and she showed him proudly the doll images of the Minx that they had made. Geoff praised them and then laughed.

"I am told that their toilet arrangements are not very adorable though and they have yet to invent a flush toilet," Geoff rolled his eyes upwards.

"Oh don't," Imogen gave him a playful push, "they are just starting out on an accelerated introduction to modernity. The ones that I spoke to were quite respectful and very refined for their evolutionary status."

"Yes, they are certainly a strange mixture, but yes, I quite like them also." Right now Geoff was feeling that he had been an absent father and husband for too long and he settled down to a concentrated period of family routine that included activities in which they could all participate.

The Passing Star was navigating through an unusual concentration of planets and stars which caught their attention and Captain Donald had opted for using the ship's sub-light poenillium engines to cruise though the cluster rather than taking a DMT jump right through it. "You never know, there may be something interesting here," he self supported his decision to the bridge crew saying that he had made up his mind to investigate.

"Hello Geoff," the Captain came through on Geoff's hucom, "Come and take a look at this, see what you think."

"Duty calls," Geoff informed his family. "I hope it is not long. "It didn't sound urgent."

"Aw," Vivienne and Sophia expressed their anguish together.

"I'm sorry kids," Geoff felt their pain. For a time they had been a tight knit family living among the tranquil beauties of Marina and now it was go here, go there, interlaced throughout with moments of anxiety as fresh dangers arose. "I promise you when this trip is over I will ask the authorities to let us all go back to Marina."

"Good," said Vivienne curtly because she always undertook to make the joint decisions on behalf of her sister. Sophia was easy going in such matters and Geoff smiled his acknowledgment to both of them. Shortly afterwards Geoff arrived at the bridge of the ship and the Captain rose to meet him as he came in through the bridge door. "I wanted you to see this and tell me if you can think what this is all about. In our approach to this cluster of star systems we have picked up some odd radio beacons but they are jabbering in an unintelligible language, interspersed with music. The beacons seem to be dotted about in a wide segment of space; sometimes they are stand alone and sometimes they are located on space rocks."

"Public service broadcasts?" Geoff's thought was projected as a question.

"No, we don't think so," Captain Donald replied. "They all seem to be sending a variety of repeated messages but at different times to each other. They may be warning beacons so as a precaution I have had the ship stopped while we fathom out a course of action."

"Leave it with me, sir," Geoff always trotted out that reassuring phrase when he felt the situation warranted it. "May I take the console over there?" He pointed to a console in a glass walled office at a corner of the bridge.

"Yes, please do, and best get the same team up here with you, the one you used to crack the Morse type language on Minx." Captain Donald's words implied the power to enable Geoffrey to purloin the staff he needed if necessary. Geoff made the gaff, however, of directly contacting the two spectre robots that he had used to break the message from the planet Minx and he received a polite but firm call from Robot Scheduling asking why he was redirecting their staff. Geoff was full of apologies when he explained what was happening and that these particular robots' now had unique skills with a language decryption system which they had devised.

"We have possibly strayed into a no go zone in space and may be in danger. The Captain could DMT out if he wanted to but he is reserving that option if things get tricky. In the meantime he wants to learn all that he can," Geoff briefed them.

"Oh well, don't damage them then," was the begrudging approval.

"I will take great care of them and I will even polish them by hand before I send them back," he laughed.

"No, don't do that; that is designer dust we put there so that everybody can see how hard we work," the Robot Scheduling supervisor chuckled.

The door to the office opened and in strolled Garry, once again ready to be a part of the team." More gibberish to be decoded," he smiled and nodded to Geoff.

"I am afraid so," Geoff confessed. "It appears that that we have gained a new annotation to our records as 'language analysts."

"After I was called in, I logged into my computer on the way here and listened to the beacons," Garry imparted. "My thoughts are that they are not warning beacons because the music in between the voice clips changes from clip to clip, whereas the vocal stuff only changes sometimes and always after a burst of music. That doesn't sound like a warning signal to me because a warning would likely be reinforced by repetition. Each beacon gives off a different message on a different frequency although that message is often repeated randomly by other beacons."

"So the most obvious solution for them being hazard warnings is probably a non-starter then!" Geoff summed up. "I think that is logical." He pondered whilst he scratched his chin thoughtfully. There was silence between them as they each busied themselves with their screens and keyboards, trying to unpick the broadcasts and occasionally using doodle pencils to write on the scribble screens that were inset in the work-stations before them.

But now the two spectre robots had arrived and they were working together and they mooted a theory, based on Earth practices, where they used beacons to denote navigable channels in shipping waterways. Mostly Earth beacons used lights on floating buoys and sometimes a small radioed clip of information was broadcast by them; but out here, they reasoned ships were much faster and required navigation data and warnings millions of kilometres ahead of them; but this didn't explain the reason for the random snatches of music transmitted by the beacons they were studying and some of the music was quite catchy sounding, so they did not get the impression that it was at all serious.

"We are not making much headway," Geoff announced abruptly. "I feel that we need a change of scene, that sometimes works. Let's go to the nearest cafe, robots as well," he added. We may all be able to spark off any new thoughts that come to us." The Captain looked at Geoff in askance as they trooped out of the office. "Cerebral break," Geoff enlightened him. "It's an enigma and we don't seem to have any leads at all yet. I feel a change of ambience is needed; we will be back in about twenty-minutes."

There was a coffee shop not far from the bridge and Geoff led them inside where they were enveloped in its' pleasant and comfortable ambiance. There were a few customers present and in the main they ignored the human element of Geoff's party but seemed amused to see the two robots accompanying them and as the party settled in their armchairs they noticed the ever present discrete background mood music favoured by the coffee houses of the ship and they relaxed to await the arrival of their order.

"It's funny how music can sometimes soothe one," Garry remarked. "It can completely change your mood." Garry looked at Geoff and they both had the same question to ask.

"The music?" they both said it at the same time and laughed.

"We have been concentrating only on the vocal parts of the recordings from the beacons. What if there is a significance to the music in-between?" Garry voiced.

"Indeed," Geoff replied enthusiastically and he called upon one of the robots to play their recordings of the music, eliminating the vocal transmissions. This they commenced to do at high volume. Regrettably they had forgotten their surroundings as the robots amplified their recordings of the beacons and they received a censure from a house robot who came over with a request to keep the noise down.

Geoff reddened and blushed sheepishly and he and Garry thereafter donned their hucoms and logged into an interface with the robots. "Are there any patterns or mathematical sequences that you can detect in it?" Geoff asked the spectres. 'Nothing of interest found,' he was assured by them although the music itself did have some resemblance to music for entertainment and similar to music used in dance halls and gigs on Ongle, they said.

"We will have to hypothesise less boisterously," Geoff grinned. "The music is random and sometimes fleeting and it changes completely from time to time but the nearest beacon to it does not change its' music at the same time, so it is probably of no significance to the wording. In which case let's assume that the music is purely intended to separate the wording but is also intended to add an entertainment value to it. That would make it sound more commercial than governmental!"

"I think we are onto something there," Garry interjected. "We need a list of the introductory words normally said before playing a piece of music for entertainment. The usual preambles are such as 'the next piece of music is by,' etc. Let's get the robots to work on that."

"Churuka!" Geoff exclaimed.

"What's that? "Garry asked.

"Oh nothing," Geoff replied with a grin, "just a word from the past that cropped up." But it had been one of those lucky incidents where the first thing you try works; and the two robots showed human desire for praise similar to humans when they announced that they had broken the structure of the language being relayed by the beacons. But when Geoff and Garry heard the transcripts they fell about laughing. This resulted in a glare from the coffee house robot to remind them that they had already been warned once, but they immediately dashed off to see the Captain to let him hear, for himself, what the messages were.

Captain Donald could easily guess that they had something important to tell him as they tumbled in through the door of the bridge, with the human element noticeably out of breath. "What have you got for me then?" He asked in his even voiced manner. Geoff fell over his words a little.

"Y-yes we certainly have got something, listen to this," and he directed one of the robots to relay the transcriptions over its' loud speaker system. "Each message is a little bit different," Geoff described.

"I am ready now," the robot confirmed in its monotone and metallic sounding voice.

"Go ahead then," Geoff answered and there was a slight crackle as the robot's speaker system was switched on.

'Welcome traveller to Fun Planet,'a message boomed out. 'Fun Planet is owned by the Firmament X Entertainments Company. Inc. and we can offer the traveller a variety of moderately priced entertainments.

Stay for just a night in a tent in a wilderness location for only ten Dupre.' Entictingly it went on to list entertainments from white water rafting, mountaineering, cave diving and hang-gliding and the various prices and add-ons and special offers for longer stays and finally the price of a full two-year ticket taking in the multitude of entertainments including trekking and all of the scenic delights that the planet had to offer. 'Stay in any one of our thirty-thousand hotels, sleep on an opiate mattress in a four poster bed, use any of our one-hundred thousand camp sites, or just go native. Be yourself, go wild, be here, there is no government on Fun Planet!'

Geoff reached forward and switched the robot's speaker off. "All of the messages are in that vein with some variations," he said, "such as you are now approaching Fun Planet, don't forget to change your money into Firmament X Entertainment Company Inc.unified Dupres, Folks, at your port of landing. If you are in this area why not pay a visit to this inter galactic renowned stop over where you will receive a warm welcome and the best time of your lives. Then, don't forget to tell the folks back home of the delights of Fun Planet when you return. There is something for everyone on Fun Planet to make your holiday a success." And soon they were all laughing. "Apparently, from what they say, Fun Planet is owned by a commercial company and not by a government or a people, as is the rule, and they are keen to tell everybody about it."

"Certainly it is a novel revelation for a whole planet to be privately owned and to be a business in its entirety,"

Captain Donald shook his head. "It is a new one on me, but good luck to them. Right, now that has been cleared up, let's get on with the mission."

They would have certainly resumed the mission but for a report that a strange craft was approaching them and it was fashioned in the shape of an animal with glowing eyes and teeth and with intricate patterns of light rippling alongs its' hull. "We are being addressed by the ship off the port bow," the Helmsman called across the bridge. "We do not recognise the language but no threat is perceived by our scanners; it has a crew of two."

"Robots," Geoff addressed the two spectres, "interpret the communications from the ship off our port bow and relay them by hucom to the Captain and to those crew assembled on the bridge." Geoffrey supervened.

"Hello, Captain of the foreign ship, may we talk to you?" A clear interpretation of what had been said was rendered by the robots. "We are executives of the Firmament X Entertainment Company Inc.and we have a special offer to make to you and to a selected number of your crew."

"Yoiks! There are salesmen with special offers even out here," Captain Donald muttered the aside before he replied to their hail. "I wonder what their BOGOF offer will be?" Then he turned to face the screen and the alien ship before he addressed his reply.

"Hello, executives of the Firmament X Entertainments Compoany Inc. That sounds very generous of you. I have directed that a empty fighter craft recess be opened in the hull of the ship opposite where you are positioned. Come near to it and stop. Grapples will automatically be extended and fixed to your ship and you will be drawn into the recess. Please wait until the red light in the recess goes out because that signifies that normal air pressure has been restored. We have already analysed the atmosphere of your Fun Planet and if you breath the same mix then you will not need closed circuit breathers."

"Thank you, Captain," the reply was courteous. "Our bodies are able to adapt to many differing atmospheres so I am sure that we will not be inconvenienced by the need to employ atmospheric enhancement."

Regardless of the friendly approach Captain Donald was taking no chances and he switched from hucoms to the ship's closed circuit system to instruct that Recess Number 109 was to be opened and grapples were to be extended to bring the alien ship aboard. 'Security,' he commanded, were to place two men in the recess and additional backups in the corridors beyond it. He next tasked the ship's Diplomatic Officer to meet the crew of the alien ship's crew and escort them to Conference Room One to meet with himself and other senior crew staff.

"That includes you," he said to Geoff. "I want you to take along one of your neat little scanners to monitor if they are in communication with anybody else outside of the ship and to position your language expert robots secretively nearby and get them to translate it if they are." Then he turned to a microphone and continued to issue instructions. Finally he advised the Security Branch that they were to mount discrete scanners to detect fissionable material, if any, that may be brought aboard with the alien ship and to eject it instantly if there was.

The elaborate security systems that the Captain had ordered in place proved later to be unnecessary as it turned out that their visitors were in close fitting clothing under which any weaponry would have been very evident. There were two crew members of the alien vessel and they were mid European looking and met everybody with smiles and handshakes as they stepped down from their ship and began to distribute brochures extolling the delights of Fun Planet.

"They seem like standard salesmen to me," Geoff addressed the Captain via his hucom.

"Yes, we are salesmen indeed," an entirely new entity came through on his hucom and one of the visitors stood before him and smiled. "Well deduced," he beamed at Geoff.

"How did you understand what I said?" Geoff was curious.

"Well, as we told you, we are very adaptable to many atmospheres; and this also extends to languages and clairvoyance. We omitted to tell you because many races shun us if it is mentioned. My name is Tony and you, I understand, are Geoff," and they shook hands once again. Geoffrey took the offered hand and welcomed Tony to the ship. Then he created an excuse that he had to attend to one of the robots in the corridor outside and that gave him an opportunity to switch his hucom to an entertainment channel and play music which he had guessed would scramble his thoughts to anyone attempting to monitor them. His purpose for the deception was also to enable him to be able to brief Captain Donald on the FXEC's ability to intercept thoughts and hucom exchanges.

"Don't be alarmed," Tony consoled via Geoff's hucom. "I have already briefed Captain Donald on that," Tony smiled genially. "Don't forget that you can always put a block in place to stop any mind probe via your hucom and that, together with the music, would make it very difficult to read your thoughts. That was inspired thinking, though!" he commended.

The meeting in the conference room commenced with the welcomes and standard platitudes and the two sales men of the FXEC made their pitch. The planet had been found and claimed by the FXEC and it had been developed as a planetary fun fair and adventure playground to serve the galaxy; and it was very popular. Each continent of the planet had been developed to cater for different interests which also took into account individual climate preferences, they said, whilst handing out roll up computers to those crew members present. When unrolled, they saw that the computers advertised Fun Planet's delights. Their interest in the Passing Star was because it originated from an entirely new sector of the universe and that led to the commercial possibility of expanding their customer base. The special offer they unveiled was two-thousand free tickets to be used now; and the remainder of the crew who could not visit on this occasion would receive two tickets each to be used at some time in the future.

One or two articles in the brochure caught Geoffrey's imagination as he studied the roll out device. A whole continent had been given over to 'wild-side-trekking.' Visitors, to this, lived in basic chalets inside extensive wired off compounds connected by corridors which frequently branched outwards and ran for hundreds of kilometres through virgin bush. En route one could rest and recover in wayside cafes and camp in secure areas in which one could pitch a tent. Outside these safety zones wild animals roamed freely and they were as gruesome as any imagination could conceive; many had been imported from other planets to a specification of 'the worst they had.' Most looked hungrily toward the campers just out of their reach and they frequently pawed hopefully at the fencing and at times quite forcefully, hoping to find a weak spot; and they loudly roared their frustration because they could not.

On another page on his tablet brochure he was taken to see a big dipper. The FXEC only seemed to do things 'large,' he noted. The dipper used natural terrain to support its track; and to access the start of the ride its passengers were airlifted to the summit of a four-thousand metre mountain where they picked up their roller coaster to embark upon what would probably be the most frightening experience of their lifetime. It looked and undoubtably would be horrifying as the track wound around sheer cliff faces and disappeared into inky black tunnels to re-emerge upside down; and then it climbed to the tops of lesser mountains and plunged down through water falls. In the last millisecond, when it seemed inevitable that the passengers were going to get soaked in icy water, a glass sleeve slipped over the car and they came through the thundering cascade thankfully dry.

Geoff flinched involuntarily when he saw at one juncture of the ride that there was an ultimate horrific event in store for the passengers and one which was almost as bad to look at as it was for its' involved passengers. The car emerged from a tunnel and, unstoppably fast, thundered round a blind cliff face to be confronted by a sizeable gap in the track; and the supporting structure could be observed leaning drunkenly away from the break. Deep below, a debris of broken trestles was strewn across the valley floor. To the accompanying screams of the passengers they were hurtled into the void and the car cork-screwed and uprighted again; and with apparent unbelievable luck it smoothly reunited with the rails of the track on the other side of the gap. Geoff raised his eyes in question at Tony, who laughed.

"It is not quite so random as it looks," he assured Geoff when he saw him studying the feature.

"There is a lot of computer wizardry taking place to ensure that it lands correctly."

"Glad to hear it," Geoff responded. "Just the same I think I may well give that one a miss,"

Geoff tapped the side of his nose.

"I am not supposed to tell you this," Tony confided,

"the passengers are, of course, aware that there is some very clever precision engineering and computers involved but in reality there are five back-up fail-safe computers locked in and any one of them could take over in an instant. If all that failed there are concealed retro thrusters, controlled by yet more computers, to ease it down to the valley floor. Geoff looked ruefully at Tony.

"It's' still not my type of ride though!"

"I don't blame you," Tony replied, "but it is Company policy that everybody connected with that ride has to take at least one trip on it. The ride I had on it still keeps me awake of a nighttime! It is a case of if you want the job you have to comply with the company; but I do sometimes ponder the mentality of the people that pay to ride on it!"

Chapter 14

DEEP SEA TERROR

With such a large crew and the fact that the Passing Star could not stay very long, they had to take what was on offer at the time when their name came up for a three day respite; and Geoffrey, Imogen and the two girls were allotted an apartment in Coral Hotel, nestled just below the fringe of a coral reef. It was tastefully laid out with picture windows looking directly onto the ocean where colourful fish and goggle-eyed monsters swam up to stare at the occupants inside. Despite their brash advertising and their less than sophisticated sounding title, the FXEC Inc.was anything but brash and they were impressed with the personal care and attention to detail they enjoyed at the hands of the company. "It is probably quite an expensive holiday in Galactic terms," Imogen declared.

The hotel guests were from a variety of races. Most had some kind of recognisable human resemblance but not all were humanoid. The Ursidae or bear like creatures were very evident but there were others, with the kangaroo types being by far the fastest at getting around. The girls were immediately befriended by two Ursidae juniors who, for want of better names, the girls called

181

Teddy 1 and Teddy 2. Their parents, looking like adult polar bears, towered over Geoff and Immogen but they seemed affable enough although their conversation was reduced to sign language; but the children had no such difficulties and they easily developed their own language based upon laughter and play.

"We are booked on a submersible tomorrow," Imogen informed Geoff. "Did you know that except for our honeymoon this is our first holiday since we were married. There were holiday like places we lived in but there were always official chores of one sort or another attached to them. This is heaven," she sighed.

"You are absolutely right, darling," Geoff caught her sentiment. "As you say, even on Marina there was always something that needed doing. Perhaps one day we may even come back here; there is lots to see."

"You are not fibbing?" She searched his face for a sign of insincerity.

"No, I am not," he broke into a grin.

"I knew I was right to marry you then, after all," she giggled and they ended up, as always, in an embrace.

A submersible was waiting in a dock for them the next morning. It was just large enough for their family as they climbed aboard, assisted by the pilot who they learned was named Geraldine.

"We have to keep these craft moving," she told them. "There are really not enough of them to meet demand, but we have two hours. I don't have the telepathic ability of some of my comrades so I do appreciate your loan of a hucom for this trip; it makes things so much easier."

"It is a two way benefit," Imogen answered.

Soundlessly the craft slipped off the ramp and they found themselves weightlessly gliding through an aquarium like ocean full of coloured fish and corals. One strange looking shoal of fish was flat faced and reminiscent of an Earth smiley sticker but unexpectedly it was at the end of its' body. Geraldine interpreted their interest correctly and explained that in their own world predators usually attacked from behind and they were more able to dodge attacks if they could see their attacker,; they also had rudimentary eyes at the other end too, but these were undeveloped. At this point in their evolution the forward eyes were only capable of detecting the plankton on which they fed. Nevertheless, it was disconcerting to see that their every movement was being gawked at by shoals of smiley faces and to know that the threat level posed by the 'Holder' family was being observed and constantly evaluated by them..

"We are just about to commence our deep sea dive now," Geraldine announced from her position at the controls; and the craft lurched nose down at an angle to point towards the not yet visible ocean floor far beneath them. "You will hear some groans, creaks, and grumbling from the ship's frame. It is of no consequence, the hull has been built to deform to cope with the increased pressures." Indeed it did groan and creak quite loudly and at one point caused Imogen to give a squeak of alarm.

Geoff, on the other hand, deliberately maintained his best placid look and put his trust in the Firmament X Entertainments Corporation's Inc. engineering, even if he did feel a little disquiet at some of the louder rumblings. "We are levelling off now, it was a little bit noisier today. I don't see why that should be; all of the strain gauges are registering within their normal parameters," she kept them informed. They had entered a grey world with limited forward vision as if a gloomy fog had descended over the sea bed and at the extremes of the misty blanket large shapes could frequently be seen to be drifting by. Some of them were disturbingly large, Geoff noted, but did not comment upon. One creature's head emerged close enough to be seen in detail but its rows of teeth could be likened to those of a great white shark on Earth but it was soon gone. A whale like creature slipped by, by virtue of its extreme length taking several seconds to pass them, and its' foghorn call to its deep sea brethren had them putting their hands over their ears to blot out the sound.

"Its weird down here," Imogen gave vent to her feelings. "I have been on many planets and I have experienced many extremes in the universe but this is quite the most scary that I can recall."

"Do you want to go up?" Geoff pointed upwards.

"No, not just yet," she replied resolutely in a controlled voice that she did not inwardly feel.

"But it is a feeling of great evil down here."

They were stopped from any further conversation as the ship gave a lurch and stopped dead and there was a slithering sound down its hull and the viewing windows blackened. The girls shrieked and Imogen's hand tightened in Geoffrey's hand.

"Look," Imogen motioned with her other hand and when Geoff did he could see that Geraldine was motionless, slumped over the controls; and the grating and slithering sounds grew more intense and from the hull droplets of water had started to drip to the floor from a pinhead hole in the roof. Galvanised into action, Geoff went forward quickly and sat Geraldine upright and he halted the thin trickle of blood seeping down her forehead with a tissue from his pocket. She was coming too and looked about her groggily and she took in the rise and fall of the ship's engines as the craft was violently being tossed about by some outside force. Intelligence came back into Geraldine's eyes and she directed Geoff to pull back on a black lever on the dashboard and hold it for a second and release it. Geoff did as bade and there was a flash of blue light and a mighty growl issued from outside of the ship and the dash screen cleared to show the sea bed; and the slithering sounds had stopped but the motors were making the high pitched sound of machines being dangerously off load and Geraldine silenced them by stabbing a red button on the instrument panel in front of her.

"What in Heaven's name was that?" exclaimed Geoff; and the explanation was taken up by Geraldine who looked somewhat dismayed.

"I think that was a Brutus Nadirer. It a good job that you were able to operate the close encounter goad; it must not have quite got its jaws fully around us or else we would have had a watery grave. Normally the ship will warn the occupants of the approach of one of those and it will automatically fire off a bright flash which dazzle and frighten them and they back off. If they come back again we give them an electric shock." Geoff was aware that, in English, there was probably no equivalent name for the beast or its' species. Thus, Geraldine had given them its native animal name in her own language and the hucom she was wearing had done its best to find an alternative name as close to a literal translation as it could manage, but it sounded ok in English.

Geraldine returned her attention to the submersible's control panel and she depressed the restart button for the engines which started up immediately but at once went into a high pitch and dangerously over revved scream before she shut them off again. "Casenfunder," she exclaimed in such a venomous tone that Geoff guessed it to be an expletive or at the very least certainly a derogatory term. "That explains why the Brutus did not gnaw at the cabin, it was busy eating the props, probably because they were moving, I expect,. but we can't get back to the top again without them."

"Ate the props?" Geoff sought confirmation of the ability of a Brutus Nadirer's ability to eat solid metal.

"Not eat as in consume," Geraldine laughed. "It will have lunged at them with its' mouth because it thought they must be alive. It is a powerful beast more than thirty-five metres in length; it is the largest creature on this planet. According to your hucom, I have found that you would describe it as a dragon, except this one lives underwater and does not breathe fire. It would have no trouble ripping the props off the prop shaft but I would hope they gave it a tooth ache."

Geraldine was quiet as she busied herself with cross checking instruments and she turned towards them rather grave faced to tell them that the ascending buoy outside had been torn from its' mounts so that they could not send it up to bleep a distress call. "That Brutus out there seems to be so glad of our company and it has all but destroyed our means of escape. We don't have a lot of options now." As if to confirm her words the ship rocked violently. The girls, absolutely terrified, screamed as the rasping sounds could be heard inside the cab - and Geraldine hit the goad switch and with a startled growl their adversary slipped away to perhaps formulate a new attack.

"Determined fella this one," Geraldine said without emphasising any enthusiasm for its' tenacity. "We have just six hours battery life and every time I use the goad it reduces the battery life by thirty minutes."

"Will they not come looking for us?" Imogen asked.

"Yes, they will, "Geraldine replied, "but we have lost the emergency buoy and down here in the deep it is a bit like looking for a needle in a haystack; you need luck for that kind of rescue."

"How about the reverse thrusters, do we have those?" Geoff asked.

"Good   thinking."   Geraldine   responded.   "The

problem is that the reverse thrusters are interlinked with the props which switch to reverse when the reverse thrusters are engaged. Because the engines are balanced by the heavy load of the main props now, when I try to use the thrusters there is insufficient load and the engines dangerously over rev. I should be able to compensate from here but for some reason that doesn't work. I simply cannot risk destroying the engines but if I use them in short bursts I may be able to at least keep the batteries topped up to use the electric goad if we are attacked. We may have to wait it out."

"They must have been a little too trusting in their technology and they have overlooked a basic fail-safe procedure somewhere. Is there any way that we can get at the balance mechanism?" Geoff asked.

"No, there is no access. It is a computer programme, this is not supposed to happen; even if we had one prop we would be ok." Just then the craft started to move erratically and they were thrown from side to side and again the girls shrieked with fear and Imogen was looking strained but trying to calm them down. There was a bang on the hull and the craft was pushed sideways and crushed to the floor of the ocean. Geraldine flicked the exterior lights on for a moment and they could see one tree trunk size arm and an ugly dragon-like head of a fearsome creature with a serpentine neck. The unseen other arm was presumably resting on top of their craft and pinning it down and as the giant head looked in at them they could see teeth, as large as farm gate posts, arrayed in its evil mouth which was yawning open and presumably about to engulf the nose cone as Geraldine applied the electric goad again.

The creature caterwauled in anguish and released the submersible and lashed out at it with its immense tail, sending them skidding bumpily along the floor of the ocean and at the limits of the range of their headlights they could see that it had turned to face them and was coming in to attack yet again and as if to emphasise their peril, the leak in the hull dripped faster and a puddle was gathering on the floor of the craft.

"I can't afford to zap it many more times with the goad," Geraldine was breathless. "We must conserve some battery power to kick start the engine." But unexpectedly there were the heads of two beasts in their headlights and abruptly the creatures of the deep set upon each other and with teeth bared they coiled their necks around each other and their thrashing tails were throwing up clouds of silt as each tried to get a fatal bite on the other's neck.

"We have got to try the reverse thrusters, it's the only option we have left. Do we have any underwater flares on board?" Geoff didn't mean to take command but his Earth-time military training asserted itself when there was a crisis.

"Yes," Geraldine said. "See that row of buttons in the panel above your head; there are six of them, one button to one flare."

"Can I press two at once?" Geoff asked

"I have never tried it," Geraldine replied. "They are very powerful and one is usually enough to illuminate a large area of the sea bed. Brutus Nadirer are afraid of them and they temporarily disorientate their vision."

"I was not aiming to frighten them," Geoff reassured her. " I want to interrupt their vision. The water is pretty murky and we may be able to get far enough away to be invisible to them. Girls," he called his daughters. "find every chair, cushion and rubberised items including your top clothing and make a heap of them there." He pointed to a spot just before the engine room. "Imogen, could you please press one of the flare buttons when I call out from the engine room; and Geraldine, at the same time, please fire up the engines and use the reeverse thrusters to get us upwards and as far away as we can."

'Cometh the hour, cometh the man,' Imogen thought inwardly. They had already subconsciously nominated him de facto captain and they set to work without question as he fired off instructions.

"I looked at the prop shafts through their glass inspection panel when we came aboard" he explained. "They are spiral shaped and they enter into a tunnel; the spiral is probably a drainage backstop to eject any excess water out of the ship. My plan is to open the inspection panel in the shaft housing below where the shafts enter the tunnel and once the engines are running I aim to drop the items that we have collected into the spirals, and they will, hopefully, churn them towards the far end. My theory is that when the stuff gets down to the end of the shaft where they cannot be forced any further it will provide a back load to the engines that will compensate for the missing load of the propellers."

"It sounds possible," Geraldine called out.

"Ready when you are." Geoff poked his head around the door from the engine room.

"Right team, lets do it," he encouraged them as the engines choked into life and Imogen pressed a button and a flare was ejected from the craft and it fizzed into life dissolving the cloak of murk which surrounded them. It was immediately possible to discern that one of the Brutus Nadirers had gained an advantage and a giant webbed foot was holding its' opponent's body pinned down to the ocean bed and it was trying to bite the other's neck. Another scuffle shrouded them in clouds of sediment again as Geraldine engaged the drive. The sounds in the engine room were appalling and the prop shafts rattled loosely along their length within their tunnel housing and the engine noise rose to a near scream. Straight away Geoff began to feed in the soft furnishing and clothing into the spiral prop shafts and they quietened. Once or twice the engines almost stalled as the load became too excessive for them to cope with but Geraldine was quick at the controls and she was compensating with responses on the throttle to the sounds coming from the engine and she was able to keep them going and they could feel the ship starting to lift as the bow thrusters came on line.

"Fire another flare please, Imogen," Geoff called. "We need to blind-side them until we are out of their range," and he turned to receive yet more material from the girls to throw into the drive shafts. But smoke was now issuing back along the prop housing as the friction between the injected material and the prop shafts threatened a fire.

"There is an exterior water sample tap over the kitchen sink," Geraldine called to Imogen. "It lets sea water in from the outside; you can find some jugs underneath the sink. Don't forget to turn it off."

Thereafter Imogen and the girls ran a relay of jugs of water which Geoffrey fed into the shafts to cool them down and to prevent a fire. They were getting to the end of material to throw into the shaft now but the discovery of a well stocked first aid chest containing packets of bandages, wound dressings and rubber tubing brought the wildly vibrating prop staff back to 'manageable' again.

Progress was painfully slow as they reversed their way back up towards the surface, first one way and then the other, as Geraldine juggled with the two front thrusters to try to maintain as straight a course as she could manage. But inevitably, the jam of materials at the far end of the pipe proved too much for the engines to cope with and first one and then the other engine gave up, four-hundred metres below the sea's surface, and the craft hung there buoyancy neutral and immobile.

"So, from the frying pan into the fire," Geoff laconically assessed their situation.

"Yes," said Imogen, then she turned to Geraldine,

"Do you think that they will have mounted a search

for us yet?" she asked. Geraldine glanced at the control panel in front of her and advised them.

"We are one hour and a quarter hours overdue. Company rules make it mandatory after one hour of no contact to mount a full search."

"How long is an hour on this planet?" Imogen directed her question towards Geoff for an answer and Geoff scratched his head.

"I think it is about two of our hours," he replied uncertainly.

"You are obviously formulating a plan?" he asked her.

"Sort of," she smiled. "It is not very elaborate but we cannot signal them and we cannot surface and they will be looking initially for any or both of those events; and soon according to my estimations it will be getting dark."

"They will still send many drones out," Geraldine interjected into the conversation. "They will be programmed to look for anything unusual."

"Good, that is an important part of my plan, such as it is," she laughed.

"What if we fired a flare upwards, say every half an hour; it would show as a great big bubble of light on the surface. They could hardly miss it."

"Indeed," Geraldine lent her support immediately. "If we do as you suggest, the initial momentum of the flare would carry it upwards for at least one-hundred metres closer to the surface and the drones couldn't miss it."

It seemed an interminable wait, but at last Geraldine announced that it was dark top-side and the ship was in a beneficial attitude to release a flare and Imogen stepped underneath the row of switches to fire it. They were relived that the flare had functioned properly because seconds later they were flooded with light from above and as it faded they settled down in the now comfortless devoid of soft furnishings in the cabin.

"Time's up," Imogen said thirty-minutes later and shestepped forward to fire another and once again they werebathed in light; and thirty minutes later she did the samething again.

"They would have been seen and recorded," Geraldine advised them. "The problem being is what will they make of it, they might just think it to be an underwater volcano." Luckily this proved not to be the case and soon after the flare had gone out they heard the thud of a grenade exploding on the surface as a signal that the flare had been spotted. They sat there in silence, waiting breathlessly, and their teeth were chattering because the comfort heating depended upon working engines and with most of their clothing gone they were left with only enough to maintain decency. They were startled by a loud microphone feedback whistle which came from somewhere outside of the ship; and Geraldine switched the exterior lights on and they could see a nodule dangling alongside them and a wire leading from it disappearing into the blackness above. A blessed, disembodied voice addressed them through the hull. 'This is a Firmament X Entertainment Company Inc. rescue vessel,' and they were asked if their ship was piloted by Geraldine and, if so, if they could not respond electronically they were to bang three times on their own hull for yes and twice for no.

Geraldine resumed her captaincy role again and unhooked a winding hand from a winch and used it to bang the requisite number of times on the hull to confirm yes. After that there followed a series of questions with the yes/no options which Geraldine answered by banging out their responses. "Right, we now understand that you have suffered damage and your ship is inoperable," and again Geraldine hammered out the affirmative signal. There was a pause, then the voice resumed. "We are sending a submersible down to you and it will attach a cable and pull you to the surface." Whereupon, the about to be rescued raised a loud cheer and occupied themselves gleefully with a lot of clapping and hugging all round.

"Many thanks, Geraldine," Geoff smiled earnestly." I feel that we owe our lives to your cool headed approach to this emergency. Many thanks, too," he turned to face Imogen, "to my clever wife who devised a method to get us noticed whilst still under water."

"Relatively cheaply too," Imogen nodded sagely. "My usual terms for rescuing people are hugs, kisses, chocolates and flowers. Geoff stepped forward and kissed Imogen demonstratively.

"That is a down payment to show that my credit is

good," he said loudly enough for their girls to hear and he grinned at their expected response.

"Mummy and daddy are always kissing," Sophia remarked to Vivienne.

"It is very unsophisticated," Vivienne replied. Geoff and Imogen laughed because they knew that Vivienne had recently picked up on the word sophisticated and it explained so much about the world to a girl approaching her teens. Sophia nodded affirmatively to her sister.

"I won't do it when I get older," she said with finality.

"Wow," said Imogen, mischievously to offend their teenage sensitivities further and she rolled her eyes for effect and said. "Your credit is accepted, kind sir" and the relief they all felt at being rescued caused them to laugh longer and a little louder than was justified by Geoffrey and Imogen's banter. A metallic clung sounded from somewhere at the back of the craft which told them that help had arrived.

"That will be the magnetic grapples," Geraldine informed them, "not long now!" In answer the craft tilted haphazardly as it started to move quite rapidly and within a few minutes they were being pulled up into the floating dock of a surface craft where a group of officials and onlookers gathered to await them disembark. It was only then, when they looked back, that they fully understood the battering that their submersible had been subjected to; there were dents all over it and gouge marks made by their adversary's teeth where it had fought to get a firm grip on its' hull.

Inevitably there followed a round of visits by officials of the FXEC Inc. and a video link with the president of the Corporation who offered his apologies for their ordeal and his congratulations that they had escaped intact. Newspaper and television interviews were end to end but they couldn't really wait until they were whisked away back to the feeling of normality and familiarity of the Passing Star and their own apartment and the luxury of their own beds. However, if they were ever to pass this way again they were now in possession of a 'Family Five month Five Continent Pass' for their use any time in the future.

"Everything is done 'big' by the Firmament X Entertainment Company Inc." Geoff said with a smile.

"Strange," Geoff's speech was hesitant when he spoke with Imogen later "I went back to the dock to use the toilet about two hours after we had arrived and the submersible was still there hauled out of the water but it already had new propellers fitted and oddly there were no dents or scratch marks on the hull so I took a. closer look."

"And," Imogen was curious. "Could it have been another submersible?"

"Well, I looked through the windows and the cabin was still in the same chaotic state that we left it in and all the soft furnishing was missing. There was a man inside the craft and he was dragging something out of the prop shaft and it looked like the blouse that you had been wearing before we fed it into the prop shaft tunnel. Speaking of the prop shafts, though, it would be a pretty amateurish set up if you could not run the props or the reverse thrusters independently. Moreover, combustion engines in a submersible! Anyway, the man saw me and held up the blouse then shrugged his shoulders and threw it to one side.

"What do you think it means?" Imogen looked at him blankly.

"There is more, too, because from somewhere in the nose cone a projector was showing a film on a wall of the dock and it looked for all the world like the Brutus Nadir that we saw. I suppose it could have been filmed as it happened to us," Geoff clicked his tongue thoughtfully, "but then again if you look at the brochure we signed, we had the option of an Undersea Voyage or Undersea Adventure. They both seemed much the same to me so I gave no thought to which one I ticked."

"Gosh!" Imogen's hand flew up to cover her open mouth. "You don't mean what I am thinking?"

"Indeed I am, we had the 'adventure' that we signed up for!"

"My God," Imogen looked aghast. "You are saying that we went through all that for nothing?"

"Well not entirely nothing," Geoff was on the point of laughing. "What we came up with were solutions to survive in what seemed to be a very dangerous situation. If it was all a hoax it was, nonetheless, very realistic to us."

"What about all the dignitaries we met and the television interviews we took part in?" Imogen asked.

"We only have their word for who they were and that it was real public television that we were being interviewed for," Geoff grinned.

"As an afterthought, I think the least said about the incident the better; we are, after all, only guessing. Do you think that we will ever come back here?"

"I will think about it," said Imogen vaguely.

Chapter 15

FORMACIDAE

"Adventures follow you around," Captain Donald remarked when Geoffrey reported back to the Bridge of the Passing Star. "You will probably find the bridge quite mundane," he teased.

"Quite probably you are right," Geoff replied, "but give me asteroid belts, black holes, comets or even singularities. I find them all quite relaxing compared to holidays with the Firmament X Entertainment Corporation Inc." Captain Donald laughed at Geoff's reply.

"Still you had better fill out a report on all you saw and did while you were down there, although I doubt that anybody reading it will be much enthused to spend their holidays there after they have read it," Captain Donald chuckled.

The next destination on the agenda of their fact finding tour was to a distant galaxy, thought to be interesting because of a pulsing blue light at its' centre. It would be tricky because there are many suns, planets, moons and asteroid belts in a galaxy. Albeit, when in the DMT, logical A to B thinking suggested that you must have passed through those stars and planets but you had not. It would be a different matter if the ship was to emergefrom dark matter in the middle of a star or solid object.The likelihood of such a mishap was not great providedthey adopted the approved procedures. Although the 'approved' procedures were often thought to be time wasting by themore impetuousbecause such disasters were almost statistically invisible.

Impatience, however, was not the way to travel in space. Visual sightings could be hundreds to thousands of years in the past and many changes could happen to a star system or even within a whole galaxy. A new procedure was to first send a DMT dart on a circular tour through the target area that they had chosen to be their arrival point. They would then be able to debrief it when it returned to them. Its' reported data would give them up to date information to feed into their pre-sets for their intended DMT jump which was 'as safe as it gets' in the often chaotic conditions of outer space.

In this case there seemed little to worry about as they computed their rendezvous. What they could not have detected from an appreciable distance was that they would arrive at their chosen destination in the middle of a minor but fast moving asteroid belt where none of its' scurrying bodies were more than a few centimetres across but it was travelling at very high speed. Multitudal Space Grit was the official term ascribed to it in their 'Hazards to Navigation' manuals. Thus, when the Passing Star arrived to lay off their objective, the noise of collisions with the hull bore the sound of a severe hail storm which indicated that it was almost certain that damage was being sustained.

There were worried looks on the crew's faces as Captain Donald, as unflappable as ever, ordered an emergency reabsorption into the DMT; but that was automatically aborted by the navigation computers.

"I find it eerie and a bit creepy that those meteorites were passing through us when we were in DMT mode." Imogen sounded vexed.

"Well, as you know," Geoff replied, "it is only the human mind that would think like that because we cannot think of nothing at all. We do not exist at all in our universe when we are in dark matter but our minds can't cope with nothing. Wherever we are, we have to have an horizon and if a horizon cannot be found our minds create one. So passing through, as going from A to B, suits our way of thinking. The reality is that we do not move at all in the DM and the space grit did not exist therein."

"Of course I know that," she replied, "it is just that I have to approach it with my human mind; I don't have another one for dark matter!"

"Oh well," Geoff laughed, "some of the space grit could well contain precious stones and gold nuggets."

"Yes, you are right," Imogen giggled. "I suppose I ought to be grateful then for the time where I may have been 'even more' valuable than I thought I was," she brightened.

"Aww," Geoff dug her in the ribs, "you are absolutely precious as you are."

"Thank you," she smiled, "you are so easy to tease!"

The ship trembled as the sub light engines were engaged to reposition it out of the meteorite stream. "Render damage reports," the Captain's intonation over their hucoms was crisp and workman like and he kept the link open so that all could share the information as it was collated by the ship's departments. The gun ports were specially hardened so they were not damaged, but there were multiple abrasions to the hull and three perforations of the outer skin of the hull which would need urgent repair. Most of the exterior EMW antennas had been damaged or torn off leaving just their stumps on the hull; but more worrying news was to follow. The DMT mesh which covered the entire hull of the Passing Star had suffered substantial damage and square kilometres of it had been torn away and that explained the reason why the Nav-computers had earlier rejected the Captain's command to re-engage DMT.

"I am thankful that the controls did abort that command," Imogen remarked. "I recall from reading a hypothesis somewhere that suggested that if the automatic lock out did not occur in these circumstances, it was possible that those parts of the ship over which the mesh remained intact would pass through dark matter, leaving the uncovered remnants where they were, a really messy business."

"Ug", Geoff agreed.

The situation did not give Captain Donald a bucketful of options, as he put it, except to stay put and carry out extensive repairs to the mesh. At the same time he was aware that the poenillium rods, that were at the heart of the poenillium fusion X engines, had shortened with use and were nearing their recommended replacement length. In consequence he took the opportunity of the enforced down time and he directed that the rods were to be withdrawn and replaced. The two procedures would take about a month and a dart was sent off to Ongle to that effect but with no request for assistance because the repairs were within the technical abilities and resources of the ship to resolve.

Minor damage to a DMT screen was not uncommon and it was usually repairable within an hour, but a full inspection found that the DMT mesh was more badly damaged than first thought and they would have to scavenge robustly to find enough copper wire to rewire the gaps to reinstate the DMT grid. Thus, the great ship hung motionless in space as humans and robots swarmed over its' hull, their repair equipment emitting sparks and flashes of light as they set about making good the damage. During this time it was necessary to switch the main DM initiators off entirely which meant that they would be out of touch with Ongle. It was expeditious in the case of large scale exterior damage for a ship's main ports and exterior access points to be left open with force fields in place to prevent atmospheric egress. From a distant view point the ship would appear to be hive-like with figures entering and exiting from the brightly lit doorways and the open hanger deck would present itself as a rectangular floodlit invitation permitting access into the very depths of the ship.

The approach of another asteroid belt had been noticed by radar but its track offered no threat to the Passing Star because its linear progression pointed to a star on the horizon. A warning shout went up when the asteroid stream abruptly executed a dog leg manoeuvre and turned towards the Passing Star. 'All personnel and robots return to the ship immediately!' The urgency of the message was reinforced by three electronic bleeps every five seconds.

The real danger did not really dawn upon them, however, until it was too late and before the last of those working on the outside of the vessel had reached a re-entry point. What followed did not seem to be threatening even though the asteroids were landing softly on the ship and rolling into the open ports and thousands more came in through the gaping hanger doors where they bounced and rolled to the far end and then into the corridors. It was at this juncture that it was realised that the fluffy, playful balls were not inert because they had continued to roll onwards and they were surging up and down the lift shafts but they were still not apparently dangerous. But Space tumbleweed, they had taken to calling it, was beginning to make a mess of the place.

Geoff was initially unaware of events because he had his hucom off and he was sitting at a work bench making some final adjustments to a wrist hucom. The device resembled a normal wristwatch even down to having a proper watch face but there was a hucom chip inserted behind its' normal watch workings and it was activated by pulling the imitation watch winder out one notch. Plugged into the side of the watch was a very thin wire which passed up inside his shirt sleeve seam and along and inside of the yoke and into the collar where it connected to a concealed transceiver pad which was pressed against the nape of his neck by his shirt collar .With the help from the medical branch they had devised a method whereby the nerves at the back of the head could be utilised to relay hucom messages to and from the brain via the pad inserted in the collar of the shirt.

Geoffrey had worked on and off at fabricating the wristcom in spare moments at the behest of the Captain who explained that his reasons were that in negotiations of a delicate nature it may sometimes be useful for the trickier bits. It was not always easy to spot the pitfalls of agreeing to or rejecting a point being raised, he confided. This was especially so in negotiations with aliens where translation of what they had to say and the meaning behind what they said was not always obvious. There are frequent occasions, he said, where there is truly no equivalent word from one language to another. Not forgetting, even if you get that right, you may not understand the full scope or limits the people you are negotiating with actually apply to a word."You know," he once said in conversation with Geoff, "I once agreed, with an outworld race of people, that I was negotiating with the term 'we' in a document without fully understanding what exactly they meant and included by the term 'we.' It was not life threatening but I later found out that the term we, to them, meant all of their possessions including their pets and farmyard animals. It was not a big problem but it illustrates how different languages can be. So if there was someone who had access to all of the sources of information in the background and who was able to advise me discreetly of the more obtuse interpretations of key words in a document or a discussion, it would help to prevent misunderstandings. It is not deceitful because it is highly probable that our opposite numbers will utilise a similar apparatus or even have a natural ability to silently consult with experts who were not evident in the negotiations".

Until the main influx of the soft, hairy, spherical-shaped space tumble weed arrived, they had been regarded as rather curious to the crew and the fluffy round objects were thought to be some kind of semi sentient seed dispersal system. It was assumed that the pods had sensed light and water on the Passing Star and that had given them the false indication of being a place where their seeds could germinate. When the numbers coming aboard increased dramatically a frisson of alarm replaced the crew's curiosity and the message was passed round to secure all entrances to the ship. It was not an easy command for the engineers at the rear of the ship, however, because the tubes from which the spent poenillium rods had been withdrawn, to make room for replacement rods, were empty and open to space and the tumble weed spewed through the inboard ends of the tubes as if it was being pumped along them. There was an instant rush by the crew to engage the mechanism to bring down the tube caps to seal them but when the electric motors whirred into life to set this task in motion the tumbleweed balls began to split open. Those near to them had expected to see a core filled with seeds. Instead, there were two ant like creatures curled crosswise around each other inside each ball and as the ball split they leapt out. The shocked engineers found they were confronted by evil looking two and a half metre tall black ants standing on their rear legs with their other four legs clear of the ground. Their top-most pair of legs ended in conventional three fingered hands and the hands carried pistols with which they menaced the engineers. Others in the group took aim at the mechanical arms lowering the tube caps and disabled them with rapid bursts of what looked like a liquid stream of fire that melted and welded the hinges of the hoist arms and splashed back in fizzing orange droplets.

"All weapon trained personnel take arms and repel invaders!" The ship's address system boomed forth and the message was also repeated over all hucoms, but the invaders did not arrive without a strategy and they came to a halt and their bodies commenced to vibrate and issue a discordant sound which rose and combined with others to become deafening. So loud, in fact, that it really did hurt to hear and it distracted the mind to such an extent that it made the use of a hucom impossible. All over the ship people were bent down or on the floor with their hands clapped over their ears trying to blot out the hideous racket.

Geoff had now been advised what was happening but he was not yet affected by the incapacitating sound so he had remained alert enough to make a quick decision to use his experimental wristcom to make contact with the engineering robot (engbot) with whom he had been conducting trials. He had no particular plan in mind, save a hunch that any additional means of communication with an outside ally may prove to be an asset. "Take instructions only from me," he instructed the engbot. "Keep this channel open."

Geoff's intuition was incredibly correct because the ants on arrival in his sector of the ship came to a halt and their lower abdomens commenced to vibrate visibly, creating a strange soporific sound that got louder until it even penetrated through walls and locked doors. Geoff's head fell forward and he was in a deep sleep and when he awakened he was to find that he was manacled to his chair by a web-like substance and his hucom was being taken from the desk in front of him by a robot. "Don't do that!" Geoff was abrupt.

"I am afraid I have to," the robot sounded apologetic. "The Formacids have taken control and we can obey no other."

"wWhat!" Geoff spluttered, "how are they controlling you?"

"They have accessed the main controls from Robot Central. I am afraid that there is nothing more that I can do, sir," it said as it dropped Geoff's hucom into a plastic sack that when opened revealed that it was already weightily stuffed with collected hucoms and it continued to look around for the possibility of hidden armaments and was heading for the door.

"Before you go," Geoff shot out the question to detain it. "Can you tell me what is happening?"

"As much as I know, sir," the robot stopped to answer him. "The Formacids are space pirates that prey upon small worlds and space craft. They first infiltrate them using various novel tailored disguises that do not initially raise immediate alarm and then they take them over. Thereafter they strip the craft or small planet of anything valuable and retreat into the void of space. They always leave sufficient provisions and facilities so that the populations subjected to their space plunder do not starve and in the case of space craft they would be able to make it to the nearest planet. They try to avoid bloodshed."

"That sounds very civil of them," a grim smile lurked upon Geoffrey's lip, "but one must not lose sight of the fact that they are pirates."

"That is very true," remarked the robot as it wheeled itself out through the doorway.

Geoff's next visitor was a terrifying upright ant. With its antennae quivering, it surveyed him as if he were a tasty grub. It did not say anything initially but it reinspected the workshop that Geoff occupied, to be satisfied that there were no small arms or hucoms evident. It then dropped down to floor level, its body glinting like polished steel making it appear even more sinister as it six-footed its way up to Geoff and grasped the strands holding his arms and legs and severed them with its' mandibles. Its' voice, when it spoke, crackled and hissed rather like it was speaking from afar down a bad telephone connection but it gave him to understand that he was not to leave the workshop until they had finished and that would be in about twenty four hours from now.

"Where are the women and children, are they unharmed?" Geoff blurted.

"We are professionals and we do not harm women and children or anybody unless they try to harm us," the creature rasped. "They are confined to their quarters and you may join them, too, when we have finished."

"What are you looking for on this ship?" Geoff asked tight lipped.

"We are looking for small, expensive portable objects; but on this occasion we have learned that your ship has some very unique inter stellar features. We had planned to take control of it and put you down on a habitable planet, but we have found that you have your sub light engines partially dismantled and your remarkable DMT facility is also inoperable. We understand that it will take many days to repair them. Needless to say our operations in space attract a lot of attention from the forces of law and order so we simply cannot risk lingering too long in one place."

"Bad luck then," Geoff opened his hands and grinned.

"Bad luck indeed," the rise and fall of rasping sounds after that statement could have been laughter, it could have been disappointment. Geoff could only guess.

211

Geoff was naturally extremely worried about the welfare of Imogen and their children but he was reassured to learn that they had not been harmed. He had already tried the ship's telephone system but it was in lock down. It was only then, as he sat scratching his wrist in contemplation, that he remembered that he was still wearing the wristcom that he had been working on before the Formacids had over-run the ship. He recalled, too, that by the necessity of its' clandestine purpose it ran on frequencies not used by normal hucoms and the exchanges over it were encrypted, thus unlikely to be intercepted and understood, and he recalled he had previously usurped engbot 351 to his personal control.

Cautiously Geoff slipped his hand down his wrist to feel that he was still wearing the wristcom. Undoubtedly, because it had been designed to look like a watch, the captors had assumed it to be one. Wary that the Formicids could be watching over the ship's internal cameras he choreographed his movements to look as natural as possible as he cupped his wrist in his other hand. Secretively he found and tugged the false winder button and a click sounded in his brain which indicated that the device had been activated.

To cover his actions further he picked up a servicing manual from a workshop bench and made out to be engrossed in reading it. "engbot 351," he broadcast the robot's identity number through the wristcom, "are you ok?"

"Hello Geoffrey, this is 351. Yes I am fine. There was a control code broadcast a few hours ago that subordinated all robots to receive instructions only from the Formacids, but if you remember you placed an override on any attempt to change my status in the chain of command, so I was able to side step the instruction."

"Where are you hiding?" Geoff questioned..

"I am in the dead space area between the inner and outer skin of the ship. I am a long way in and it is sometimes a very tight fit. I do not think that they will find me," 351 sounded triumphant at his success at remaining undetected as if he was engaged in a game of hide-and-seek.

"Well done 351. How are your power levels?"

"No problems with power," 351 replied, "there are numerous power cables between the hulls. I am able to use my induction coils to top my resources as required."

"Stay topped up then and I will see if I can find a way out of this messy situation," and Geoff closed the link.

"Are you there 351?" Thirty minutes had elapsed since Geoff was last in contact with the robot.

"Yes, I am here and my electrical storage capacity is now one-hundred percent. Do you have anything in mind?"

"Yes, I have something of a plan now. What I would like you to do is to make your way between the inner and outer hulls to a spot adjacent to the storage bay where we keep the DMT darts. Let me know when you are there."

"That is eight-hundred and fifty metres from my present position," 351 advised, "it will take me about fifteen minutes to get there."

Geoff waited apparently engrossed in the servicing manual that he was pretending to read until he got the message that 351 was in position.

"Listen through the wall," Geoff commanded, "if all is clear use your welding facility to fashion a hole in the inner skin to where the DMT darts are stored and then go in and bring one of them back to your hiding place and re-patch the plate behind you." Ingenious design the engbots he mused. When it came to welding the plate back on it would put its' welding finger to the plate to be refitted and melt the metal and then let the weld cool so the plate would now be welded to its' finger. It would then draw the plate back after it, then seal it in place with the welding finger of its' other hand. "Once you have done that, move away from the DMT storage area so that even if they did detect the weld they would have a devil of a job finding you with the whole of the double hull to search. Let me know when that is done."

"All done, what are your further instructions?" 351 advised. Geoff grinned, it seemed that 351 was becoming involved with the plan at a personal level.

"Good," Geoff's relief was clearly conveyed even by his wristcom. "What I would like you to do now is to download to the dart a full report on all that has happened since the Formacids invaded and took control. You may have to open the input flap near the nose cone to do that."

Another nail biting delay ensured but it was de-stressed by:-

"Task complete," flashed through by 351.

"Brilliant 351," Geoff enthused. "Now please manually set the DMT dart bias controls for Ongle, then cut a hole in the outer skin of the ship and push the dart through the hole but keep a hold of it. When you are ready, using my authority, remotely re-initiate the ship's DMT field for about two seconds. It is quite safe to do this but that is as long as we can dare, bearing in mind it is not connected to the shield so you must first create a localised DMT field around the dart. At the same time push the dart out into space and it will disappear. Don't forget to seal the hole in the skin as quickly as possible afterwards," he added. "It will have triggered an atmospheric pressure drop alarmand if you seal it quickly they will probably put it down to a computer glitch but, just in case, get away from there as far as you possibly can."

Even by Ongle standards the response was fast and a scant forty-minutes later the giant Star-Class cruisers, Shooting Star, Lone Star, Home Star, Far Star and a dozen smaller planetary class craft materialised into being around the Passing Star. Smaller craft such as destroyers and frigates were joining them every minute until there was a formidable array of ships gathered. They were reinforced unexpectedly by blacked out, needle shaped, alien ships which arrived using sub-light engines and they then formed phalanxes fore and aft of the Passing Star.

The crew of the Passing Star were not aware of the

events happening outside but the usurping Formacid pirates certainly were. If the crew could have heard and seen the exchanges and conversations between the Ongle fleet and the newly arrived alien fleet they would have learned that they were an echelon of the Formacidae Space-Police and that they had been hunting this particular group of pirates across the galaxy. Nonetheless, it was a stand-off because the Passing Star had been buttoned up completely by the pirates and neither the Ongle or the Formacidae police could open fire for obvious reasons. With the Passing Star in its' present immobilised state and the space police now in control of the pirates' vessels, the only negotiation that the pirates could expect to discuss was their surrender and they were understandably reluctant to agree to taking their chances in the Courts of law on their home worlds, so it was an impasse.

The lack of up to date intelligence did not, however, apply to Geoff who was back in contact with 351 who kept him abreast of the news as it developed by eavesdropping on the Passing Star's hyperlinks. The knowledge gave Geoff a new train of thought. "351," he mentally whispered and then laughed inwardly because he realised there was no whisper facility in wristcom communications but the furtiveness of his action seemed to calm his own nerves somewhat.

"Here," 351 responded.

"Stay on line. I have a new plan that we can try. Can you get below the floor joists of Robot Central? If you can I want you to try to get there."

There was chit chat between the pair of them as they worked out the best route; and 351 would have to take and enter by burning his way through the inner hull at a point intersecting the floor space underneath Robot Central and the ceiling of a store room below. The between space there had been left deliberately large during construction to facilitate the cable ducting necessary and to provide room for engineers to work when attending to the complex cabling beneath the computers above. It was a time consuming task and Geoffrey sat in his chair and dozed away for two hours, but he came immediately alert when 351 told him that he was in position.

"I hate to tell you," Geoff admitted, "that I have sent you on a mission without a cause, but somehow I thought from that position we could possibly interfere with the operations of the Formacids. Can you come up with anything better than simply snipping the computer cables which was what I had in mind?" Geoff explained his dilemma.

"That could possibly work. It would certainly hamper their operation but conversely also our own ability to regain control, too. I have been exploring the possibility of something discrete but more useful because we would regain the use of Robot Central computers. Please wait a moment and I will run a few checks .351 out."

"What other options do we have then, 351?"

"It is simple really. The central computer and its auxiliary backup computer work together with the backup computer being constantly updated with what the main computer is doing. If any one of these computers goes down, the other takes over with no interruption and continues to run the system. The Formacids did not have the time or ability to re programme the computers so they have installed a temporary code to control the Robot Central computer. Temporary codes are lost entirely if power is interrupted to the main computer and its' auxiliary simultaneously. The trick is to disrupt the power sources to both computers at precisely the same time and for not less than ten seconds. After a ten second outage the fail-safe back-up capacitors which could conceivably provide fleeting reserve power to the computers will have been deactivated because I will have shorted them out. I will then restore both computers back on line. When I have reactivated the two computers and the Formacid code is wiped out, you can work through me to them via your wristcom and then subvert all AIs to your command via the Robot Central computers.

"Let's do it then," Geoff was on the edge of his seat when he realised that his actions may give something away and eased to loll back on it again. The door to the room where Geoffrey was, slid open and a Formacid came in and glanced over Geoff and picked up the manual that he had been looking at. Seeing nothing suspicious it put it back down and left the room which confirmed to Geoff that he was, indeed, being watched through the ship's internal cameras.

"There is a snag," 351 was back on the air ."I have to tell you that I have found that I cannot assist you in your endeavour unfortunately," 351 made the surprise announcement. "My fail-safe protocols will not permit me to execute your plan to disable Robot Central and take control of the AIs."

"Protocols?"

"Yes, I have to be authorised before I can take part in such a venture myself but I understand you are one of the four people on this ship who have a code to over-ride AI protocols. It will not work for the Robot Central computers though because they would block it as suspected malware. The malware filters can only be bypassed by direct input via an approved keyboard."

"Have you an approved keyboard to hand?" Geoff asked.

"Yes, I have. There are engineering keyboards down here," 351 replied.

"I hope that I can remember the code,"Geoff muttered to himself. Then it came to him in a flash. "Stand by, it sounds daft but here it comes 'Unzip8359point4holder' I have assumed emergency control." He confirmed it over again.

"You have assumed control," 351established, "what are your orders?"

"You are to carry out the plan discussed previously and deactivate both of the Robot Central computers for a period of not less than ten seconds and then reconnect them simultaneously. When this is effective you are to broadcast the UNZIP code that I have given you to all

Robots and AI devices on this ship."

There was a fifteen second break before 351 returned to announce:-

"It is done, Geoffrey."

Ship-wide, on all decks, robots stopped in mid-activity and stood with fixed gazes that drove the Formicids to distraction; but for all of their hissing and agitated waving of feelers they singularly failed to make any impression upon the robots. Out of frustration they tried physical violence but it was pointless because the robots they attacked just fell over and they stayed down where they had fallen. Triumphantly they tried to reintroduce their alien cookie to regain control of the robots but the Robot Central computer, itself an AI, passed their attempts via 351 to Geoffrey for confirmation before they could comply. Thereafter, Geoffrey revised his plan and he instructed 351 to sabotage the power links to Robot Central's computers entirely. In a counter move the Formacids despatched a party to Robot Central. But by using 351's ability to connect with other robots, Geoff had them seal off doors and lifts. It would take the Formacids an hour, at least, to blast through doors or climb the innumerable stairs and ladders. In the meantime, Geoff could now access the short wave radio channels and was briefing the commander of the flag ship, the Lone Star.

"All robots," Geoff's message was going out across their interactive peer to peer networks, along with Geoff's UNZIP code, "proceed at once to open hull ports and hanger doors and initiate their atmospheric conservation fields. Switch all external illuminations on. If you encounter violence you are to resist it to a conclusive outcome." The Formacids were dismayed that their previously loyal robot force, wherever they were, turned on heel or dolly wheels and headed for the corridors and lifts. Moreover, even semi intelligent equipment stonedwalled Formacid's attempts to control it. They tried to intercept the robots in the corridors to prevent them opening the ports in the hull but sheer numbers of robots was a deciding factor. Of now, the human crew were progressively regaining their freedom and using tissue paper in their ears to thwart the mind controlling, sleep inducing, soporific discord created by the Formacid abdominal vibrations.

The human crew did not have weapons at the moment but the word was flashed around that the Formacids were vulnerable to insecticides. In the course of a normal day there was always the possibility of bringing back some minute insect or insect eggs from a planet that they had visited, so all of the ship's departments had insecticide sprays to hand objective to preventing cross planet infestations. The Formacids were too big to kill with one can of insecticide, nevertheless, insecticide seriously incapacitated them to the point where they could not control their limbs. It also irritated their eyes to the extent that they could not focus properly which resulted in them staggering about like drunks. By now the the hapless beasts were facing a barrage of insecticide as the humans fought back and there were deaths on both sides.

As the Passing Star's wide ports were thrown open, dozens of smaller Ongle craft came over to land on the ship's hull and they discharged their military crews in battle order, making for the entrance points, whilst other ships flew right into the hanger decks. A superficial attempt at defence was made by the Formacid pirates but they were trapped in space on a dead ship. They had a number of hostages to trade that was true, but the Formicidae Space Police were in possession of the pirates' space ships so hostages were pointless if there was no escape route to trade them off against. They also knew that their own police force would be merciless if harm was done to hostages .

Absolutely nothing was working for the Formacids, even the inboard space runabouts and fighter aircraft belonging to the Passing Star, by reason of their heavy dependence upon AI, were unresponsive to any attempt to activate them. Little by little the Formacid pirates were forced back and collectivised where they darted furiously to and fro making agitated clicking sounds to each other. In the end they did prove that they were the professionals, as they had claimed themselves to be and they surrendered to their own police force who took them away.

"What will happen to them?" Geoff broached the question to an obvious senior member of the Formacidae space police who took them away.

"Those that inflicted death or injury will be punished, like for like he was told. The others will be found useful supervised work for as long as the Courts deem necessary, to fit their crimes. Tending the hive's eggs is a favourite with the judiciary, tunnelling is another.

"How will you know who committed what?" Geoff feared they would be tortured. "I only met two of them while I was a captive but they weren't threatening."

"You are a humanoid," came the rasping answer, "we are different. Our species are unable to withhold information because we are all a part of the hive and all information is communally shared. As soon as we have them back on our ships they will be reconnected back into the collective and we will be able to sift through their individual activities."

"That is clinical." Geoff was in a learning curve. "I am not so sure that I would take to being a member of a hive."

"Each to its' own; it has advantages especially where law is concerned. The case will be already judged because we know the details. The Judge merely sets the sentence according to the severity of the offence." The Formacidae raised and dipped its antennae in a way that some how comically mimicked a human raising and lowering their eyebrows.

Geoffrey had already passed his authority over to the robots and the AIs to the Captain who had then used his own over-riding command code to unlock Geoff's control over them and he had restored them to the control of Robot Central. Apparently the Captain had been locked in his quarters with a substantial guard outside of it. Messages of commendation and praise deluged in via Geoff's hucom and he was a bit embarrassed by it all. He pointed out that he was in the right place at the right time and that it was mostly engineering robot 351 that had formulated and carried out the successful plan. Later, when he spoke to the Captain about suitable recognition for 351, they were both at a loss for a solution as to what could possibly be considered a reward for a robot.

So it happened that Geoff raised the question of a reward to 351 and asked him if there was anything that he particularly wanted to do but was restricted from doing so by his present circumstances. 351 was surprised to be thought worthy of any reward but did mention that he had always wanted to try his hand at fly fishing. "My word," Geoff chuckled; "I am sure that can be arranged; and a dart was sent back to Ongle with the unusual request. Word came back that the Lone Star which was presently co-located with them, was due to commence a three week picquet duty around the Ongle planet Sara, said to be the best fishing waters in the system. Engbot 351 was henceforth assigned to the Lone Star with the special instructions that it was to be transported down to the best fly fishing area of Sara for the duration of their stay, with a tongue in cheek proviso that if he needed any assistance to bait his hooks they could nominate a person from Ongle. No guessing who that person would be, Geoff laughed. 351 took the information, as robots do, without any facial indication of delight but Geoff noted that its' responses via hucom communication were somewhat quicker than was normal and a few times in conversation there were misplaced nuances. At a guess, Geoff reasoned, these were clues to a level of increased activity within 351's core processor.

Chapter 16

THE LAST POST

Following upon the episode with the Formacid pirates, the continued journey of exploration by the Passing Star was curtailed and the ship called back to Ongle for a refit because the Formacids had, for the purpose of theft, dismantled many thousands of parts of its' technical apparatus. The news, when they heard it, left Imogen and Geoffrey greatly saddened. The earlier damage to the DMT screen of the Passing Star had also caused a re-think at the Ministry of Defence who felt that the incident had shown that, albeit very rare, the DMT mesh was vulnerable to multitudal space grit so the screen was to be upgraded along with the refit. When works were completed the Passing Star was to become the Flag Ship of the Ongle fleet and the QvO was to be paid off.

Geoffrey and Imogen were devastated by the news, but through pod casts they learned that the QvO was simply too expensive to run. Of course they already knew that but it had been the first capital ship ever built after the human slaves had over-thrown their Rap masters. Back then they had wanted something mind boggling and a statement of their emancipation which could prowl the universe on their behalf and lay claim that Ongle was now under new management. There were tears in Imogen's eyes as she digested the news.

"I love that ship." Her voice was broken.

"I know you do and so do I" Geoff sympathised.

When they next saw Captain Donald on the bridge of the Passing Star he had further news to impart about the QvO and he explained. The decision was equally based upon safety, too. It would have been just too expensive to fit an upgraded DMT screen around the QcO. Originally it had taken the Ambrocognians two and a half years to put the present mesh on the hull, but the new method was to bury the DMT mesh in the ship's hull and given that the QvO had a rock hull it would not be cost effective and it would take years to complete."What I can tell you is that the QvO is to take one last grand tour and will replace this vessel in our present deep space exploration and there is an open invitation for any previous crew who may wish to man it for its last voyage. You are both invited, I am told. Admiral Berry and his wife Janice will be on board, too, but another Captain will be in charge. The ship will also carry a random selection from society as well as dignitaries from our government."

"Oh, lovely," Imogen brightened up, "but what is to happen to the QvO?"

"I was coming to that." Captain Donald was pleased to answer her question because he knew it would be reassuring to her. "The ship is to be entirely preserved and it will be placed in a fixed orbit in the Ongle system and it is to become a museum and also a lecture centre for recruits; and it will also house The UoSS, (University Of Space Studies) and become a training centre for apprentice space crews. People will be able to visit it and be informed of its' history as a part of their tour," he addressed Geoff. "They will be able to visit the 4D printer room and see the table which you were beamed onto and a hologram will re-enact your arrival. Needless to say," he refocused his gaze on Imogen, "your cottage in English Village will also be a star attraction." The relief that Imogen and Geoff felt was measurable by the breadth of their smiles and their light hearted small talk .

The QvO was provisioning with water, fuel and food for what could be a long time away from base; and when Geoff visited its' bridge three days later there were familiar faces and hand shakes and a little back slapping. For a while they stood around yarning about trips and their adventures that they had experienced during the times when they had crewed the QvO. "Do you remember when....?" and.... "Do you recall...?" "What about when .....!" As each story was recalled with its' shared experiences it often had them all in fits of laughter.

Newly promoted to the rank of Admiral, the Admiral and Janice Berry, Geoff learned had to live in the sparsely laid out but beautiful landscaped approximation of the Swedish village of Stensjo. "They only built Stensjo a year ago on the QvO," Imogen told Geoffrey, "because they had realised that there were quite a lot of people of Scandinavian origin in the Ongle system of planets but they were unrepresented on the QvO. Ongle had spent some time hunting around for television and travel programmes about Sweden and they came across Stensjo among them and they have recreated some of the water scapes and low hills that surround it. It is quite beautiful there. The Admiral," strangely she still referred to his military status even though she was his niece, "recently undertook a genealogy profile test," she continued, " and it established that he was originally of Scandinavian descent and was probably descended from a settled Viking family in England."

"That, I imagine, probably accounts for your own flaxen hair and pale skin," Geoffrey observed.

"How strange," Imogen looked pleased, "I had never thought how that applied to me. I don't mind being Swedish one little bit."

"That kind of relegates me to being a Viking captive then," Geoff fashioned a glum expression.

"But an appreciated captive at that," she nudged him with the palm of her hand.. "Now get me a coffee, Englishman," she teased..

The QvO sat contentedly like a mother duck that swam in limitless space surrounded by her ducklings, represented by the smaller Craft fussing around her as they transloaded passengers and stores for the journey. Geoffrey was already on the vessel and he came down to the dock to meet Imogen and the children; and as they disembarked from one of the runabouts the girls were full of appreciation and squealed with delight when they saw the cottage where they were to live in the English village for the next few months. "Why is all that straw on the roof?" Sophia asked .

"Well, it is a traditional weather proofing used before people could afford slates or tiles for their roofs," Imogen clarified. "It keeps the house dry."

"I wouldn't think that rain was much of a problem in here," Vivienne registered.

"Oh, but it does rain in here," Imogen was amused, " they need it to water the gardens and the grass around the village pond and village green. They could do it all with sprinklers but rain is more authentic for the era so it rains to a schedule, usually during the night. "It keeps the dust down too," she added.

"Scheduled rain, how peculiar!" Vivienne laughed.

"Listen up, please," the ship's public address system came to life, proceeded by an unexpected feedback whistle. "This is Captain Proctor. I will be your Captain for this voyage, so let me welcome you all aboard. I can tell you that we will shortly be transiting to see the planet Earth. Regrettably it can only be from a distance because we fear being detected if we come too close. After that we are going to visit our good friends in the Ambrocognia Mundi Colligate and spend some time visiting their planets and meeting their people. I hope you all have a happy and interesting trip which, by the way, is about to commence right away, so standby for a DMT jump right now!" They didn't feel a thing, of course, and there was no sensation of travelling. "Its beautiful," the girls said in unison as they saw the real Earth for the first time "and to think that daddy once lived there," Vivienne added to the conversation.

"It is all blue." Sophia was stunned. "Is the air there blue, too?"

"Not really," Geoff explained, "the sky looks blue but it is to do with light wavelengths and the way some wavelengths are dissipated in the atmosphere. It is the same as the light you see here."

"Oh" said Sophia, not sounding really convinced, and for a while afterward she quietly scanned her father with her eyes to reassure herself that he radiated no, hitherto, unnatural blue light that she may have failed to notice in the past.

"From here," Imogen joined the conversation and pointed to the Earth against the backdrop of blackness, "it looks like it is so vulnerable and unsupported. One almost feels that they could pick it up and put it in shopping bag."

"No, don't do that Imogen," Geoff retorted. "The water would slosh about everywhere." The girls looked at him in dismay but Imogen laughed.

"Daddy is just being silly," Vivienne said to Sophia and they nodded their wise teenage heads sagely.

The Ambrocognia Mund Colligate was, of course, a whole system of planets and the QvO wound its' way steadily around them, stopping here and there to let sightseers off at various points and receiving visitors back up from the Colligate. Next on their bucket list was a visit to Fun Planet and the ship remained in orbit around it for a whole month and parties went down to experience the delights provided by the Firmament Entertainments Company Inc. But, before long, that became a two way exchange as people from Fun Planet came up to see the QvO. So many, in fact, that the Captain received a visit from the company directors and the development managers of Fun Planet who asked if they could reconnoitre the ship so that they could replicate the parts of it that so interested their clients when they had visited the ship earlier. "We will add them as yet another experience to our extensive range of sites and entertainments," they told him. "I really didn't think that we would ever come back here," Imogen announced, "but now that we are here I don't feel any compulsion to revisit it but perhaps while we are here we ought to drop in on Geraldine. It may seem rather rude if we did not."

There was no need for Imogen and Geoffrey to invite their two girls along because they had already buddied with another group of teenagers from their on-board school and they were down on Fun Planet from breakfast to dinner time. "We hardly get to see them since we came here," Geoff joked to Imogen.

"It's developing into a bed and breakfast relationship," Imogen observed,"but they are with their school teachers so I guess there will be a measure of control over the safety aspects. Anyway, lets go down to see Geraldine, she is going to meet us at the hotel where we stayed."

When Geoff and Imogen arrived Geraldine met them with a wide smile and a hug and they retired to the coffee lounge of the hotel but Geraline apologised that there had been a set back and she now had to pilot an earlier scheduled deep sea adventure due to the illness of the scheduled pilot. Laughingly they went over their escapade and towards the end of the conversation Geoff became more serious and asked Geraldine if it had really happened at all. "What on earth gave you the impression that it had not?" Geraldine smiled and Geoff appraised her of his suspicions.

"Well, it certainly seemed real enough to me," she giggled; and then the conversation reverted to friendly banter and the extended invitation for Geraldine to join them for a holiday on Marina, which she accepted with excitement. Then it was time for Geraldine to leave to go on duty but just before she left she stood in front of them and in the final moment before she turned to leave she put her head on one side and she said. "A deep sea adventure awaits me." She drew out the word adventure - seemingly emphasising that it was a word out of place. With a wink that encompassed both of them she left.

"There you are," Imogen interpreted the exchange. "I think we just got our answer."

Since the accident of the Passing Star and its unfortunate materialisation into a space grit storm there were new regulations on the use of DMT by any ship, such as the QvO, that had not had its' DMT screens 'hardened' against space clutter; and of now they had to resort to some pretty old fashioned safety procedures. Before any DMT jump, regardless of distance, they were obliged to release a DMT dart to recce the selected intended point of arrival and only then, if satisfied, in ship's jargon that it was 'clean space' were they permitted to initiate the manoeuvre.

The next visit was at the request of Geoff who wanted them all to see the planet of the spirits and once again Geoff and now his family, as well, were enthralled by the intricate dances and alluring siren voices of the spirits. The girls, of course, loved it and they danced with them, but Geoff became alarmed and called for them to stop their activities when he saw that the nearest spirits had ceased their gyrations and they were gathering silently and sinisterly around the two girls. "It is a problem with other life forms" Imogen ventured an explanation to the girls. "We can never be quite sure how they operate at an emotional level. For all intents and purposes they may have felt that they were being insulted, so don't ever do that again."

"Certainly not," Vivienne retorted, "it was scary."

"I don't like them any more now," Sophia pouted.

The voyage was scheduled to include ports of call and in one the DMT jump appeared to be a copybook arrival. But that was their initial opinion, for within two hours they were surrounded by a large fleet of vessels and the Captain let the exchanges with them to be broadcast to everybody on the ship and they were certainly not receiving quite the friendly greeting that they would have wished for.

"Quakasite vessel," they heard the challenge. "You have entered Donale restricted space. Standby to be boarded."

"This is not a Quakasite vessel, what ever that may be," the Captain replied cooly. "We are from the Ongle system of planets and we are on a peaceful recreational visit and far from home."

"Balderdash Quakasite, you have tricked us before and we will not fall for that again. Prepare to be boarded!"

"I see," the Captain replied unflustered, "I would agree to receiving a small delegation from your ship and we could, perhaps, establish with them that we are friendly with no hostile intent and they could also bear witness that we are not Quakasites ."

"Negative!" The spokesman of the threatening alien fleet was plainly irritated. "We have fallen for that, too, and our delegation ended up as your hostages; we had to pay a ransom for their release. If you do not surrender within the next two minutes you will be fired upon by superior forces. We require you, at once, to open all of your exterior access ports and permit our Donale Military Space Guards full access to your ship or you will be obliterated."

Geoff, thinking that he would be needed, put in a hucom call to the bridge of the ship. Despite being busy it was the Captain who answered in person. "I was just wondering if I would be needed?" Geoff came to the point with haste. "That is kind of you, Geoff, but it is all under control up here. We have assessed that their ships are only capable of sub-light speed and any projectile that they may fire at us can be taken down before it arrives. I am a bit miffed by their rude demands though; I may teach them a lesson. I will have you patched through to the helm so that you can watch.the proceedings."

Geoff returned to their lounge and switched on a master screen and right away a picture narrowed down into the sight of the ship's bridge and it was obviously in a state of alert; and he was just in time to hear Captain Proctor rebutting the Donale fleet with an icy "I cannot agree to your demands. We are on a peaceful mission and we are entitled to move through space without interference or hostility from you or anybody else. Your demand is refused!"

"Be it on your own head then," the reply carried the nuance of finality to it and the alien fleet turned towards the QvO. But, before their eyes, the enormous QvO flickered out and disappeared, only to reappear behind them. Urgently the alien fleet chaotically rounded to face the QvO again but once more it flickered out to appear at the side of them and then in front of them and then behind. The captain kept this cat and mouse game up with them for near twenty minutes, leaving the alien fleet in total disarray with its' ships pointing inwards, outwards, backwards and at all angles of up and down.

"I think that will be enough of a lesson in the art of good manners for today," he said. "Perhaps, one would hope, they will not to be so rude to visiting space craft in the future." Captain Proctor's face beamed.

"I like him," Geoff laughed to Imogen, "he is not at all stuffy. I imagine the Donales will be scratching their heads over this for years to come yet; and he didn't employ brute force for a single moment."

"Boys will be boys," was Imogen's response.

"What does that mean?" Sophia had overheard the conversation.

"They never grow up sometimes," was Imogen's enigmatic retort.

For this trip the QvO had been let off its virtual leash and they were free to go anywhere and visit any area where it was considered safe to do so and ports of call came and went. They all benefitted from the many experiences and societies that they met. An acute business sector, Colligate, had managed to wangle its way aboard as passengers and were benefitting in other ways and rejoicing over their full order books for when they got home. For others it was also a voyage of nostalgia and previous crew members often viewed the voyage with regret. For as long as they could remember the QvO had been ever present and barely a week or a month had gone by when it had not made the despatches. The QvO was a part of their lives and now it was to be pensioned off. But their present journey had taken the QvO to the very edge of the known universe, albeit one that was a human boundary. It was not the end of the universe because there were still clusters of stars and galaxies stretching ahead until they became dimmed out in the distance of the unknown.

Admiral Berry had more or less been cast in the role of being a passenger although Captain Proctor briefed him from day to day on events as they happened. He had, nevertheless, tactfully kept off the Bridge so that Captain Proctor could get on with running the ship and not, metaphorically, having to glance over his shoulder to see if the Admiral approved of his every action. But the Admiral was about to reveal a covert mission. That surfaced when he invited the Captain to lunch, in his quarters, with him and his wife. Geoff and Imogen were also present because they were members of the family and in the role of observers who might, from a more detached perspective, be able to see any flaws in the plan that was about to unfold.

The dinner had gone very well and as previously, for such occasions, Imogen helped Janice to prepare it. The Admiral then took the opportunity after the dinner to divulge the important news that he had to impart. The matter was classified so it could not, for the moment, go beyond the room. The message that he had to convey was of the growing concern in the Supreme Council Of The Ongle System of planets. The object of their concern centred around the growing use of dark matter transit by the known planets in their part of the universe. It meant that given the right equipment a marauding force from a yet unknown galaxy could in the blink of an eye arrive on their notional doorstep. In this area of the cosmos they had the benefit of the AMC - Ambrocognia Mundi's weather 'DMT beacons' secreted within dark matter itself. This enabled them to also detect the ships coming through the DM and to report their headings. It was cutting edge technology and it was probably not available to any other species in their sphere of interest. With exception of the

Donales, who they met a week or two back, no other species had ever displayed instant hostility towards them. "We do not know the rights and wrongs of their conflict with the Quakasites and we are pretty sure that we are capable of defending our home worlds from an attack launched from anywhere in our quadrant, but space is unlimited. If anything, the brush that they had with the Donales did illustrate that all of the communities in space are not necessarily friendly. "Which brings me to the real point of this meeting,"

The Admiral reached out for the glass of water in front of him. "Ongle does not know what lurks beyond our known boundaries and what is yet still further beyond that. So another purpose has been added to our mission. They have especially selected the QvO because it has the best all-round protective hull of any vessel of the fleets of both Ongle and the AMC. We have been directed to cross the known boundaries and penetrate deep into the space beyond them and to learn what we can. I have pointed out that we have non-combatants on board and they have responded by directing other craft to uplift the non-combatant passengers. At the moment we are very near the edge of what we know and in two days' time I propose that we push over the threshold as directed, but warily to start with, and then expand our understanding further if we meet no opposition." He looked toward Captain Proctor who instantly recognised the subverbal order and he rose to face the Admiral.

"Yes, we are prepared enough to do that," he smiled. "If I may, I'll take Geoff back onto crew if he is willing.

He has certainly proved to be an asset on many occasions on other vessels in the past and perhaps we may need to unlock that potential yet again!" Geoff looked towards Imogen who didn't look particularly enthusiastic but she made a hand movement and gave a look that unmistakably conveyed to him that it would be hopeless to refuse. "Thanks for that introduction," Geoff smiled at Captain Proctor. "I will do my best and may I thank you for asking me."

Notably not many of the non-combatant passengers availed themselves of the option to discontinue the voyage. Most said that they had joined the QvO for its' last hurrah before becoming history. They wanted to be able to retell that they were on it, up until it was finally paid off. On balance, they also expressed a collective opinion of why should space on the other side of an unmarked line be any more dangerous than the space that they were already in. Ongle agreed that they could remain but, to dot the Is and to cross the Ts, they would have to be sworn in as crew members for the duration of the voyage.

The instruction issued by the Ministry of Defence was to reconnoitre the unknown. It was to be achieved by short leaps and a DMT dart was to be sent ahead to scan five-hundred light years ahead and if it looked to be safe the QvO was to initiate a follow-up jump to the co-ordinates determined by the dart. Accordingly, all jumps were to be made employing these parameters until, by steps, they had penetrated deep space to a distance of twenty-five thousand light years beyond the known boundary, after which they were to return.

From the offset of their extended deep space expedition they could see that there was much to offer and to see, but physically it was not so different from what they had just left. Here and there dinosaur type creatures were the top of the food chain; on other planets there were humanoid people and on another giant spiders ruled. There was nothing to suggest that this unexplored area of space held any particular dangers to them and to any future missions. They reported their findings back to Ongle and the AMC after each step into the unknown, but presently the QvO was motionless as new preparations were underway for their next extension of deep space knowledge.

Now with Ongle's permission they were poised for a further five-hundred light year leap and the dart was being made ready to launch ". ......three ..two.. one," Captain Proctor's voice intoned, followed by "What the heck?" and a click as he switched his microphone off. Geoff was on the bridge at the time and he, too, had witnessed what had surprised the Captain. The dart was offering no technical reason why it would not comply with the launch code and it remained mutely in its' launch cradle. Geoff moved to switch on the diagnostics readouts but they all confirmed that the dart was fully serviceable and operational ready, yet it failed to move on command. When Geoff conveyed the read-outs for the dart to the Captain, his decision was obvious and he ordered that the dart be removed from the launch cradle and it was to be replaced by another dart from the DMT stores. When that failed, too, they turned to investigating the launch mechanism and the computer controlling the process and again they drew a blank. Everything was working properly but nothing was happening. Some delay followed as they brought another computer on line and they installed a different launch cradle and then another.

"It's plain weird," Geoff said aloud. "Everything tests to perfection but the harsh reality is nothing works. I wonder if there is some kind of local effect. It doesn't follow that space is uniform throughout, after all we have already picked up some interesting rock samples out here which contain elements that we have never yet found in our own quadrant. I cannot help but think that it is something external which is interfering with our systems; there is nothing showing up on our test equipment though!"

"Indeed, we can't see it, but that is not a sufficient reason to discount it," Captain Proctor agreed with Geoff's thoughts. "If that is the case then I do have some leeway. I can do a short direct DMT jump forward to an observable point in space where we have made accurate visual predictions regarding the safety of the ship on arrival. Let's try that and see if we can leave behind what ever is tormenting our systems." For a while the Captain spoke into his microphone to keep the crew up to speed with the prevailing difficulties and he also asked Admiral Berry if he would come to the bridge.

Admiral Berry arrived to handshakes all round and he commenced to study the readouts from the failed launch attempts. "To tell the truth, there is nothing for me to look at in the down loads," he verified his conclusion. "They all show model efficiency for all the the ship's systems," he continued. "I think your idea to see if we distance ourselves from the cause and effect may be the best solution, a jump of about one light year will be safe enough, I am sure."

"Right," Captain Proctor was secretly relieved that the Admiral had reaffirmed his own interpretation. "It will take at least twenty minutes to get the raw computations fed into the nav computer."

"Don't rush it at all, a few more minutes could make all the difference between arriving in clean space or in pieces on the surface of a planet or an asteroid." Admiral Berry nodded.

"At least all of our other computers and systems are working," Captain Proctor volunteered, "so we will get a very accurate map of the target zone from them, fingers crossed." He held up his hand to show them and Geoff and the Admiral laughed that even in the days of super computers there were still a few personal safeguards that could be taken which enhanced one's feeling of security.

"I'll stay here, if you don't mind?" Admiral Berry asserted but disguised it as a fake question.

"Comforting to have you here, sir" the Captain was genuinely pleased.

In the meantime, sensing that this could end up as a long session, Geoff had taken the opportunity to send for a coffee dispensing robot which was now trundling in through the bridge door and those not directly involved with taking computations for DMT gathered around it to offer their views to each other.

"Well, things look good. We have a particularly uncluttered segment of space keyed in and we are ready to give it a go," Captain Proctor said in the direction of Admirable Berry.

"Go ahead," and the Admiral both said and nodded his reply and everybody who would now have a job to do hastened to their work stations; only the Admiral and Geoff stood legs apart looking at the forward screens. They saw the count come all the way down but when it reached zero and they should have done a DMT jump they saw, instead, the words 'DMT devices deactivated' zoom into focus on their monitors and they heard an expletive from Captain Proctor.

"Recheck systems and recommence the DMT countdown," the Captain ordered; and they repeated the full procedure several times before the Captain gave up and called in the technicians to carry out a top to tail scrutiny of the DMT and all of its associated equipment. This they did but found nothing untoward.

The status of events was now rapidly realigning and moving from 'anomaly' to a full blown 'crises' and in the circumstances the Admiral assumed command and he began to issue instructions but was mindful not to reduce the status of the Captain; and to him he made only polite suggestions which the Captain knew were buffered orders. "Ok," the Admiral kept it sounding informal, "do you think that we could try the poenillium fusion X sub-light engines? We have be too able to move away in case we are in some kind of damping field."

In due course the poenillium engines came on line and the Admiral left it to the Captain to call for them to be engaged - but when they were engaged they still made no progress as step-by-step they cranked them up to full power. Even so, they remained in situ, the engines straining but going nowhere as if they were enveloped in an unyielding morass. Then, at the Admiral's suggestion of "Give it everything," the engine power control levers were pushed through the red gate to the position of 'Emergency Last Resort.' They had to be shut down almost immediately because the very floor they stood on started to vibrate alarmingly because of the sheer power being applied to the ship's structure through the engine restraints embedded in it. It was then that Geoff made an observation that as they had come in one way perhaps they could go out that way. Although not fully convinced that it would work, they used the bow thrusters to turn the ship around and were relieved to discover that they could, indeed, move in that direction and the poenillium X engines propelled them out of their predicament. Now it dawned on them that nothing was technically wrong with the QvO. Indeed, everything was working as it should now that they were heading for an invisible exit.

"Well well," Admiral Berry patted Geoff on the back, "you seem to have got us out of that one. Have you got any more suggestions of that nature?"

"Not many," Geoff replied, "a lucky guess really, but

it certainly seems to point to a mysterious force which has prevented us from going any further in that direction. If I may make a suggestion, we could try and side-step it and move a light year or so to the right or left and then try again."

"That seems to be a good suggestion," the Admiral addressed the Captain. "Should we give that a try?"

"It's as good a plan as any," Captain Proctor agreed.

The new manoeuvre was achieved in under ten minutes and they stood off and launched the dart and this time it did submerge in the DM and returned with a clear picture of space for them to emerge from after the jump; and this time the jump did go well. "Would you like to sit in this chair?" Captain Proctor joked to Geoff, but he spoke too soon because the lights of the QvO dimmed and then went out and the standby lighting turned itself on. Hurried conversations ensued with the power room staff and on the bridge they were stunned to learn that the main generators were still engaged and that their meters were registering that power was being produced but the physical truth was that although the indications were normal there was no power actually being provided by any of the generators.

"Not any of them?" The Admiral questioned. "You mean none at all? Huh", he said as he finished his conversation. "There are sixty-five high power generators spread about this ship that are deliberately disbursed to reduce the possibility, due to an accident, of the ship losing all of its' electrical power. They have bought them all on line and of now we should be enjoying ten-times the power that the ship requires.. They have all worked fine except none of them have produced power and now the poenillium engines have shut down too, so we are dead in the water. Without sub-light engines we cannot even reverse our route as we did last time."

"It is almost as if we are being played with," the Captain mooted.

"Assuming that is the case," Admiral Berry postulated, "then let's sit here and do nothing at all to see if they get bored with their game." The ship was quiet with barely a sound as they sat there mostly in silence before one of the crewmen pointed to a pinpoint of light in the centre of the Bridge and later reports confirmed that the same apparition had appeared simultaneously in all of the inhabited parts of the ship. The pin point expanded and it radiated rays of light and they could see that at the very centre of it stood a figure three metres tall and dressed in a white Arab Thobe.

"Greetings to all the people of the Ongle system of planets and those of the Ambrocognia Mundi Colligate and those on QvO" a voice filled their minds. "We are addressing each and every one of you at the same time and everywhere on your ship."

"Are you responsible for this?" The Admiral was on his feet. "If so, who are you and why are you interfering with this ship?" Admiral Berry did not sound best pleased.

"Please be seated and we will restore your electrical power and explain," the voice continued.

There was no audible change of sound as the ships's generators reassumed their task of powering the ship but in the meantime the glowing figure had grown in height to a full four metres tall and it was still radiating white light; and a feeling of calm and peace settled upon everybody as it commenced to speak again. "We have no bad intentions towards your ship, Admiral," it smiled. "We tried to stop you going any further earlier but you have proved yourselves to be tenacious, which we admire, and an exception has been made in your case. In answer to your question, we are the ascended future of humanoid mankind. It does not matter what different names that humans attribute to God, provided that he is the Creator and is a just and peaceful God. They are all one and the same in eternity. Sadly you are not ready yet to join us. The humans in your universe are still largely unaware of each other and are often engaged at war with one another, even on their own planets. You cannot ascend until your have matured and that may be thousands of years to come. Only then will you be permitted to cross the barrier that we have erected and we will be as one. I must say that we have been astounded because you are the only race that has ever been allowed to enter the empyrean prematurely, as you have done today. You will be returned now to your home space and we implore you to go back and unite the people of your cosmos and we will await you when you have reached your goal. We thank you for visiting us, and farewell, and God will be with you always." The figurine did not fade out, it simply disappeared leaving each one of the   stunned crew knowing inwardly, and collectively, that they had just met an etherial being.

"We are just off Ongle, now," the helmsman announced. "I didn't touch a thing but here we are."

"This is certainly going to take some explaining." Admiral Berry cleared his throat and asked a crew man to arrange a shuttle for him.

"That man is probably carrying the most important message ever carried by any member of mankind. " Captain Proctor pounded his desk absently. "Well that and the hands of God incident, when the Rap-Terrabot fleet attacked Earth, is going to change everything. I am glad that I was a part of it."

Chapter 17

WORLD WAR III

O n Earth, tensions were running high because of an increase in Chinese activities around their artificially dredged up islands in the South China Sea. The islands were built in international waters. Clearly the Chinese believed that they would confer upon them an extension of their territorial waters and enforce their claim to the disputed Spratly Islands and so make the South China Sea their own. The Chinese were adamant on this point even though it infringed international law and their expansion in this area threatened the security of neighbouring states who feared their forceful annexation by China; but from the Chinese point of view their ownership of the China Sea would enable them to enlarge their military presence in the far East and thence into the Indian Ocean.

The Indian Ocean was regarded as a Western bastion against Chinese expansion. India, ever wary that the Chinese may one day gain control of the entire Indian Ocean, immediately threw in its' lot with Brunei and set up an Indian Airforce base and a naval dockyard there. In the meantime, the United States continued to overfly the South China sea objective to maintaining that it was

249

international waters. In short, things were politically messy but had descended into a calm but glowering stance between the nations of the far East. Sensing a possible calamity, the United Nations called for peace and for nations to ease tension through dialogue.

To some extent dialogue became the favoured option, the alternative being a nuclear war which did not really appeal to anybody. Yet, one small mistake or an over-reach in confidence and the present watchful stand-off could render the South China Sea unnavigable to any fleet for thousands of years to come. There was the distinct possibility of military cascade, too, which would be certain to follow by reason that even a localised nuclear war would trigger programmed escalation; and pre-emptive counter strikes would follow - in the main because of the automatic implementation of the many mutual protection treaties that abounded between nations. Thus, once the mad logic of war took hold there would be no stopping it and Russia, the United States, Great Britain, China, India, and France would not survive intact because each side had the total annihilation of its' enemies in mind All this could blow up (sic) over a few man-made islands in the South China Sea which, in retrospect, the survivors if any, would come to regard as a senseless war.

Tacitly, the Chinese still permitted ships and aircraft of other nations safe passage through the South China sea but they maintained a strong military presence there because they believed that they had historic rights and they had their own arguments based upon their in-house perceptions of what constituted national security and sovereignty. In particular, they objected to Indian expansion in the Indian Ocean which they saw as provocative with the deliberate intention of isolating China from the geographical West. The Indians, of course, pointed to China's unnecessarily aggressive posture and the build up of their military and naval capability; and it developed into a race to expand militarily into areas that the scowling sides each termed to be their spheres of political influence.

All this was of major concern to India who commenced to beef up its' presence in the Andaman Islands. They also made a treaty with the Maldives to be able to use the old RAF base on Addu Atoll. The Chinese felt that they had to act before the expanse of the Indian Ocean became an Indian lake, backed up and stiffened by the American base on the British owned islands of Diego Gracie in the Indian Ocean and other Western assets in the Gulf of Arabia.

Previously, India had already acquired military rights to Assumption Island in the Seychelles. There was little chance that the government of the Seychelles would kick India out of Assumption Island because India had made a pact with the Seychelles Government for rights to its' use. Giving away these rights had, at the back of them, the fear by the militarily weak Seychelles that in times of international stress their nation could be taken from them by force. So they needed a more powerful protector; and the Chinese sensed an opening to exploit. To subvert the Seychelles, the Chinese approached the problem in a traditional and tried and tested way. They badly wanted a

251

base on the African side of the Indian Ocean so they clandestinely poured money into dissident groups in the Seychelles and, latterly, Russian weapons, too, which they had purchased elsewhere in the world to reveal no breadcrumb trail to China. Later matching of weapon serial numbers showed that these weapons had been exported from Russia to Brazil, although nobody believed that Brazil would wish to arm a dissident breakaway party in the Seychelles. Thus, regardless of subterfuge, the finger of suspicion pointed accusingly at China.

It was a long term strategy carried out by the Chinese, but they knew that in a poor country money buys political allegiance and it was with their case loads of money that the Chinese were eventually able to undermine the Seychelles government. The latter flatly refused dissidents' totalitarian demands to enforce democratic principles because they had noted that the 'democratic rights and principles' demanded had been selectively redefined as being only those implements favourable to the dissidents.This led to rioting and the arrival of armed terrorists on the streets. In many respects the terrorists were better armed and better trained than the Seychelles defence force which succumbed; and many defenders committed treason by throwing in their lot with the terrorists. Of course this did not go unnoticed in the world; and America, Great Britain and France, for military and historical reasons, began to rattle their sabres. The new Communist government of the Seychelles claimed that they felt insecure and invited the 'friendly' Chinese to defend them, thus the Seychelles became a vassal state subject to Chinese manipulation. Regardless of the change of regime, the Indians published a document signed by the previous government of the Seychelles which gave them the rights to own and operate a military base on Assumption Island for a period of 99 years. They had no intention to leave Assumption until the due date specified in the treaty.

The events on the Seychelles spooked the government of Mauritius and they revived a treaty they had with Great Britain; and the British once again sailed in to the Indian Ocean and reactivated their old maritime headquarters on Mauritius. The Australians, alarmed at the military game of chess going on to the North and the West of them, remilitarised their Cocos Island in the East of the Indian Ocean and started to use the Mauritius base along with the Royal Navy; and they formed a joint task force operating from there. South Africa, feeling very vulnerable in the circumstances, asked the British and the Dutch to provide defence and aircraft support.

Thus, step by step, tension was ratcheted up, and the Chinese saw an opportunity, in the event of war, to check mate the Madagascar channel and Mombassa - which was used as a port by the British navy. With the Indian government refusing to vacate Assumption Island, the Chinese capitalised on the impasse. They persuaded the Seychelles government that it was absolutely vital to their national security that they give way on Aldabra Atoll and permit the Chinese to build an airfield and a small resupply port for Chinese nuclear submarines there. With Aldabra being a world heritage site, it is needless to say that this caused an international uproar but there was no indigenous population on Aldabra. The seasonal work force on the atoll was comprised of Seychellois natives, so there were no fundamental rights of an indigenous population to factor in to the argument against the Chinese plan.

The dominos continued to fall when a secret NATO meeting expressed alarm that if the Chinese controlled Africa, or surrounded it, they would with Russia to the North to all intents and purposes have politically split the world in half. The British, with a small fleet and not able to cover all of its' Atlantic islands possessions on its' own, offered bases to NATO nations on Ascension Island, Tristan da Cunha and South Georgia. A British aircraft carrier and escorts ploughed south to the Falkland Islands to counterbalance an emerging Chinese courtship with the Argentine.

A military manoeuvre by the Chinese massed troops along the border with Myanmar and a hurried treaty of mutual support, in the case of aggression, was concluded between the Myanmar Government and India. Thereafter, India poured troops into Myanmar where they took up entrenched defensive positions, along with the army of Myanmar, facing the anticipated Chinese routes of attack. Malaysia also signed the same treaty. Thus the scene was set with the nuclear powers of America, India, China, Britain, France and the unknown nuclear allegiance of West Pakistan jockeying around the Indian Ocean seeking to check mate each other's military moves; and that contained all the ingredients of disaster for the world.

Needless to say, diplomatic wires were red hot.

Mysteriously, in another move, the sophisticated underwater submarine detection apparatus across the Northeast gateway to the Atlantic Ocean ceased to operate overnight. Western alliance strike aircraft were also taking off and landing at dispersal airfields which it was hoped were not scanned in for a pre-emptive attack by China and Russia. The Royal Navy missile submarines also moved out to their secret hiding places around the world. Submarines, of course, were the ultimate deterrent against pre-emptive nuclear strike because they could continue to prosecute a war long after there was nothing much left on land to come home to. The Royal Navy hunter killer submarines were already in place in their specified locations. But, before any of these submarines set out, they were attended to by divers who attached additional spoiler plates to their propellers to change their underwater disturbance signature of their props to mimic those of Russian submarines.

At the edge of space, both Russia and America were busy readjusting the tracks of their orbital nuclear bombs objective to hindering surface based predictors from knowing exactly where they were at any given time. These nuclear devices, upon the reception of an activation code, would explode and yield an electro magnetic pulse, (EMP) which would be strong enough to destroy 'un-hardened' electrical equipment all over the world, including mobile phones and personal computers, and more importantly, their enemies' radar and guidance systems. These EMP explosions could also be repeated at intervals for as long as the stock of nuclear weapons in space lasted. As a last resort it had been rumoured, or perhaps deliberately leaked, that China had constructed a Doomsday version of the hydrogen bomb. This bomb was encased in cobalt and if it was detonated it would be an act of national suicide that would over time also spread deadly radioactive poisoning to the rest of the world, too.

The scenario was horrific; but one could still cling to the hope that sanity might prevail. Would they really wish to destroy all life on Earth, including their own? People looked at each other questioningly. If only one politician would say ' This is silly, it is not worth it;' but they did not. From their bunkers those same politicians issued threats and taunted each other and made military gestures which resulted in such a fine balance that a misunderstood move by either side could result in full scale war.

After a time, things began to ease up a little, but national ambassadors still lambasted each other across the floor of the UN. But reason was returning until the tipping point was reached again. What caused it this time was that an Indian warship was practicing torpedo training off the coast of Brunei and they had broadcast the necessary notice to shipping to stay clear of the designated area. For the purpose of the exercise, a real torpedo would be fired at an old motor torpedo boat (MTB) that was rigged to operate under guided control from the shore. For realism it would dodge and weave as a ship would if it sensed it had been fired upon. The torpedo when fired from an Indian destroyer would automatically follow the twists and turns of the MTB until it caught it up and then detonated against its' keel. The exercise was to be filmed, so the torpedo had been fitted with a proper warhead to create a maximum explosive effect for the cameras. Things were going to plan for the Indian destroyer and it moved into position just off the shoreline and the MTB was performing perfectly under guided control. The torpedo was set and when fired it would home in on the MTB's propellers and a zigzag trail of bubbles would show on the surface of the underwater path that the torpedo was following.

To schedule, the MTB roared into the bay and the torpedo was fired and it commenced to hunt down the MTB and was following it, move for move, and closing fast. Then, at the anticipated moment of impact, the person controlling the MTB from the shore put the MTB, 'for its' speed,' into an impossible sharp turn and it flipped over. With no keel underwater for it to collide with, the torpedo sped underneath the upturned hull and like a liberated barracuda headed off in a straight line towards open water. It continued on for about a kilometre and then there was a dull underwater explosion. Briefly the stern of a Chinese submarine with churning propellers came clear of the water and the vessel stood nearly upright for a moment and then slid into the water in a near vertical dive. Another explosion from deep down caused the sea surface to foam and a column of water gushed upwards into the air and cascaded back into the sea. The results of that explosion soon started to pop up on the sea surface and could be seen as papers, plastic cups and bodies.

Despite profuse apologies by the Indian government, there were orchestrated anti Indian and anti West riots in

Beijing. The Chinese government announced that India would be punished for attacking one of their submarines that had been going about its lawful business in Chinese waters. The Indians refuted that and said that it was in Brunei coastal waters and that they had broadcast warnings for four days before the live torpedo firing was scheduled to take place in that area. The real reason, they said, that the submarine was there at all was probably to spy on the Indian naval exercise. In the meantime, the rest of the world's populace made a dash for the supermarkets and topped up on water and tinned foods and being just before a weekend the sound of digging and hammering could be heard in Western suburbia with men furiously fashioning underground shelters in their gardens. Four days later, an Indian destroyer struck a mine off the Andaman Islands and sunk with all crew. Nobody admitted to planting a mine there. The Chinese press reported the Indian destroyer was dropping mines in the the waters off the Andamans. Their comment was that the Indian navy had already demonstrated a cavalier attitude with munitions with its' runaway torpedo in their waters. The probability, therefore, was that it had probably struck one of its' own mines or had mishandled one and it had exploded onboard. A day later, a Chinese vessel struck a mine in the South China Sea and was all but vaporised by the explosion.

The response from India and America was to suggest that a Chinese weapon had blown up spontaneously on the Chinese ship that was carrying it. Detailed articles appeared in the Western and Indian newspapers describing previous, but never published, incidents resulting from the faulty trigger devices on Chinese weapons and how these had led to many accidents in the Chinese navy.

In desperation, the United Nations called for calm and negotiation but things had already gone too far. The next event was by persons unknown. In the dead of night, people had come out of the sea at Cocos Island and they had broken into a 'closed for the night' Australian military operations centre from where they had liberated its' desktop computers. The computers were replaceable, the information stored in them was delicate! A British frigate, on patrol off the Cape of Good Hope, reported that it had tracked a Wolfpack of five submarines skirting Antarctica, thence into the Atlantic Ocean. After that it disappeared without trace. The French navy detected a submerged submarine approaching their nuclear submarine facility in Brest and chased it away with depth charges. Hastily relaid sea bed microphones reported that submarines were moving from the Barents Sea in to the wider Atlantic and the rush to war began in earnest.

Peripheral war really commenced when an undersea nuclear explosion out to sea created a tidal wave that wrecked the Chinese nuclear submarine base in Pakistan. India ignored the accusations levied at it. Another incident, for which the culprit nation could be reasonably guessed at, had seen the opportunity of international mayhem to settle old scores. Thus, a nuclear tipped missile emerged from the depths of the Mediterranean Sea and came down to demolish Tel Aviv. Israel, a country even in normally circumstances known for an incredibly short fuse, made no secret that it would retaliate in kind. It followed that Tehran, Damascus, Beirut, and Tripoli disappeared in respective mushroom shaped clouds. Now the Mutual Defence Treaties, in case of attack, were dusted off. As in the past, various treaties had provided the rationale for two world wars from which the world had learned no lessons. Russia had a mutual defence pact with Iran, Syria and Libya. Likewise, American, had a similar treaty with Israel. Pakistan really didn't have proof of who had triggered the tidal wave which had wrecked the Chinese submarine facility at Karachi, but India was their odds-on favourite for their reprisal.

Ever since the Rap-Terrabot defeat in the solar system, the Ongle government had maintained a small scout craft for surveillance purposes in the Solar System and reports from it were coming in thick and fast to the effect that a nuclear war on Earth was inevitable. It was only political hesitation on the part of the larger countries that would be most involved that was preventing it; and things were so knife-edged that the very next mishap would tip the balance. Indeed, they said, warnings of what to do in the case of nuclear war were already being broadcast by Earth's radio networks. Stern military men had come on air to discuss the blast damage and the radio-active consequences of nuclear war and to tell people to take cover preferably below ground level and that they should take ample supplies of water and food with them because everything above ground would be irradiated. There followed the advice on how to survive the nuclear winter which would result from clouds of debris sucked up by nuclear explosions. In truth, one could see that it was all morale boosting and there was little hope for anybody who could not live underground and survive for years on what they had taken down with them.

The military Last Talk networks, over which the appropriate commanders would issue the last orders to their troops once the war had 'gone nuclear,' were activated. Their message would be to their forces thanking them for their outstanding service and that they might now go home to their families. A NATO early warning airborne command aircraft, eternally circling over Iceland, succumbed to a missile fired from the unexpected direction of above. The worlds largest aircraft carrier, the USS Midway 2, at five-hundred metres long and affectionately known as Route 66B, left the Hudson River importantly, at speed, with the intention of being morale boosting for newsreel cameras and sightseers. A British hunter-killer submarine lurking under the North Pole icecap was engaged by a Russian submarine and she sunk it. It was only that, todate, not a single nuclear bomb had landed on the soil of any of the main protagonist countries which had caused them to hold off from directly attacking each other.

On Marina, Geoff had been watching it unfold on recorded television and he guessed that Ongle would act quickly. They had not, he reasoned, defended Earth in the battle with the Rap-Terrabot fleet only to see their ancestral peoples commit hari-kari in a turf war. There was always the possibility of a last minute Divine touch on the tiller as they had witnessed in the Rap-Terrabot war. But this was was different. It was a self-inflicted, home grown mixture of protectionism, national interest and a desire to be the top dog among nations that was being played out. Humans had the gift and the intelligence to stop this at any time; but if they wished to waste everything for nothing in a nuclear war then, if not now, with no change of heart or direction, they would certainly do so in the future.

The call to arms came through almost immediately to Geoffrey and a shuttle had arrived even before he had finished the call. He was to report to the the Passing Star, the flagship of the Ongle system, and work under the direction, once again, of Admiral Of The Fleet, Peter Berry. The mission was to be a show of strength and an illustration to the people of Earth that there were forces even more powerful in space than those on Earth; and they were prepared to use their vast technologies to prevent Earth from committing suicide.

Once again Geoffrey swept Imogen up in his arms and said goodbye to her and the children. "Well, I married a hero," she laughed, "the downside of that is that he is always off somewhere to save worlds and civilisations from Armageddon."

"Oh, I am sorry, darling." Geoff was serious. "I think I will resign from the Space Force when I get back. How is that?"

"Well, you have certainly done your bit for Ongle and the planet Earth, but there is no other way even if you were not a Space Force Officer. As. before, against the Rap-Terrabots, the only Earth man on Ongle cannot dissociate himself from the prospect of the demise of the planet Earth; so you are excused this one." Imogen and their two girls stood and watched his craft take off in a silver flash as it headed for outer space, wherein it engaged DMT and arrived just off the Passing Star a moment later. An electro magnetic grapple shot out on a line from the hanger of the Passing Star and clamped itself onto the recovery plates specially designed for that purpose and they smoothly drew the shuttle into its' voluminous depths.

It was nice that Admiral Berry had come down to the hanger bay to meet Geoff and he commenced to brief Geoff right away that it was not an invasion fleet. Its purpose was to prevent and intimidate. The objective being to educate the nations on Earth that no matter how big they thought thought themselves to be, in reality they were infinitesimal compared to the universe in which they lived. "We are only going to take three hundred ships, together with their fighter escorts, and our first business is to stop the war and fully illustrate who we are and what we represent and the capabilities that we have at our disposal. Thereafter, we aim to bring the leaders of the largest nations up to the Passing Star. We may have to knock their heads together to get them to see common-sense. We want you to speak to them first and I propose to land you back at Greenbrook with me. That will cause a stir, if nothing else. From there we would like you to liaise between the fleet above and the Earth's Centre For Space Studies Initiative and convince them that we mean them no harm, but we will not allow them to have this world war."

Chapter 18

23.59 HOURS

The fleet arrived around the blind side of the moon and straight away isolated Earth's new internationally manned moon base by surgically taking out its communication links. The Passing Star, being too big to approach the Earth, sat between Earth and the moon. The rest of the fleet spread itself thinly around the Earth's circumference. Their timing was fortunate because they were split seconds early. China had fired three missiles at Indian military facilities in the Indian Ocean and an Indian submarine had responded in kind by launching three nuclear tipped missiles at similar Chinese military assets. Russia, more in tune with China than it was with the West, came in on the Chinese side and set wheels in motion for all-out war by launching a pre-emptive strike on America and Europe simultaneously. On board the Ongle ships, they watched as the awesome barrage of ICBMs rose above the Earth's atmosphere and started to arch back down towards their selected targets.

The World was truly seconds from oblivion. "All ships engage and destroy missiles." The command was given from the Passing Star. The reaction was instantaneous because their weapons were already locked

264

on and they were capable of self selecting, aiming, and firing their bolts faster than a machine gun. As the orange tracer-like balls of the poenillium canons reached out from the Ongle fleet and criss-crossed Earth's upper atmosphere. There were no explosions when they despatched the ICBMs because, when struck, theatoms of both the missiles and their war-heads were transmuted to become stable orphaned atoms. At most there was a puff of what looked like smoke but it soon dispersed. Then the fleet turned its' attention towards the orbiting nuclear bombs and they, too, suffered the same arbitrary dismissal, as did a multitude of cruise missiles. On Earth, they did not know what to make of it. They knew that there were unknown objects in the skies above but each nation had put that down to either their own secret weapons or those of the enemy.

The next nuclear strikes were to have been made by aircraft but that was a failure, too, because the Ongle escort fighters were everywhere and coloured laser fire came at them from out of the sky and ruptured their wings while they were still on the ground. The remaining weapon capability, namely fired from submarines, were eliminated as soon as they emerged from the ocean. For the participating nations they saw it as a disaster; all of their years of planning for just such an event had gone completely awry. But at this stage, they did not know that the same fate had befallen the missiles of their enemy and their stomachs churned as they expected the enemy missiles to arrive; but they were met with silence where there should have been heat and shockwaves from exploding nuclear bombs.

On airforce bases, the crews looked glumly at their ruined aircraft.They knew that they would surely be wiped off the surface of the planet before they could hope to repair any number of them. Each side, therefore, cringed believing that they had lost the war and that retribution, meted out to them as the losers, would surely follow. The civilian populations, where they could, remained crouched in their cellars and air raid shelters and even in ditches and caves, but nothing happened and a palpable feeling of unreality swept through them. Some of them had portable radios and televisions or even their mobile phones but they were inoperable.

The civil authorities did have hardened communication links to regional command centres and they were aware that no bombs had actually fallen, but it was not a planned for situation. They had reams of information about what to do in the aftermath of a nuclear war. But they had no guidelines explaining what to do if a war was unexpectedly called off. Bit by bit some of the braver citizens left their shelters and looked skywards. There were strange craft up there, they observed, and they hovered silently. In the bushes the birds twittered normally. Over London there was a cloudless sky, but dominated by a very large stationary object centred over the Thames. It started with a whisper and words spoken behind their hands, then it grew to a hubbub and then to shouts and singing. Soon everybody, all over the world, were telling each other again and again that 'the war is over.'

In China, they reasoned `that all of their missiles

must have been destroyed by a secret enemy weapon and that there was nothing for it but to set off their doomsday bomb but, yet, everybody there was alive and there had been no reports of any nuclear bombs falling on mainland China. In consequence they were finding it difficult to make the decision to kill everybody on Earth.

The Chinese Doomsday bomb was one of the very first nuclear bombs they had made during their nuclear awakening. It was quite crude and did not resemble how one imagined a nuclear bomb would look; instead it consisted of a jumble of wired up chunky parts mounted on the bed of railway freight truck. The fact that the bomb had started to leak radiation did not matter too much to them because it was kept deep underground in a lead lined bunker. When budgets permitted it was scheduled to be replaced by a sleek new design. The plan today was simple, it was to be detonated in situ. Once it had been exploded, the Earth's atmosphere would do the rest and spread the lethal radiation around the world. As a preliminary, the bomb had been towed out on the railway track that led into its' underground cave. Fortunately, at that point, the decision was made for them. Two orange balls of fire tore down from the sky and the doomsday bomb and its' truck bed vanished.

World - wide confidence was growing increasingly and radio and television stations were, where possible, reopening and mobile telephones started to work again. Politicians shook their heads and wondered why that which could have been settled diplomatically or have been ignored had been built up into a hysterical madness and a race to make war. It was was not quite over yet because each side was accusing the other of harbouring a secret weapon which they had not declared to the UN for inclusion in the non proliferation treaties. Realisation came later when it became apparent that each side's nuclear strike capability had been deactivated, but how? Had they lost the war or won the war? Nobody could answer that question.

At this point the plan 'B' of the Ongle fleet went into operation and Space runabouts, or fighters, appeared and came to hover over every major city of the world. Most countries interpreted this to be the invasion stage of the war and within their technical means, they loosed off anti-aircraft missiles at the vessels hovering ominously above them; but beams of light from the ships above intercepted the missiles which then vanished. Where there were no static ships hovering over smaller towns and smaller cities, other Ongle craft cruised slowly past them so that everybody could see and understand the message that was to follow was not a hoax.

"People of Earth," so began Geoffrey's message translated by his hucom to all languages. 'Greetings, my name is Geoffrey Holder and I am an Earth man. Please go outside and look and you will see above your cities that there are craft of a design and size that you have never seen before, but they will not harm you. We come to you in peace and to stop the disastrous war that you are engaged in. Please resume your normal day to day business. We will not harm you. Our mission of peace will land at Royal Air Force station Greenbrook in the

South of England tomorrow and all will be explained."

Perhaps Geoff could have phrased his message a little more carefully because his broadcast caused immediate traffic jams made by those fleeing the South of England which they now saw as the potential site for a military conflict. Conversely, the brave and the curious were coming the other way in droves with the intent on witnessing the first contact with the aliens for themselves. Adding to the chaos were the military which, as a precaution, were trying to manoeuvre tanks and field guns into the vicinity, along crowded, vehicle packed country lanes. Then the police arrived, took one look, and shut off all the country lanes and turned around the potential spectators and refugees and sent them back home.

Nevertheless, there were still a lot of people who had made it to Greenbrook and they sought out vantage points in the surrounding fields and hill tops from where they could see over the airfield. When Ongle came, it was with a show of potential force for which the Passing Star had emptied its entire space-fighter compliment to accompany the long, bladed, arrow shaped, shiny white space runabout which silently came in to land gently at the intersection of the two runways in the middle of the airfield. Above it, the Passing Star's complement of five-hundred dart shaped fighter aircraft hovered in diamond patterns to be seen against the blue sky over most of the South coast of the UK. The crowds on the hills stood spellbound and those who had binoculars told them that a stair case had dropped from the belly of the landed vessel and a lone figure was descending it towards the tarmac.

269

'He is carrying a flag,' the whisper went around. 'It is the Royal Air Force flag' somebody observed, as Geoff Holder put a foot down on the once familiar ground of Greenbrook. Again, as he had on the day when he had been accidentally transported from Greenbrook to the QvO, he could feel the airfield's history rise up from the damp soil and he was conscious that yet another extraordinary chapter was being added to it.

As he looked he could see that it was a much modernised Greenbrook. Gone were the olive drab colours of war and smart looking buildings and houses had replaced them. A village had sprung up where the old staff dormitory had once been for the Iris Net personnel. But it did not now house airmen but the civilian boffins of the new Space Studies centre. Carrying the Royal Air Force flag had been Geoff's idea. "It might seem a bit OTT," he explained, "but I think it shows that we are aware of where we are and we come in friendship."

The next person down the steps was Peter Berry wearing the full regalia of an Admiral of the Ongle Fleet. 'I will be in my posh suit' he had previously remarked to Geoff At the top of the steps were Imogen and the two children who had been especially and secretly brought to the ship without Geoff's knowledge so that they, too, could participate in Geoffrey's home coming.

Two Royal Air Force all terrain vehicles edged cautiously forward across the grass area of the airfield to the intersection of the two runways and stopped before the Ongle vessel; and an elderly white haired man, sporting a handlebar moustache, alighted from one of them. He was

Squadron Leader Ben Southwick (retired) but he had been urgently co-opted by the Ministry of Defence to be there to meet ex Corporal Geoffrey Holder and to vouch for his identity.

Ben Southwick, who still bore a demeanour of command about him, was suffering as wheels of his mind were turning frantically and desperately trying to recall a mental picture of corporal Geoffrey Holder; but as he approached he remembered him instantly. Ben came forward smiling and with his hand outstretched. "Yes, I remember you now. My word, you certainly must have a tale to tell. Welcome back to Greenbrook!" Geoff smiled.

"It is good to be back, indeed, and I am delighted to see that Greenbrook has been saved."

"In a way you saved it yourself when you got hit by the bolt of lightning. We call it lightning because that is what it resembled to the witnesses who saw it, but I guess that another word for it will now have to be added to the English dictionary. We got the note, by the way, and the diamonds and the disc you sent and that is what saved Greenbrook."

"It is good to be back on Earth and at Greenbrook," Geoff couldn't help repeating.

By now Geoff had become aware that Imogen and the girls were behind him and they were all ushered towards one of the vehicles that had come to meet them and Admiral Berry was invited into the other one. Helicopters whirred overhead as dignitaries were flown in, including the Prime Minister of the United Kingdom and the ambassadors of the USA, Russia, China, France, India, Germany, Japan, Brazil, Australia, Canada, Spain, Italy, and the larger Muslim states. Each was eager to get first hand reports and flash them back to their own heads of state and Admiral Berry immediately went into conference with them.

The children who were with Imogen were fresh out from Marina only an hour earlier and they had just covered billions of kilometres of space in the blink of an eye. Of course, when compared, no functional airfield could ever aspire to complete with Marina. But the manicured, emerald green grass captured their imagination and the route of the vehicle took them past a children's adventure play site and they perked up immediately. For the next two days their world was a whirlwind of studios, meetings, discussions and questions, not only from Great Britain but with emissaries from around the globe.

Finally, Admiral Berry disclosed that they proposed to hold a meeting between all heads of state of the planet Earth. The meeting would be held on Passing Star, above the moon, and transport would be provided at pickup points around the world. The purpose of the meeting was to set the conditions for Earth to join with the Ongle System of Planets and the Ambrocognia Mundi Colligate system and to exchange an envoy and trade with them and to become a part of a mutual defence force against any fresh intrusions by unknown life forms bent upon Earth's subjugation or destruction.

Stunned by the hysteria which had so recently set

them on a course of nuclear oblivion, the politicians had sobered up and there were many to be seen engaged in back-slapping with people who only two days ago had tried to bomb them out of existence.

On the third day after their arrival, Ben Southwick invited Geoff and his family back to his treasured Lock View Cottage for refreshment and a brief respite from the constant publicity to which they were exposed. In the circumstances, the RAF was most certainly not going to refuse to supply a helicopter to make the journey. It was slow by Ongle standards but it flew low down mostly along the canal leading to Lock View Cottage, making it a delightful journey.

At the sound of the helicopter's approach, Ben's wife came out of the cottage to wave to them as they came across the bridge; and for three relaxing hours they were able to sit in the garden with the placid water-lily strewn canal in view. There were ample cakes and pots of tea and coffee, making it a welcome respite indeed. Earth, it seemed, had scored very favourably with Geoff and Imogen's two girls when it came to cream cakes.

"Oh dear," Imogen sighed as she sipped her coffee,"I can see that you lied to me. Our coffee is nothing like this," and Geoff grinned.

"I have got used to yours and I quite like it now," he assured her.

A future date was then announced by Admiral Berry for vessels to come down from the Ongle fleet to pick up every head of state on the planet and convey them to a conference. Due to the number of attendees the main hanger of the Passing Star would be cleared and the assembled heads of Government, each with two permitted advisors, would be addressed by the First Minister of the Supreme Council of the Ongle System. Apart from being transported through space, the heads of state were also astonished at the sheer size of the Passing Star and the technical wonders it encompassed. Many found the ubiquitous robots especially interesting and the way they interacted with their human inventors. Most astonishing to them was that they were self standing in many things and attended to their duties, going from one to another without any apparent human instruction.

The great hanger had, of course, been quite spruced up for this meeting and there were even cut flowers, fountains and trees evident in a fake foyer. After a brief introduction, Ongle's First Minister rose to speak and he told them of how the ancestors of the people of Ongle were captured slaves from Earth who had eventually liberated themselves from slavery. He told them that although there were nine inhabited planets in the van Ongle system, there was only one government and how electronics had made this possible and all military forces and police forces came under the direct control of the central government. Albeit, he said, it was centuries since the first human had set foot on the Ongle system but they still regarded the Earth as the Mother planet.

Then, to a surprised audience, he revealed details of the attack that had been attempted upon Earth by the Rap-Terrabot fleet and how the Earth would not have stood a chance against the sophisticated weaponry and space ships of their attackers. It was clear, then, that the Ongle fleet even when combined with the space ships of the friendly AMC were so outnumbered by Rap-Terrabot fleet that the Earth would have surely been lost. The audience murmured quite loudly when they were shown a video taken by the Ongle scout vessel secreted in a crevice in an asteroid. From that position it was filming the enemy build up Were it not for the event which followed, it was clear that planet Earth would have been left a toxic lifeless ball and riven by volcanoes left behind where the alien weapons had exploded deep within its' crust. Then, inexplicably, the Rap-Terrabot had started to truncate and was gathering up into a ball and the evidence suggested that they were trying to break free of the what-ever force that was pulling them together. Finally, at a critical moment, there came the intervention of the 'hands of God' which both Ongle and the AMC attributed it to be. Two massive plasma streams had left the sun and had curled around behind it to encompass the Rap-Terrabot fleets. The plasma changed shape and became glowing hands, millions of miles across, which had come together in a celestial clap within which the Rap-Terrabot fleet had perished. On Ongle and in the AMC they had unquestioningly come to believe that it was Divine intervention that had undoubtedly saved the Earth.

That of course, he reminded them, was an attack from external forces. Internal strife on planet Earth was self made and was an act of 'free will.' As such, intervention by the superior power was restricted, not only because it would have been necessary to take sides in a dispute but because humans had been given the right to free will that effectively included the right to pursue self inflicted injury. War of the nature that they had so recently tried to prosecute was but an extension of that principle. The audience sat more upright on their seats when he told them of dark matter transit and how it was possible to be anywhere in the known universe within one second of keying the required destination into a computer controlling a ship's DMT grid. This led to unexpected dangers. You could never know exactly how many races there were in the universe or of their intentions towards other civilisations. Right now, the planet Earth is very insecure because of the newest advances in dark matter transit which had rendered it a safe way to travel. Hitherto, he told them, they had decided that until Earth had caught up both socially and technologically they would not introduce the planet to the universe. Recent events, though, had morphed a change of mind. Regardless that the people of the planet Earth did not at the moment demonstrate that its' people had the social maturity to deal with the situations that unrestricted space travel would demand of them, they had decided it was necessary to bring forward the first contact.

Nobody likes to be told that they are backward, especially Earth's politicians and the assembled shuffled uneasily in their seats. But he continued and warned them that you cannot export your petty rivalries into space. By luck and happenstance, Earth had been saved from voluntary self destruction. There could be no winners in a nuclear war and no country could have claimed to have won the war if the end result was that their own country was left just as devastated and uninhabitable to human life as that of the presumed losers. If Ongle and the AMC were to help the Earth and propel them into contact with the vastness, the riches and the diversity of the universe, they would have to grow up very quickly. Again there was some obvious dissent. They, after all, possessed the concept of democracy and they could not foresee that any life form, wherever it was, could do better than that!

"The reality is," he resumed, "that we are not going to impart technology to you if you are only going to use it to pursue petty religious, political, racial or colonially motivated wars among yourselves. In any event, the exploration of the cosmos is beyond the financial reach of nation states. Even your mightiest warships are toys alongside deep penetration spacecraft. The power required to move this ship, the Passing Star, through space exceeds by a long way all of the available horse power of all of the navies on Earth. Space travel is, therefore, expensive and it could only be contemplated as a joint undertaking by a united Earth. If we are to help the Earth then it begins with the people of Earth helping themselves. You will only be accepted by us if you dissolve your nation states and centralise and install one government for the whole world which would also control all of your defence forces." This was greeted with a gasp of dismay by the audience representing the larger countries, but with undoubted feelings of relief by smaller island states.

He hesitated briefly for his words to be digested and then resumed. "The idea that pervades Earth thinking is that one piece of land or a people are ascended over another; or that one religion is the only true religion, ignoring the fact that people are basically genetically the same everywhere as, too, is the land they live on. Any supposed differences, especially religious differences, are entirely artificial and an allusion created to justify personal power over a group of people by instilling in them that they are unique or superior to their neighbours in some way. As a result of one of our journeys in inter stellar space, we have learned that there is only one God; but religion has been used by mankind to divide communities rather than weld them together. Provided the God you worship teaches justice and honesty and does not support wars and excess, he is both one and the same person.If you make the changes that we ask of you, we will welcome you as equals in the universe and advance your civilisation by five thousand years. You must ask yourselves, do you want Earth to die by its' own hand without its' people ever reaching social maturity, denying them the wonders of the universe?"

The First Minster beckoned the Secretary General of the United Nations and indicated that he should take the microphone. The grey haired, distinguished man took to the rostrum and he thanked the First Minister of van Ongle and its' people and the Government of the Ambrocogia-Mundi Colligate for its' defence of Earth against the Rap-Terrabot revenge attack; and for stopping the recent military confrontation from developing into World War Three. He noted that the people of Earth, in space terms and maturity, were but children for whom the possession of the weapons of mass destruction were dangerous. "In the light of what we have seen today," he said, "quite simply, I agree. Mankind has a lot of growing up to do. Let us make a start right now" he urged. "In one week's time I propose to invite the head of every nation on Earth to attend a week long meeting at the United Nations headquarters to lay the foundation for a one nation, one people world and to ready ourselves to take our place in the universe. Lets do it, what do you say?"

The audience rose as one and applauded their approval. As the meeting broke up, the leaving heads of Governments were talking face to face with each other, although they realised that they still had their own electorates and their opposition parties to win over. Approval at a meeting, of course, was a long way from planetary approval but you could see instantly that politics on the planet Earth could never be quite the same again.

Where Geoffrey is now

EPILOGUE – THE ANSWER

Marina had by now been declared safe and Geoff had decided to take the opportunity to resign his Commission with Space Fleet and retire there with Imogen and the children. "You have certainly served them well," she confided, "and I will have the man in my life at home all of the time." Things could not, of course, ever be quite the same on Marina because the Ongle government had decreed, for safety reasons, that there were to be two new military encampments on Marina. Although they were some distance from the Grande Lodge they did keep in touch with each other on a day to day basis. "It is for the best," Imogen sighed, "but I loved it when there was just the family and nature here and we had it all to ourselves!"

But before Geoffrey could leave Spaceforce he had to sign his discharge papers on Ongle; and he also used the time to go around and visit the people he knew in their offices and to say good bye to them. His last port of call was to he Biological Laboratories. A branch of which, since he had first arrived on the QvO, had been studying the possibility of human transportation. From time to time, he had dropped in on them at their request to provide them with yet more tissue and blood samples for their research.

"Yes, we had heard that you were leaving," the director of the Department came up to him and shook hands.

"I feel it in my bones, it is now time to retire," Geoff smiled.

"Well, I hope that we will see you from time to time when you pass through Ongle," the director cupped his chin in one of his hands and looked at Geoff thoughtfully.

"You know we have investigated every aspect that we can think of to try to learn how you managed to get beamed up to the QvO. In the long process we have managed to beam across just a few flies whose legs were fleetingly twitching which was probably as much to do with rigour mortis because they were otherwise stone dead. Perhaps we were being over optimistic or were even vain enough to think that we could do it. We should have been more sensible. Even if it were possible to beam up a body and keep it alive, what about its' memories and stored information? What about the blood that would surely runaway as the body was been reformed? The person would certainly die from that well before they had fully materialised. Then we have to factor in the ever present radio static in space. That would undoubtedly interfere with any transporter beam. In the circumstances, the specimen being transported could arrive, for example, gruesomely headless, et cetera, or with bits of space debris embedded in it."

"There are other considerations, too. In our enthusiasm we had entirely over-looked the social price of success. Just suppose it were possible to teleport people, together with their memories; we have since envisaged the real human problems that may create. Supposing a rich person is facing death or is simply seeking immortality or his, or her, lost youth. It would be a great temptation to them to use their money and approach the criminal world to find a new host body. You can imagine the scenario yourself. A young man accosted, dragged off the street, drugged and transported to survive not in the persona of the person that they once were. Instead, they would only know the memories and character of their new owner. So the victim would have been murdered for its' body. Vagabonds, too, may well seek to escape justice by beaming themselves elsewhere in the universe and into another body. Personally I think, on reflection, that we can congratulate ourselves for being so fortunate to have not been able to unveil the secret."

"So what do you think happened...?" Geoff's eyebrows puckered a little.

"Heaven knows," the Director answered as they parted. But as he watched Geoff walk away the Director pensively fingered his ear lobe and added aloud to nobody in earshot, "And that may well be the answer," he smiled and nodded.

THE DARK MATTER ENIGMA

I see it not, but I am aware,
I know there is something there!
It is the something that fills the voids
Twix you and I and asteroids?

It cannot be measured in feet or metre,
nor even by mile or kilometre.
What is its' use, I wonder why
It lurks unseen in a clear blue sky?

Is it the glue that binds together
Saturn's rings and Scottish heather?
Is this the place where spirits thrive,
the place we go when we are not alive?

It is the flux between the stars
from way out there and Earth and Mars.
It is the path, as we evolve,
that beckons us on and on to solve.

What future then awaits mankind?
If only we are not so blind.
Are our differences just so great
that world war III we contemplate?

Side track not-then our ultimate role
for irreligious or political goal.
If we can survive as the human race,
wonders galore await us in space.

By V J Yarker March 2019

Printed in Poland
by Amazon Fulfillment
Poland Sp. z o.o., Wrocław

51555781R00174